THE WAR WITHIN

L. G Campbell

NOTE TO THE READER

I started writing The War Within before the Pandemic and I, like so many others, found myself struggling at times. Personally, I struggled with my health for a while, and then most of my plans were cancelled.

I have decided that while 2020 may not have been the year that you or I were dreaming of, rather than seeing this year as a write off, a complete disaster, I am choosing to see it as one that will be remembered forever.

Through it all the love and support from friends, family, and the book community has been amazing. We have come together and shown love towards everyone and anyone that needed it. We came together when we needed to and we will never forget that.

Let's continue to support each other. When times are hard and the world around you is just too much to handle, just remember, a book will always offer you that escape, whether you are reading or writing your own.

ACKNOWLEDG-MENTS

Book community friends, old and new, your support has been nothing short of amazing; I'd honestly be completely lost without you.

Robyn, my PA, thank you for doing everything I hate so I can focus entirely on my writing. Thank you for sharing my books and helping to spread the word. Honestly, you're a bloody godsend!

Fay, you are an absolute diamond for supporting me, for helping with my readers' group, and for helping me to spread my books. I can't thank you enough.

To my readers, you guys continue to astound me, your love, support, and appreciation means the world and more. You make this ditsy, dyslexic, gin loving author extremely ecstatic!

To my family who read my books, I'm sorry for scarring you with the steamy scenes. Love you!

To my friends who read my books, enjoy you fellow filthy minded buggers!

PROLOGUE

"I swear man, when we get out of this shit hole, I'm going straight to Karly's and we ain't leaving her bed for a week." I hear Joe sigh behind me as we crawl low behind a wall. I hold up my hand, halting him. We turn, our backs flat against the wall, keeping low.

"When we're done here you won't last five minutes, let alone a week. How long has it been since you've seen her?" I asked.

"Eight long, painful months. I swear man, my balls are so blue I'm starting to think I'm turning into a damn smurf." Joe snorts at his own joke.

I smile and shake my head. Joe is my brother and my best mate. We joined the army at the same time and we've progressed together through the ranks. Even though I'm his senior, which I like to remind him of just to piss him off, we're both special forces: a specialised team. We don't fight in ordinary wars. Hell, we fight the wars you don't see on the news. I like to think we're sent in to clean up the trash. We deal with the terrorists, gangs, and traffickers: the people behind the wars, usually the people with an extreme amount of money and power. We work under the radar, we go unseen, and we will never repeat what we see or what we do.

"Well, I hate to tell you this brother, but at nearly nine months pregnant I don't think she's going to be in the mood for a sex marathon."

I look down the scope of my rifle and frown in confusion. This doesn't make any sense. I look at the co-ordinates given to us and double check. Sensing the change in my mood, Joe looks over his rifle and down his own scope.

"What the fuck?" He mumbles under his breath.

"I know, it makes no sense. It's just a small village. I can see kids playing football, people going about their business. There's no sign of the Mexican Cartel. This was supposed to be where the head of the Cartel was hiding out. We have strict instructions to get in and get out, damn it! It was supposed to be a quick take down. There was no mention of damn civilians." I seethe through my teeth.

"I can't get no response or signal to contact base either. I say we get the fuck out of here. They never get the co-ordinates wrong. Something in my gut is telling me we need to get the hell out of here." Joe says.

He's right, something is off.

"You're right, but let's scope the perimeter first and make sure this isn't just a smoke screen and behind it all is what we're looking for." I suggest.

"Yes sir, let's get this over with so I can get back to my woman." Joe says.

We're just about to leave when a dark truck comes speeding into the small village. It doesn't slow, or even swerve to avoid people. It mows down anyone and anything in its way. Eventually it hits a small house. Women and children are screaming and crying. It all happens so fast, and then a second truck comes speeding in. This time there's a guy on the back of it with a machine gun, shooting at the people. My body tenses, watching the innocent women and children be gunned down.

"Holy fuck, we have to stop these mother fuckers." Joe growls.

I nod and signal for us to move out.

We split up and move around. We stay hidden and shoot and take out the men that are killing these innocent people. I think the cries and screams of the women and children will forever be ingrained into my soul.

I'm just about to turn and find Joe when I hear another truck approaching. This time it's the Mexican police, followed by the army. I sigh, relieved that there will be some control over this village, and grateful for the backup.

Joe stands and waves the trucks down. They come to a halt and the police get out and walk up to Joe. I'm just about to start walking towards them when the police officer raises his gun and shoots Joe straight in the head. My steps falter, and my breath catches in my throat. Pain surges through my chest as I watch Joe's lifeless body fall to the floor.

More gun shots ring out, snapping me out of my dazed state.

A woman runs towards me carrying a young child in her arms. She is crying and shouting at me in Spanish. Without warning she dumps the child in my arms.

"¡Por favor, vete! ¡Toma a mi hijo y vete!" (*Please go! Take my son and go!*) She cries.

I look down at her lifeless son in my arms. I look back into her pleading, desperate eyes. I don't say anything; I just nod. For whatever reason she has trusted me, a complete stranger, to get her son out of here.

She lets out a relieved sob, and leans forwards, talking in Spanish to her son. She kisses his head. She reaches up and places one of her hands over my heart and the other over hers.

"Tu eres fuerte, mi angel guardian. Cuida a mi hijo." (*You're strong, my guardian angel. Take care of my son.*) She speaks quickly before turning and running away.

I watch her run. I'm about to call out to her to stop, she'll get herself killed, but I'm too late. I watch as she collapses to the floor.

I grit my teeth, and swallow back my emotions. I look down at the small boy in my arms: he's unconscious but still breathing.

With one last look at my best friend, my brother in arms, Joe, with one last look at his lifeless body lying there, I turn and run. I run and run. I ignore the pain and the need to rest. I won't stop until I get this boy to safety.

I vow never to return to the army or special forces. We trusted them. Joe lost his life because somewhere in the ranks there was a mole, a double crossing son of a bitch.

Today will live with me forever; it will plague my dreams and every single breath I take.

CHAPTER ONE

Axel

I'm sitting in the corner of a strip club, hidden by the darkness with my bottle of Jameson for company. I watch as the girl on the stage dances, sticking her arse and tits out to the guys around the stage waving their money to get her attention.

I down my drink and quickly pour another. I'm not here for the strippers. I'm here for the peace. I'm hiding from my family, hiding from them looking at me with worry and concern in their eyes. They think I don't see the disappointment in their eyes. I do, every damn time.

I need to be as far away from them as I can right now. I can't face them. I can't face Rose, not after what I did to her.

I close my eyes and feel rage pulsing through me. Rage and anger at myself. I'm disgusted at what I did, grabbing her by her throat and squeezing. I didn't even see her. It wasn't her throat I was squeezing. My mind was back there. I was back in the depths of hell.

I shake my head, not wanting to go there. I can't go there; that place haunts me. I down my drink again and relish in the burn it causes in my throat.

"Hey there handsome, you want some company?" I turn to the voice and see a bleached blonde girl in stockings and a corset with fake tits spilling over the top. Her face is covered in make-up. I curl my lip in disgust.

"No." I answer and turn back to my drink.

"Oh come on honey! Anything you want is yours. We give you extra at this club." She tries to sound sexy, but she just sounds cheap and trashy.

"Not interested." I answer, ignoring her.

She leans forward and starts running her hand up my thigh. I grab her wrist, stopping her, and push it away.

"I said I'm not fucking interested, now

fuck off." I growl.

She huffs and storms off. I carry on drinking.

I stay for another hour and then decide to leave. I take my bottle of Jameson with me.

My family don't know I'm renting a warehouse apartment. The apartment is not in Mufftown, it's just outside. No one knows I'm here and that's the way I want to keep it.

I pick up my suit jacket. I'm still wearing my suit from Rose and Rip's wedding. I get up and walk towards the door, and as I'm walking through some guy walks into me.

"Hey! Watch it cunt!" he yells.

That's all it takes. I swing round and my fist connects with his jaw. His head whips to the side. Before I can give him more I'm dragged from behind and pulled out of the club.

Two guys have me on the ground. They're kicking me and hitting me. I welcome the blows. I can't explain why, but the pain feels good. I smile at them, almost goading them to continue.

The guy I hit comes out, takes one look at me, and kicks me hard in the head. Stars cloud my vision as I fight to stay conscious.

"What the fuck do you think y'all doing? I've warned you shitheads that if you start trouble I'll ban your damn asses. Now fuck off!" I hear a big guy yell next to me.

"Oh fuck! Tank, get me some napkins or the first aid kit or something." I hear a female barking orders.

"First aid kit?! Fuck me! Patty, Vinnie's idea of a first aid kit is emergency lube and a pack of condoms." The big guy roars with deep laughter.

"Just grab me something I can use! A cloth, ice, just move your ass Tank!" She barks.

"Alright Patty, calm down. Jeez, if you were anyone else right now I'd be putting you on your ass." The guy called Tank grumbles, slamming the door behind him.

I blink repeatedly, trying to focus. Patty comes into view. I instantly recognise her and by the look on her face I know she recognises me too. My gut tightens and I feel ashamed. I look away.

Groaning I move slowly, trying to sit up. I wince in pain.

"Easy, there's no rush." She says, I look at her concerned face and brush off her hand on my arm.

"I'm fine." I grumble.

I slowly make it to my feet and sway unsteadily. I watch as she reaches out to support me.

"I said I'm fine!" I snap.

She blanches like I've slapped her. I immediately feel guilty.

"Sorry." I grumble an apology.

"It's fine. Um, it's Axel, right?" She asks nervously.

I give her a tight nod.

"You probably don't remember me, I'm Patience, Maddie's mom." She says. There's a sadness in her eyes at the mention of her daughter.

"I remember you."

My head is throbbing. I reach up and feel wetness. I pull my hand down and look; blood covers my fingers.

Patience walks over and takes my hand in hers. Pulling a tissue from her pocket she wipes the blood away. I just watch her.

At that moment Tank comes barrelling through the door.

"Right, here's the damn first aid box. Ha! I damn well told you. See, that's a bottle of lube and about five condoms. There is also couple of antiseptic wipes and a bandage, so that's something I guess." He shrugs, going through the box.

Patience takes out the wipes and opens one.

"Um, could you either sit down or lean forward? I can't reach the cut on your head." Patience says with a small smile.

I don't say anything. I lean forward a little so she can reach. As soon as the wipe touches the cut I hiss in pain. I watch as she nibbles on her bottom lip, concentrating on what she's doing.

Her eyes flicker to me and she gives me an embarrassed smile.

A strand of her dark black hair falls across her eyes. I don't even think, I reach up and slowly tuck her hair behind her ear. She freezes and sucks in a shaky breath. Her eyes meet mine and in that moment I feel things stir inside of me.

I don't like it. I feel like she can see into the very depths of my dark and broken soul. I break eye contact and step back.

"I'm fine, I have to go." I state as I reach down for my bottle of Jameson I dropped earlier. I stumble. Tank reaches out for me and steadies me.

"Easy there big guy." He booms in his deep voice.

"Come on, I have a truck, I can drop you home." Patience says from behind me.

"I don't need no ride home." I snap back.

"Hey man, don't be a prick. Patty is a good woman. You've had too much to drink and you've had your ass handed to you, just accept a lift home. Don't be a damn fool. She will only worry and get upset, and I don't like seeing Patty upset, no one does!" Tank warns me.

I sigh and nod, giving in. I don't want the hassle, and there's no doubt Tank could probably kill me with his pinkie finger.

"Thanks Tank, I'll be back for my shift soon. Cover for me." Patience leans up and kisses a smiling Tank on the cheek. She turns and takes my hand, leading me to the truck. I try not to stumble. I also try to ignore the way her hand feels in mine.

We get in her beat up old truck and she pulls out of the car park.

"You staying with one of your sisters?" She asks.

"No, I'm renting a warehouse apartment, in the old cotton mill factory." I answer.

"Oh I know where that is. Not too far from here." She answers, smiling.

"You haven't got your bike." I state, remembering her pulling up on her bike, looking hot as hell.

Her face turns sad.

"No, I err…had to sell it today. I've had a few money problems. Austin has promised that once things pick up again he'll buy me my dream

Harley." She says smiling.

"Austin?" I ask.

"Austin's my boyfriend." She answers with a sigh.

It's not how you would expect someone to answer when talking about their partner. I don't comment or make any more conversation, I just want to get back and drink until the world goes black.

She turns down the long dirt track to the mill and pulls up outside.

"Thanks." I mumble under my breath and jump out.

Before shutting the door I turn to her.

"Keep it to yourself yeah?" I ask.

"Sure. I won't tell anyone what happened tonight, it's not like I see anybody all that much anyway." She shrugs.

"No, I mean don't tell them where I am, where I'm staying. I want peace and if my family find out that I'm here, I won't get any." I say, starting to feel agitated. The last thing I want is my family knowing where I am. I just want to be left alone.

"Sure. Don't worry, your secret is safe with me." She says smiling and doing a zip action with her fingers across her lips.

I don't smile back. I give a brief nod, slam the truck door, and walk inside.

I hear her pull away as I make my way to the bed. Laying down with my bottle of Jameson, I take a drink and close my eyes.

Images of screaming women and children running scared flash before me. I immediately open my eyes to push away the memories.

I lay here, drinking and staring at the ceiling. The silence of the apartment only welcomes the memories of their screams. It gets louder, the sound of gunfire and screaming. I down more drink.

"Arggh!" I yell into the empty room. I get up and walk across the room and turn on the sound system, the loudest it will go. Slipknot's 'Before I Forget' fills the room, drowning out the screams.

I walk to the bathroom and open the cabinet, taking out the bottles of pills the army doctors prescribed me.

I look at myself in the mirror; my eyes are sunken, surrounded by dark circles, the sleepless nights visible. I look back to the bottle gripped tight in my hand. I could take these now and it would all go away. The flashbacks would stop forever. I could fall into a world of blackness and peace.

Lily comes into my head. I think about the day she found her best friend dead. I think about what that did to her, the pain it has caused her through her life. I can't do that to her again, I can't be the one to cause her that pain.

I drop the bottle and clench my fists in anger. I'm angry at myself. I've been to warzones, I've killed people, and I've lost brothers before. But this, what happened, is something that I can't shift. It haunts me. It wasn't a warzone, it was a fucking ambush.

The one thing you're told as a solider, as special forces, is that you should feel safe and comfortable that what you're fighting for is for good, that the ones you put your life on the line for are the ones that'll have your back. They didn't.

I watched as Joe was brutally murdered, shot at point blank range. I watched as he fell to his death. I watched a quiet innocent village be destroyed, killing innocent people, and for what?

Joe's wife has lost her husband. Joe will never get to see his baby son grow, and his wife will never know the real truth behind it.

The truth is the ones responsible for it all were the ones we were fighting for.

Letting out a loud roar in pure frustration and rage I rear back and slam my fist into the mirror. I welcome the pain as I watch it shatter.

Panting I reach for the bottle and take two pills, swallowing them down with my Jameson. I don't bother to check my hand, even though I can feel warm blood running down my knuckles and dropping to the floor.

Carrying the bottle to bed I lay down, this time not closing my eyes. I drink some more, the sounds of Slipknot's heavy metal music drowning out my thoughts. Well, not all of them, there's one thought as my eyes become heavy. It's the only thought I welcome in: Patience.

CHAPTER TWO

Axel

I wake to a pounding on the door. I groan and rub my face. I squint my eyes open to see the daylight shining brightly through the blinds.

Rolling over I look at the clock; it's just after eight in the damn morning.

There's another bang on the door.

"Alright! Just wait a fucking minute!" I yell.

I pull on my jeans, not bothering to do them up.

I walk to the big metal warehouse type door

and swing it open.

I'm surprised to see Rip on the other side of the door. He looks me up and down and shakes his head.

"How the fuck did you find me?" I ask.

Rip smirks.

He points to his patch.

"We're the Satan's Outlaws motherfucker, ain't nothing we can't find out. Also, this property belongs to Fury's sister. Didn't exactly take much to figure it was you when she mentioned she had an English guy renting it." Rip smiles and shrugs.

I sigh and place my hand on my hips.

"Fuck." I groan.

"I just wanted to be left alone, now the lot of them are going to be coming round getting in my business. Don't suppose I could talk you into keeping this bit of information to yourself?" I ask.

Rip throws his head back and roars with laughter.

"Fuck me, have you met your sister? Hell, I like my balls, if I kept this from her she would have them in a damn vice. Anyway, after what you pulled at the wedding grabbing her like that, just be fuckin' thankful I ain't knocking you the fuck out. I get that you have some shit going down and whatever it is, it's winning. You look like shit." Rip points out.

I don't miss the way his eyes change when threatening me, he means every word. I may be crazy, but I like that. I like that Rose has a guy that will protect her like that. Truthfully, I wish he would knock me out. The guilt of doing what I did to Rose consumes me. I deserve to have my arse handed to me.

In the distance I hear a truck approaching. Rip looks over his shoulder and smiles. He turns back to face me and leans in.

"You have to take what she has to say to you, and she ain't gonna be nice about it. You need your family. I get that you don't want them all up in your business, so I've convinced Rose to keep it to herself for a while. She's agreed, but only for the rest of this month, after that she's ratting you're ass out." Rip states.

I grit my jaw and nod, it's something at least. I know Rose will kick my arse. Sometimes I think she has bigger balls than most men.

"Oh and another thing, you ain't alone in this. You ain't the only one to have PTSD, at least half my brothers are ex-military. When no one else was there for them or no one else understood, the Satan's were there. The brothers are always there." Rip says low, his eyes pinning me, making me listen. I give him a brief nod and grit my teeth.

I look up to see a barrel of dust and a truck come speeding in. It skids to a stop in font of us.

Rose jumps out and stomps her way over, clearly pissed off. I look to Rip. His eyes light and he doesn't even try to hide the smile on his face as he watches my crazy pissed off sister making her way over.

Rose comes toe to toe with me and tilts her head back to look me in the eye. She punches me hard in the gut.

I let out a grunt and clutch my stomach.

"You utter arsehole, how dare you worry the shit out of us all! We've been wondering where you've been. The army said you've gone AWOL? You mister bloody GI bloody army action figure! Why would you hide from us?! We're your family. We love you even when you're being a bit of a dick. You had mum worried sick! You had me worried too! All of us! Don't even get me started on Lily! Do you think she needs this shit being so heavily pregnant?! What did Daisy do to deserve this? Nothing, and she's the nicest one out of all of us." Rose yells poking my chest hard.

Rose is fuming. I can see the anger in her eyes but also the hurt lying behind it. I hate that I've hurt her.

Rip reaches up and gently squeezes her neck. He leans in and whispers something in her ear. I watch as some of that anger disappears.

"I'm sorry Rose, I am. It's just I'm not in a good place right now. I need to figure some shit out and I need to do it alone." I apologise.

Rose snorts back her laughter.

"Well I can see that, you look like shit. But what you're forgetting is in this family no one gets left alone to face demons. It's what we do, we are always there for each other no matter what. So suck it up buttercup because I'm not going anywhere." Rose informs me, placing her hands on her hips.

I pinch the bridge of my nose, and wince, the pain reminding me of my fight last night.

"Now dear brother, tell me who in the hell kicked your arse so I can go kick theirs? More to the point, why did you let them? Or are they in a worse situation than you are right this second?" Rose asks.

Before I can answer Rip jumps in.

"Woman, come up for air and let the damn man speak! Stop asking him twenty questions, he'll tell you when he's ready." Rip snaps.

Rose spins to face Rip, raising her eyebrow in question. Rip's lips twitch, fighting back a smile.

"Don't tell me what to do. He's my brother! I will ask him whatever I bloody well want! Do not piss me off Rip." Rose warns.

Rip just smiles.

Rose fights her own smile and rolls her eyes.

"Look guys, this is all very nice and you two are cute, but I'm not in the mood to talk. I don't want to talk. Now if you don't mind I need to take a piss and then I'm going back to bed." I move to close the door. Rose barges it open and storms past me. She stops and looks around the place.

"Sorry bro. You may not want to talk, which is fine, but I could smell you a mile away. You stink of skank and booze, plus I can see you've let your place turn into a shithole. So while you have a shower I'm cleaning up and then making you breakfast. You're going all skinny and you need to eat." She orders.

I'm about to protest and tell her to get the fuck out when her sad eyes meet mine. I can see the worry behind her eyes. I can see that me doing this means a lot to her. She needs to do this. I sigh and give her a brief nod.

Rose smiles brightly.

"Go on then. I'll clean this lot up for you. How bad is your bathroom? I can clean it up after you're done." She says walking towards the bathroom.

I reach out to stop her but it's too late. She freezes and looks at the shattered mirror on the floor, the drops of dried blood, and the knocked over pill bottle. She picks up the bottle and reads it, her eyes brimming with tears.

Of course being a nurse she knows exactly what they're prescribed for.

"Rose…I…"

Rose sniffles, shakes her head, and gives me a small smile.

"It's okay, no talking remember. Let me clean this up before you get in the shower. Afterwards I'll check over your hand." She walks towards me and wraps her arms around my waist and rests her head on my chest, not saying anything, just holding me. I wrap my arms around her and hug her back. I swallow back the emotion.

She sniffs and pulls away and claps her hands.

"Right, let's clean this crap up." She says forcing a smile.

She walks off to the kitchen and I turn around, clenching my fists. I look up and see Rip watching me. He doesn't say anything, he just gives me a nod. It's a nod of understanding.

Once Rose has cleared up the bathroom, I take a long shower. I stand there with both hands braced, leaning with my head hung under the shower.

Flashes of images from that day explode behind my eyes. I open my eyes and shake my head. I reach for the shower gel and start washing. The events of that day won't plague me if I keep busy, if I keep my mind from going there.

I get out of the shower and get dressed, my body starting to ache more form the beating last night. I notice my hand is dripping blood again.

I grab the towel and wrap it around it.

As I walk into the main living area I'm greeted with the smell of bacon. My stomach rumbles. I haven't eaten properly in days.

"Hey, you look better. Here, I made you some bacon, eggs, and toast. Also some fresh coffee." Rose says as she places the plate and mug on the breakfast bar.

I take a seat and dive in, starving. It doesn't take me long to eat.

"Wheres Rip?" I ask, taking a swig of my coffee.

"He's got some business he has to see to. You finished? I can see to your hand now if you like?" She asks, looking at the blood stain towel.

"Sure." I answer.

She grabs her bag which has some of her equipment in and starts to clean up my hand.

"I'm going to have to stitch it. The bit you've

cut is right on the crease of the hand, when you move your hand you're just opening it back up again."

I nod to Rose as she sets up her stuff and starts to stitch the cut.

I don't wince or flinch in pain. I like the feel of the pain. I deserve the pain.

After she's done she packs up her stuff and gets ready to leave. I walk her to the door, and she stops and turns to me.

"Ax, I won't tell mum or any of the others you're here, not yet anyway, but I can't keep it from them forever. You need to talk to someone. I can give you the number of the counsellor we use at the centre? Promise you'll call me if you need anything." Rose pleads.

I nod.

"I promise, no number for a shrink. I'm okay, I can deal with it." I try to reassure her.

She nods.

"I will pop by in the week, okay?" She reaches up and kisses my cheek.

CHAPTER THREE

Axel

I sit around in the apartment for a while after Rose leaves. I flick through the TV and through some local tourist magazines that were left behind.

Fed up of the deafening silence and not wanting the flashbacks to invade my thoughts, I get up and look at the time. It's after 12pm. I know Passions, the strip club, will be open. It'll be quiet, only the hardcore weird guys go in at this hour. I'm guessing that I'm classed as one of those guys now.

I grunt to myself, annoyed at the fact I can only find solitude in a strip club.

I grab my wallet and head out. I walk there, the journey only taking me around twenty minutes. Only 2 cars pass me.

I walk up to the door of Passions and before I can swing it open someone is stepping out.

"Woah there man! I nearly took you out." Tank bellows.

He pauses for a moment and then realises who I am.

"Oh it's you! glad you're okay. You're early. None of the girls start until after 2pm, it's just the bar open." he informs me.

"I'm here for that reason, just a drink. Not interested in the dancers." I answer.

Tank throws his head back, laughing like I've just cracked the funniest joke.

"Sure and I'm a pretty little girl in a pink tutu!" Tank roars with laughter shaking his head.

His huge hand clasps my shoulder.

"Hell! You Brits are funny guys. I'll catch you later if you're still here, maybe you can tell me some more jokes." He shouts over his shoulder.

"It's not a joke! I like the bar!" I yell back, trying to prove I'm not a dirty bastard wanting to be in a strip club all day.

Tank's loud rumble of laughter follows behind me as I walk in.

I can't help but smile and shake my head. Tank is definitely one big character.

I order a coke, I don't feel in the mood to drink right now. I don't know if it was seeing Rose earlier, but I know if I don't stop the drink now and slow down that's one road I don't want to end up on.

I look around the club. Apart from a few cleaners and some of the dancers practicing, no one else is here.

"Fuck you Patty! I'm telling you that shit ain't mine."

I hear yelled from behind me. I turn on my stool and see Patience with a small bag of powder, looking pissed off. The other woman throws her hands in the air and stomps her feet like a brat.

"Gigi, we found it in your locker! It was in your make up box! You know it's the first of the month, and you know we do random searches! Do not try and play dumb with me. You know the damn rules. Get your shit and get out." Patience says sternly.

"I'm telling you it ain't mine!" Gigi whines.

"Okay so someone planted it did they? Lets go to the clinic and have your blood tested, shall we? Maybe I should start piss testing all of the girls! What do you think?" Patience snaps back.

Gigi goes quiet and avoids looking at Patience.

"That's what I thought. Get your shit and get out. Don't you dare step foot in this club again, you hear me? Damn girl, you've just lost yourself a damn good job for a little bit of blow. You'll see just how good you had it hear, no other club in any of these town looks after their girls like we do." Patience throws the bag of drugs at her.

"Go."

Gigi bends down, picks up the bag, and shoves it in her pocket. Pushing her shoulders back she storms off, flipping the bird over her shoulder.

I look back to Patience and watch as she leans her head back and lets out a long breath.

She turns and her eyes fall to me. She smiles and heads over to me.

"Hey Axel, what are you doing in a strip club in the middle of the day?" She asks, smiling.

My eyes fall to her mouth, she really does have a beautiful smile. I shrug.

"Just wanted to get out of the apartment. I like that it's quiet here. It's not like a normal bar or club where people try to talk to you," I state.

She takes a step back.

"Oh, I'm sorry, here I am talking to you. I will leave you to have your drink in peace." Patience states, giving a little wave as she walks off.

I don't call out to stop her. I don't correct her. I don't tell her that her talking to me for thirty seconds has been the highlight of my day so far.

I turn back around and focus on my drink.

It has been a few hours now and I've just ordered a burger and fries. This is probably the only strip club I've ever been to that serves food.

"Shit man, that don't look good." A guy points out next to me.

I turn to the guy to see why he has such an issue with my food.

I'm about to tell the guy to piss off and leave me be when I recognise him.

"Err Rebel?" I ask

"Rubble." He corrects.

I nod and continue eating my fries.

"So, you been ordered to come here to keep an eye on me or something? Making sure I ain't causing no trouble?" I ask.

"Fuck no. I couldn't give a shit what you're up to, I'm hear checking in on Firecracker." Rubble nods towards the stage.

I turn, expecting to see one of the strippers

performing, but he's looking at Patience.

"Patience?" I ask.

"Yeah, Firecracker is her road name. She has one hell of a temper when pushed; she goes off like a darn firecracker!" Rubble snorts.

He turn to the barman and orders a beer.

"Okay, so why are you keeping an eye on her? She seems perfectly fine and safe here." I ask confused.

Rubble looks to me for a moment, clearly deciding whether or not to tell me.

"Fine, but listen, this shit doesn't go no further. I'm only telling you because it is family business and you're family, well, kinda. Firecracker has stopped coming to the bike club. She has given up having her daughter Maddie full time, she only sees her for an hour or so at bedtime and on weekends now. Her folks Big Papa and Raven are worried. They've tried talking to her but she just tells them to back off." Rubble pauses, taking a large swig of his beer.

"Anyway, long story short is Patty met this guy, and he's a tool. He's a real manipulator and a complete dick. She loves Maddie and she's a great mom, so for her to give up having Maddie full time, well, we all know she must have her reasons. She knows I come here to keep an eye out. It's expected that the Satan's Outlaws take care of their family. We're just making sure she doesn't get hurt, and waiting for the day that she wakes the fuck up and kicks his ass to the damn curb." Rubble finishes.

I sit with my eyes glued to Patience. The fact that she's with a guy like that makes me angry; she deserves so much more.

"So the burger, is it shit?" Rubble asks, completely changing the subject.

"I've eaten worse." I shrug.

"Well that's enough for me. I'm so damn hungry I'd eat just about anything." Rubble says, patting his stomach.

He sits with me, eats his burger, and has another beer. We chat about random shit.

"I gotta go. Listen, I ain't interfering or anything, it's just, well, I've been where you are right now. We all deal with our shit in different ways. I get it. You want to be left alone because deep down you don't want your family seeing you this way. Am I right?" Rubble asks.

I don't say anything. Rubble continues talking.

"PTSD will eat you up and takeover your damn life. Now you can either be a pussy and let it, or man the fuck up and let some people in to help. I had my brothers, and I needed that. I needed them. I ain't the only ex-military brother in Satan's Outlaws. You ain't the first or the last to go through this. You ain't alone." Rubble claps me on the shoulder hard and walks off.

I want to punch Rubble for knowing but the other part of me wants to thank him. Either Rose has told him the club, or I'm not hiding it as well as I thought I am, and it is transparent to everyone.

The club gets busier as the evening falls. Deciding to leave, I head to the gents toilets.

A guy comes in as I wash my hands, I don't pay him any attention. He comes to stand next to me.

"Yo man, you new round here?" He asks.

I turn to look at him. I take him in. He has tattoos, a shaved head, and by the looks of his expensive watch and clothes, he has some serious money.

"No offence man, I ain't interested." I say and go to walk past him.

He reaches out and grabs my arm. I freeze and every muscle in me tenses.

"I ain't no fuckin' fag! I seen you about. I heard my woman gave you a ride home. I'm warning you to stay the fuck away from her." He growls.

"Get your fucking hand off my arm right now." I warn in a low threatening tone.

I can feel that I'm about to lose it. My fists are clenched tight, fighting the urge to knock this guy on his arse.

The guy laughs.

"And what the fuck are you going to do about it? You English cunt!" He continues laughing.

That's it. I grab the guys wrist and quickly remove his hand from my arm and twist it behind his back. I push him hard through the doors and don't stop until he's hit the wall opposite. His face connects hard and I hear his nose crack and see the blood splatter. I have him pinned.

"What the fuck man?! I'm going to fuck you up!" He yells.

It's my turn to laugh.

"Back down, you have no idea what you're dealing with. Now, if Patience had any fucking sense she would leave your sad, pathetic arse. I don't normally give warnings, but don't come near me or you'll find out exactly what I am capable of. See this as your lucky fucking day."

There's a noise from down the hall I turn my head in that direction and see Patience. Shit.

I push him away and walk off. As I pass Patience I lean into her ear and whisper.

"You're worth a lot more than that piece of shit."

I walk out of the club and back to the apartment, not feeling sorry or guilty for handing that guy his arse.

I shake my head. I really don't understand what a woman like her sees in a complete waster like him.

CHAPTER FOUR

Patience

I watch Axel storm through the club and out the door. I'm not really sure what to make of his words. *'You're worth a lot more than that piece of shit.'*

"Patty!" Austin yells.

I jump and look to him. He looks pissed off. He storms towards me.

"You stay the fuck away from him. I don't like him. He just needs to count himself lucky that I kept my calm and didn't kick his ass." Austin states.

I snort back a laugh and roll my eyes.

Austin's eyes narrow.

"You laughing at me baby Treasure?" He asks.

I wipe the smile from my face and shake my head.

"No, I was laughing at something else." I answer lamely.

Austin leans in and kisses along my neck and nips my ear hard.

"Ow." I yelp.

"Don't ever laugh at me again Treasure. Remember, I own you. You're mine. You owe me." He whispers.

I nod, not arguing back, I can't. He's right I owe him. Who knows what mess I would be in right now without him.

"Good. I'm meeting Paco and his boys so I gotta shoot. Don't expect me home tonight, he's having a big party." Austin states, looking down at his watch. He leans in, kisses my cheek, and leaves.

I hate Paco, he scares me. I hate that Austin works for him, but if it wasn't for Austin working for him I would still owe Paco.

People don't understand why I stay and put up with Austin, but the truth is he saved me. He helped me when I was at rock bottom. So I can take it. Truth is, without him I'd probably be dead. There's one thing that turns my stomach and that is Austin's pet name for me, Treasure. He says it's because of my emerald eyes, but it just makes me feel like an object.

I sigh, I know what Paco's parties are like. There will be a lot of blow and naked women. I shake my head, not really wanting to think about it. Austin swears he has never done anything at the parties and I have to trust him, even when he comes home the next day smelling of other women's perfume.

I get back to work organising the girls for their upcoming performances. It's a fairly quiet night which makes it easy for me to sort. When it's crazy busy and we have stag parties or 21st birthdays it gets packed out and the girls stress more, and maybe even add extra routines in. At times I've had to get on stage and perform, but I try to avoid that at all costs if I can.

The night is rolling down and I'm clearing up the dressing rooms, packing away the girls' make up and switching all the lights out, getting ready to leave. My mind has been elsewhere all night. All I can think about is Axel and what he said to me. He's not the first person to tell me something like that, so why are his words sticking?

"You nearly done Patty? I want to get my

ass home to my woman, I'm a man waiting on a promise, and when you have two little cock blockers under the age of five, you don't risk missing a damn promise." Tank yells after me as I grab my purse.

I laugh, shaking my head.

"Okay! I'm on my way out now. Does that mean you're gonna be happier at work tomorrow if you're getting yourself some?" I ask, laughing as I walk out the club and lock up with Tank behind me. He always makes sure all of us girls are walked to our car every night and never leaves me alone to lock up.

"What in the hell are you talking about woman?! I'm a tall glass of chocolate milkshake! Smooth, sweet, and people always want more of me." Tank wiggles his eyebrows playfully. I burst out laughing.

"Oh shit Tank, you're gonna make me pee my pants! Go home to your wife; you don't want to keep her waiting." I say wiping the tears from my eyes.

"You get your ass in your truck, then I'm going, because my woman is waiting at home thirsty for her chocolate milkshake." Tank shouts over his shoulder walking to his truck. I am roaring with laughter as I jump in mine.

Tank beeps his horn, waiting for me to pull off. He won't leave until he knows I'm on my way home. I beep back and pull off.

On my way home I wonder if I should swing by to apologise to Axel for Austin's behaviour earlier. I'm sure that's why I can't get my mind off of him or his words. Clearly Axel is going through some shit, he didn't need Austin giving him more shit on top of that.

Without even thinking I'm pulling up outside Axel's. I don't think twice, I jump out of the truck and knock on the big metal warehouse type door.

It's when I'm waiting that my brain seems to kick in.

"Shit, what the hell am I doing?" I say to myself.

I start walking back to my truck.

"Of course there's no answer Patty, he's probably in bed. You idiot!" I chastise myself.

"Patience?" I hear from behind me.

I spin round and do a little wave.

"Uh, yeah, hi." I answer.

I walk back towards him, and nearly stumble as I do.

He's standing there, arm outstretched, holding the door open. He has no top on and his jeans aren't even done up, they hang loosely on his hips. His well defined muscled body is on full display. My eyes travel the full length of his body. I take in every inch of his ripped and defined body.

I notice a long scar on his lower abdomen and I wonder how he got it.

"Erm, I got that fighting in Afghanistan." Axel informs me.

My brain decides to work again, and I realise I'm running my fingers along his scar.

I gasp and pull my hand back like it's been burned. I feel my face heat with embarrassment.

I look up at Axel, he doesn't look amused.

"Shit sorry, I err, well, I erm. Sorry, I'm just gonna go." I say as I start backing away.

"Patience. Why are you here at two in the morning?" He asks, crossing his arms and leaning against the door.

Fuck! He looks even hotter like that.

I shake my head to get my mind out of the gutter.

"Well, I am sorry. I guess I'm so used to being up at this hour I just assume everyone else is too. I, well, I just thought I would apologise for Austin's behaviour earlier. He means well. He was just looking out for me, but he can be a little overprotective sometimes." I say, relieved I managed to get a whole sentence out without stuttering.

Axel lets out a grunt.

"I'm sure he is. You don't need to apologise for nothing, you shouldn't have to go round apologising for him. He's a grown man, I'm sure he could do it himself if he wanted to. It's your choice. You decided to date a complete prick. I'm guessing you either secretly love the drama that comes with dating someone like that or you're one of those women that thinks you can fix him." Axel says with disgust.

His words piss me off. Sure, it's two in the morning and I'm sure I've woken him, but I've driven over here to be damn well been polite and apologise to him.

"There's no need to be a complete ass about it! I was being polite and came here to apologise. You know what, you can shove your god damn apology up your mother-effing ass! I don't even know why I came here. So much for trying to be nice and do the right thing." I fume.

Before I know what's happening Axel has grabbed me and pinned me against the door. His arms surround me and I'm completely caged in by him.

"I guess this is the Firecracker I've heard about?" Axel says, his voice low and gravelly. His face is so close to mine I can feel his breath across my lips.

I take in a shuddering breath and lick my

suddenly dry lips. His eyes drop to my mouth. He brings his mouth closer to mine and I can feel the feather-like touch of his lips. I close my eyes, waiting for it, wanting him to kiss me.

But he doesn't. He pulls back. I immediately open my eyes, confused.

"Go home Patience." He grits.

I'm a little confused at his quick change in mood.

"What?" I ask.

"I said fucking go home!" He yells.

I jump and practically run to my car. I stop and turn around before getting in.

"Fuck you Axel! Your moods swings are like a fuckin' hormonal teenager! Do me a favour don't come near me again. Asshole!" I yell as I jump in my truck and slam the door.

I put my foot down and wheel spin myself as fast as I can out of there.

On the drive back to my apartment I try to figure out if I said or did something to cause that reaction, but I know I didn't. It's probably for the best that he stays away from me and I stay away from him. I don't need that kind of complication in my life; I need my life to calm down. I need to focus on getting my baby girl back home.

Jumping from one unstable guy to the next is not going to do me any good at all.

I walk up the steps to my apartment, I can hear the neighbours shouting at each other again. I walk quickly past number eight, hoping he doesn't hear me. The guy in there really creeps me out.

Apparently though I'm not so lucky. His door swings open, making me jump. I keep walking to my apartment which is just down from his.

"Hey there cutie, I've just opened up a bottle of whiskey. How about you come and join me and my friends here for a night cap?" He asks sleazily. He looks me up and down, not hiding where his mind is going.

"Thanks, but I've just got in from work and I'm tired. Plus Austin will be home soon." I lie.

"Well, I ain't seen him around today and I'm thinking he ain't coming by at this hour. I hate to think of you all alone. I'm happy to keep you company." He smiles.

I give him a tight smile and shake my head.

"Thanks, but I'm good. Have a good night." I quickly open my door and slam it behind me, sliding the chain across and double locking it. He really gives me the creeps.

I lean against my door and look around my tiny little apartment. It's not much, but it's home. It's my first home away from the club. I paid for this myself with no help from the club. I furnished it and made it the best I could for Maddie and I. I made it our home.

I walk to Maddie's room as I do every night. I look around her room and see her little bed filled with her teddies. I lay down on her bed, take her pillow, and breathe in her smell, her adorable smell.

I call her my little cupcake because she always smells sweet, and her kind heart is so full of love for everyone. I'd always say to her 'cupcakes make people happy and everyone loves a cupcake. My little princess Maddie, you are my special little cupcake.'

The tears start falling. My heart aches for my baby girl. I know she's safe and loved and I'm thankful I still get to see her, but it's not enough. She belongs with me. We're a team, me and her. I've made many mistakes in my life. She was made by mistake, but she was my absolutely perfect mistake. I wouldn't change having her for the world.

I got myself into this situation and I have to keep trying to get myself out of it. It wasn't safe for her here, Austin yelled at her when she wasn't being quiet. Plus the people he works for scare me, and I grew up with bikers. She wasn't happy here, and I can't just kick Austin to the curb after what he's done for me.

I'm lucky that Maddie wasn't taken away from me permanently. So as much as the pain kills me, and as much as my heart breaks, I know that this is the best it can get.

I cuddle Maddie's pillow and wish I have her in my arms.

"Night night my little cupcake, your mama loves you so much. Sweet dreams baby girl." I whisper into the dark room.

CHAPTER FIVE

Axel

I decide to go for a run. The sun is barely up, but I had a shit nights sleep. Not being able to sleep is nothing new to me but the reasons for this shit night's sleep is something completely different.

All I could think about was Patience. The spiteful way I spoke to her, the way her hurt showed on her face when I said those things to her, and the way I pinned her up against the door. Her smell, the way her eyes searched my face, and damn it, the way she licked them fucking plump pink lips. Shit! I'm getting hard just thinking about it.

I pick up my pace running. It's only around eight in the morning and people are getting up and leaving for work. It's probably the most people I've seen about since I've been living in the apartment.

I run for miles until I see a small street up ahead with a convenience store. Feeling the Texan heat, I decide I need water. I run into the shop and grab a bottle. Not paying much attention to anyone around me, I line up to pay.

"Please Sam, can't you just add it to my tab? I need these bits. I can pay you tomorrow when I get paid." A voice says up front.

I immediately snap my head up, recognising her voice. I move to the front of the line. I stand behind her. The clerks eyes come to mine. I hold up my water and point to Patience's stuff too. I hand him the money. He smiles and nods, taking it.

"Wait! What the?" Patience says spinning around to see who's paying for her stuff.

Her eyes widen, then just as quickly narrow as she crosses her arms over her chest.

"Sam, do not accept that money. He is not paying for my darn stuff." Patience says, her eyes not leaving mine.

"Err, sorry miss Patty I've already rung it through the till." The clerk shrugs.

Patience spins round and grabs her things.

"Fine. Here are you things." She shoves her shopping in my hands.

I don't have much choice but to hold it. She storms out of the store.

"Wait!" I run after her.

"You're really going to give me your shopping? You were just saying to that clerk that you needed it. You asked him to put it on tab for you! Oh but when I buy it for you, you'd rather go without?!" I ask.

She stops at her truck and spins around to face me.

Her eyes flare with defiance and I like it.

"I didn't ask you to buy that for me. I can choose if I damn well want it or not. I don't want your charity!" She seethes. She crosses her arms under her chest which pushes her breasts up in her ACDC tank top. My eyes momentarily flicker down and of course she notices.

"Oh hell no! My eyes are up here buddy, you do not get to look at me that way. Pervert." She yells, poking me hard in the chest.

I raise my hands in surrender.

"Okay I'm sorry, but I'm only human! I'm only a man. A man, I might add, who notices when there's a beautiful woman standing right in front of him." I defend.

Her eyes soften slightly, and a slight blush taints her cheeks. Fuck! I like that too.

"And any man would notice when a woman pushed her beautiful breasts up like that. Any straight guys eyes would flicker to look, even a man of the cloth." I state.

Shock then anger descends across her face. Her eyes, I swear, turn to fire. They are alight with anger. Fuck, I like that look a hell of a lot.

I can't hide my smile. I watch her eyes flick down to my mouth; they soften for a second before the fire blazes behind them.

"Are you kidding me! You think this is funny. You think you can openly insult and stare at a woman's breast?! Jesus H Christ! I should have known you're a complete jerk and let them guys carry on kicking the shit out of you!" She fumes.

I don't think, I just act.

I step towards her, pinning her to her truck. She gasps, not sure what to do. I reach over through the window and drop the shopping on the passenger seat, still keeping her pinned with my body. The smell of her and the feel of her pressed up against me makes it really hard not to kiss her and see if she tastes as good as she smells. She smells sweet like strawberries and cream.

I press my face alongside hers, breathing in

her scent. I graze my lips slowly along her jaw until I reach her lips. I pause and look at her. Her eyes are closed, her beautiful plump lips slightly parted, awaiting my mouth.

"Open your eyes beautiful." I say softly across her lips.

Her eyes flutter open and right then her eyes are alight; they are burning with desire. I close my eyes and lean my forehead on hers briefly before looking back at her.

"You don't need me, you don't need this on top of whatever it is you have going on. I will only make life harder for you and you don't need that. Focus on you and your baby girl. Get shot of that jackass. You need simple, you don't need any more complications. Baby, I'm just one big fucking complication, that I can't even solve. I'm one big fucking messed up puzzle with broken and missing pieces. Go. I won't come by the club again, I will leave you alone. Take the fucking shopping and just get on with your life." I finish.

I kiss her forehead and turn and leave. I leave her leaning against her truck. As I jog out of the parking lot I hear a 'fuck you!'.

Everything in me is screaming to go back to her. I can't. I can't bring my nightmare, my hell, into her already fractured life. She's better off without me.

I just need to focus on me and stop taking the

meds. I need to get back to myself. I just don't have a fucking clue how to do that.

When I get back home I stare out of the window, looking at nothing, thinking only about him.

I walk to the wardrobe and pull out the shoe box. It's where I've put my stuff from the military. Important things. I see the bit of paper with the number on. I grab my cell and dial the number.

"Hello, Oak House, how can I help you?" An elderly woman's voice asks.

"Um hi, I, err, was just wondering how Miguel was doing?" I ask.

There's a pause.

"Sir, can I ask what relation you are to the child?" She asks.

"I'm not...I...shit. Oh god I'm sorry...I was the one that found him and brought him in." I finally answer.

My heart is beating a million times a minute, my hands are clammy, and I can still hear his mum begging me to take him, to save him.

There's shuffling on the other line and a door closing.

"Sir?" she whispers.

"I'm not supposed to say anything for confidentiality reasons, but I can hear how much you care for him. If anyone asks, this call never happened dear, okay?" She asks.

"Yes of course, thank you." I sigh, relieved.

"Miguel is, um, still suffering from the trauma of whatever it was he went through. He doesn't speak or talk to anyone. He doesn't play with the other children. He just sits at the window and stares outside. It's like he's waiting for someone to come and get him. Honestly I've never seen a three year old behave like this before." She whispers.

I rub my hand over my face. My heart hurts at the thought. I thought him being in a children's home, a nice children's home, would help him. I thought it would give him the chance of having a family again.

"Sir, I really shouldn't say this at all, but I've seen the envelopes that come in with money for Miguel. I have a feeling that they come from you, sir. And, well, please don't think I'm speaking out of turn, but that boy needs a home. He needs someone like you who cares for him. I would beg you to consider this as an option. I would have him at mine in a heartbeat, but I'm eighty-five now dear. No authorities are going to hand him over to me." She states.

At her words I take in a sharp breath and

shake my head.

"No, I couldn't I...err...fuck! Sorry. I have stuff going on. It's complicated. Just trust me when I say that the home is the best place for him right now." I answer.

She sighs on the phone.

"I understand sir, but can an old lady give you some advice?" She asks.

"Sure."

"Well sometimes, in fact, most of the time, children have this way of bringing out the best in us. In turn, we bring out the best in them. Children have a way of making you see the world differently; they bring beauty and light into it even through the darkest of times. They make adults be better. Well, just by talking to you sir I think you're just as broken as poor Miguel. Given time together I think you could both heal each other and have a bond like no other. So please, just think about it sir." She begs before disconnecting.

I drop my phone to the floor and lay on my bed, staring up at the ceiling.

Miguel, like me, is broken. Taken away from his mother, his family, his home. All of it is gone, dead. I thought that with him being so young, he would heal. I thought that he would be adopted, that there could be a fresh start for him to go on to and live his life. After all, that's why his mother begged me to take him. That's what she wanted for him. She wanted him safe, loved, and cared for. I guess that is what he is, but a children's home is no place to grow up. No matter how much money I send for him, he needs a family, and he needs to heal.

I jump up from the bed and head to the shower, determined to figure out a way to fix this. I owe it to him, I owe it to his mother. But I can't just take him in and adopt him. I'm not fit for him right now. I couldn't add that to what already feels like the weight of the world on his small shoulders.

If only those mother fuckers hadn't set us up. If we hadn't been there Miguel would've still been a happy little boy growing up with his mum and family.

"Fuck!" I yell, and slam my fist into the tiled wall. There's so much pain and frustration running through me. I close my eyes and Joe's face enters my mind. The memory of him laughing, the memories of when he found out he was going to be a father, the memory of his lifeless body lying there. All I can see are his eyes staring through me.

"I'm so fucking sorry man, so god damn sorry." I grit, the emotion and the pain too much to contain. Tears sting my eyes.

I need to save Miguel, I need to take him

away from that home, for Joe. I wipe my eyes.

I hear a loud knock on the door. I step out and wrap a towel around me, walking to the door, wondering who could be knocking and praying it isn't one of my meddling sisters.

I reach the door and swing it open ready to give my sisters some shit.

But I stop. It isn't any of my sisters, it's Patience. She's standing with her arms crossed looking really pissed off, but I don't miss the brief appreciation that flickers across her eyes as she takes in my close to naked state.

CHAPTER SIX

Patience

I'm raging the whole way to his place. I swing by my apartment and empty out the little bit of savings I had hidden for emergencies, but I only had thirty dollars in there. It's meant to be purely for if I need fuel, or to put towards a bill. I would rather have a damn hard time and scrape by than have him swoop in and save the day, thinking he's some kind of prince charming, rescuing this poor girl.

"What a jackass!" I yell to myself in the truck.

I speed all the way there, my mind going

over it in my head. The more I think about it the angrier I get.

Then there was the way he brushed his lips over mine, the way he warned me away from him! I saw something pass across his eyes in that moment, and for a brief second I actually thought I might like him! Ha!

"Don't be a dumbass Patience, get your head outta your damn ass!" I chastise myself.

Screeching my truck to a stop outside his I jump down and storm across to his door. I clench my fist, knock hard, and wait. I tap my toe impatiently with my arms crossed, feeling ready to tear him a new asshole.

The door swings open and I swear to Jesus every thought just leaves my brain. He's standing with a towel wrapped low around his waist, droplets of water running down his broad muscled chest. My eyes follow them.

"Holy fuck, I don't think I've ever felt thirsty and soaking wet at the same damn time." I mumble.

There's a cough of laughter, bringing me back to reality.

I feel a blush hit my cheeks.

"If you're thirsty I can get you some water." Axel smirks.

I shake my head and remember why I'm

here in the first place.

"Ha-ha. Listen, here's the money for the groceries you paid for earlier. I am not a charity case, and I don't need your help. I am perfectly capable of looking after myself. You don't need to come into my life pretending to be my prince charming and thinking you're coming to my rescue! And now you're flashing your voodoo body all up in my face!" I rant.

I hold my hand out with the money, looking everywhere but at Axel. I feel his hand grip around my wrist as he pulls me to him. I slam into his bare chest and all of the air leaves my lungs. He doesn't let go of my wrist, holding it to his chest. I struggle and try to pull back.

"Stop Patience. Stop and just bloody well look at me." He says, his voice low and commanding.

I reluctantly look up at him.

"I know you don't need my help. I know you're strong and I know you don't need rescuing. It was a nice gesture, a gift. You accept gifts, right? It's rude not to accept gifts. Now, the only reason I can think of why you decided to come all the way down here is because you wanted to see me and my voodoo body." He smirks.

"Ughh you pig! Let go of me now!" I snap back.

Axel leans in and whispers in my ear.

"You want what you can't have, you just refuse to admit it." He nips my ear, making me gasp.

I push back and look at him. I really look at him. He has such a darkness behind his eyes, a broken sadness.

"Have you been crying?" I ask.

His whole face closes down. He lets me go and pushes me back slightly so he can shut the door. I grab hold of it before he can close it.

"I see it. I see the sadness behind your eyes. You're broken and you're stuck in the darkness. I've been there and it does get easier. It's okay to be broken, it doesn't make you weak to speak to someone." I say empathetically.

"Sure, and you're the person that's going to fix me? You're going to be that one person I confide in, that I bare my soul to?" Axel says sarcastically.

"Sure, be a dick about it, hurl shit at me if it makes you feel better. Just remember that you ain't the only one going through shit." I say as I turn and leave.

Before I jump in my truck I flick him the bird over my shoulder.

I hear a small rumble of laughter and the sound warms me. I smile to myself on the drive home.

It all makes sense now. Something big has happened to him, enough to make his mood swings give me whiplash.

God this man is going to drive me insane, I know it. I know it won't be the last I see of him. If I'm completely honest with myself, I don't want it to be the last time I see him.

I pull up to my apartment and jump out.

"Hey there pretty lady!" Is yelled across the parking lot. I look up and see Mr Wheeler, my eighty year old neighbour, waving me over.

I walk over smiling.

"Hey Mr Wheeler, how's your day been?" I ask.

"Well, it's all the better now I've seen your pretty face. Got time to play an old man at some chess?" He asks, pointing to his board that's all set up. He's been waiting for me to come home. He's become lonelier over the last year since his wife passed away.

"Sure! For a handsome man like you, I have all the time in the world." I say smiling and taking a seat ready to play.

His face lights up. He lets me win every time. I know he lets me win because I'm a really crappy chess player.

We sit for a while playing when a car comes

screeching into the parking lot. We both look up from our game and see Austin stumble out of the back passenger door.

"Adios!" He yells laughing and falling over his own feet.

"You know I'm an old man and darn it, I am eighty years old, and even I know when I see a damn fool. Lady, you are worth so much more than that. I just wish you'd see it." He says patting my hand.

I place my hand over his and give it a gentle squeeze. I lean over and kiss his cheek.

"Until next time Mr Wheeler." I say standing. He smiles and shakes his head.

Austin spots me.

"Hey my Treasure! Come get that fine ass over here and take care of your man." He yells.

I smile a tight smile. The sun isn't even down and he's beyond trashed.

He puts his arm around my shoulders and leans his weight on me as I struggle to help him up the steps to my apartment.

I manage to get to my apartment door with Austin barely holding his weight. We stumble inside and I drop him on to the couch, panting and out of breath.

Austin starts laughing and pointing behind me. I turn to see what he's laughing at. I jump back, my sleezy next door neighbour is leaning against the doorway smoking. He smiles and my stomach recoils.

"I'm just doing my neighbourly duty. I came to see if you needed a hand with your man here." He states, his eyes looking me up and down.

"No. We're all fine thank you." I reply.

"See he's been partying a little too much and a little too early. Now who's gonna be looking after you huh?" He says walking towards me. I back up to the wall.

"Oh hell! He likes you! That's my damn woman man! You can't go around touching another man's woman without asking." Austin says laughing, like it's one big joke. He isn't drunk. He's not slurring his words, he's on something.

"Oh my bad, my man. Do you mind if I touch your beautiful lady here? I shall make it worth your while." The guy says winking and holding out a small bag of white powder.

My parents always taught me how to protect myself, especially my Pa. He wanted to know that if I ever needed to defend myself I could. I also usually carry a gun, but at this moment in time it's locked away in my nightstand.

I watch Austin think for a moment and then laugh. He takes the bag of drugs that's offered to him. My eyes widen in shock and I curl my lip in disgust at him.

"Now, where was I?" He says, dropping his cigarette to the floor and stamping it out on my carpet. That alone makes my blood boil.

He starts running his hand up my stomach and over my breast. It takes everything in me not to be sick. I have to be smart, I have to get to my gun.

"Um, sir, I don't even know your name." I say coyly, fluttering my eyelashes. I watch as arousal flashes through his eyes.

"No need for names cutie pie, you can call me sir, that'll be just fine."

I smile and he starts to kiss my neck. I reach for the belt buckle on his jeans. He grunts and I feel him smile against me, happy at what he thinks I'm about to do.

I grit my teeth and fight back the bile as I reach in and grab hold of his dick. At first he moans in appreciation which soon turns into screams of pain as I tighten my grip, dig my nails in, and twist.

His legs give out from under him and I let go as he falls to the floor crying and wailing, holding his dick. I quickly run to the sink and wash my hand. If I had the time I'd bleach it.

"You fucking bitch!" He screams, rolling around on the floor.

Austin isn't making a sound. He is dazed and high, staring at the ceiling. I run to my room and grab my gun. I walk back, take aim, and shoot.

He screams.

"What the fuck?!"

"Get the fuck out of my apartment. If you don't move, the next shot will be your dick. My pa taught me to shoot and I have damn good aim. That first shot was just a warning. I never miss my target. So I suggest you take your pencil dick and get the fuck out." I threaten.

I don't take my eyes off of him. I keep my gun aimed at him. He slowly gets up, still whimpering in pain, and hobbles to the door.

"You fucking crazy bitch." He spits before leaving.

I move quickly and slam the door shut and lock it. Turning I lean against it and try to calm my crazy heart.

I look to Austin who is still high and dazed on the couch. I feel hurt but only because of how little he cared. I feel stupid, and angry with him for bringing drugs back into my apartment. I need to get out of here and away from him.

I don't waste any time. I grab my bag and stuff it full of my things. I grab another bag and fill it with Maddie's things, not forgetting the dog teddy I bought her for her first birthday. I grab some food and drink. I don't leave a note or anything for Austin, he doesn't deserve an explanation.

As I leave I aim my gun at the dickhead's apartment in case he tries anything.

I load up my truck and drop a note into Mr Wheeler. Then I'm off.

I don't look back and I have no idea where I'm going to stay, but every mile I put between myself and Austin, adds to the relief I feel.

CHAPTER SEVEN

Axel

I'm watching some shit on TV and not really paying attention. I just keep picking up my phone to dial the children's home and then chickening out before actually calling them. Frustrated with myself I throw my phone onto the couch and go and pour myself some Jameson. Just as I'm about to drink it there's a knock on the door.

I frown and look at the time. It's late, too late for any of my sisters to be driving out here. I reach for my gun and make my way to the door.

I open it slightly and see Patience.

"You gonna open the door properly or just stare at me through the crack all night?" She says sarcastically, rolling her eyes.

I pull open the door and gesture for her to come in. She does, and I watch as she nibbles on her bottom lip nervously. The one thing I never thought Patience would be is nervous.

I put my gun down on the counter, grab another glass, and pour her a Jameson.

"Your Ma teach you to always be that welcoming with a gun and a glass of whiskey?" She asks sarcastically.

I grunt in response. Picking up my glass I drink my whiskey. We just stare at each other, but not in an uncomfortable way. The only way I can describe it is that I can't look away, she has me completely captured.

I watch as she picks up her glass and downs the whiskey in one.

I grab the bottle and pour her another while she crunches her face up.

"Your mum ever teach you to savour a good whisky? This isn't a shot of tequila." I point out.

Patience crosses her arms and raises her eyebrow at me.

"Yeah, because you really savoured all them bottles you were wallowing in at the club?" She smirks.

I hate being called out on my shit, but more importantly hating the fact that she has seen me in that state. She's seen me at my lowest, at my most vulnerable.

"If there's no reason for you to be here, there's the door. Don't fucking let it hit you in the arse on the way out." I bite back.

I down the last swig of my whiskey and walk off into the lounge area. I sit down and flick the TV on.

Patience walks over. I notice she's doing that lip nibbling thing that she only does when she gets nervous.

"Look, I'm sorry. I didn't mean to bring that shit up. It's just, well…" Patience sighs and rubs her face.

She looks uncomfortable, tired, and stressed.

"Spit it out Patience, why are you here?" I say sharply, not meaning for it to come out that way.

"Can I crash here for a little while? Just until I can get enough money to get a new place." She rushes out, her eyes pleading. She looks ashamed to be asking me.

"Sure." I answer.

Patience jolts in surprise at my response.

"Sure? You're letting me stay just like that with no questions as to why or what happened?" Patience asks in confusion.

I shrug my shoulders.

"It's not any of my business. If you wanted to tell me you would've. As much as you may think I'm an arsehole, I don't make a habit of letting women sleep out on the street when they clearly need somewhere to stay." I answer back, getting up and heading to the front door.

"How in the hell do you know I'm desperate?" She asks.

"You haven't gone to your family. You haven't gone to the Satan's Outlaws, and you haven't gone to any of your work colleagues. For whatever reason that may be, you are desperate enough to come here. It's not like we've exactly seen eye to fucking eye." I point out while putting my boots on.

"Where are you going?" She asks.

"To get your stuff out of your truck, keys?" I answer holding out my hand.

She fumbles getting the keys out of her pocket and hands them to me. I don't say another word. I take them and walk out of the door, leaving her looking lost.

As I grab her things from the back of the truck, I can't help wondering why she's here. I bet my fucking left nut it was to do with that twat bloke of hers. If it wasn't, she would have said. In the short time I've known her, I know how stubborn Patience is. She would rather struggle and suffer than cry for help. That's why she's here and not with her family. It's because they'd be asking questions.

I walk back in and close the door and chuck her keys on the side. Placing her stuff down I look up and see her at the kitchen sink washing up dishes.

"What the fuck are you doing?" I ask.

Not fazed by my abrupt tone she just rolls her eyes.

"Cleaning the dishes that were sat here. What does it look like I'm doing?" she asks back sarcastically.

"I don't expect you to do dishes or any-thing else. Just because I said you can crash here that doesn't mean you owe me shit." I point out.

"Easy there, you need to chill out. It's just a few dishes. This ain't no repayment, this is me pulling my weight around here. Now I know it's like nine at night and I don't know about you, but I'm hungry. You eaten yet?" She asks, not looking up from the sink.

"I haven't. We can order in." I say, reaching for the menu off the fridge.

"No, I will cook. I looked in the fridge and I can throw something together. We can save some money." Patience shrugs.

"You don't have to." I answer.

"I know, but I want to." Patience looks over at me and smiles.

I swear when she looks at me like that, with her face so carefree, I'd cut off my dick and hand it to her if she asked for it. I'm in serious fucking trouble.

"Fine, I will get you some clean bedding." I say as I walk off.

I start stripping the covers off of the bed and replacing them with clean ones. I'm tucking it all in when Patience walks in.

"Wow, I can tell you were in the army. Hell, not a crease in sight and look at those damn perfect corners!"

I look from her to the bed. She's right of course. I don't even think about it anymore. It's ingrained in you from the first day to the last.

I don't realise my jaw is locked tight and my hands are balled into tight fists at my side. My breathing has escalated and I can feel anger flaring through my veins. Images flash through my mind of Joe, of Miguel.

I feel a warm hand touch my arm.

"Axel? Axel, are you okay?"

I snap out of it and look at Patience. There's concern written all over her face.

She moves slowly and wraps her arms around me. I freeze, not sure how to react to it.

"It's okay. You're safe. I got you." She whispers quietly, her hand placed on my chest.

I slowly wrap my hand around her, holding her tighter to me.

We just stand together. I inhale her sweet scent and it calms me. I swallow nervously.

"I…err…I just…"

"Shh, there's no need to explain. Let's make a deal. We don't need to reveal shit to each other unless we completely want to, or our lives depend on it." Patience says, leaning up and smiling at me.

I don't think, I let my body take control. I slowly move a strand of hair out of her face. I cup her face, lean in, and take her mouth, softly and slowly kissing her. Patience kisses me back, and that's all my body needs. I groan and deepen the kiss. I feel her grip my shirt.

I walk her back until I have her pressed up against the wall. I trail kisses down her neck, nipping and sucking.

"Axel." Patience says my name and my head

snaps up.

"I don't think this is a good idea." She breathes.

Her plump lips are swollen from my kiss. I run my thumb across her bottom lip. Her words don't match what her body is saying.

She closes her eyes as if she's using all of her self-control to resist.

"I'm sorry." I apologise.

Patience's eyes snap open and she holds my hand and shakes her head.

"No, no, don't apologise. I wanted it just as much. Maybe more. I still do. It's just, I can't right now, there's so much going on and..." She fumbles.

I watch the frustration and the struggle that's raging in her.

"Hey." I take hold of her chin. Those beautiful green eyes of hers connect with mine and the sadness in them is like a punch to the gut.

"Remember the deal, there's no need to explain. It's probably the smartest option. You have your shit and, well, I'm clearly fucked up." I reassure her.

She smiles and it takes everything in me not to kiss her again.

I step back, giving us distance, and I immediately miss her body pressed up against mine.

Patience lifts her hand and holds it out.

"To being two fucked up people. To being fucked up friends." She says.

I can't help but smile back at her. I take her hand in mine and we shake.

"To being fucked up." I agree.

She laughs and the sound does something to my messed up heart.

Before either of us can say or do anything else, the smoke detector starts going off.

"Fuck! The casserole!" Patience wails and runs out of the room.

I don't move. I look around the room and then back towards the doorway.

"Fuck me." I say to myself.

I know I'm screwed; she's got me. I've had a small taste of her and now I want more. I want all of her.

CHAPTER EIGHT

Patience

After eating a slightly burnt pasta casserole we watched some TV. His couch is really comfy and for the first time in a long time I actually feel relaxed. I feel myself start to fall asleep.

The next thing I know I'm being carried.

"Hhmm? I'll sleep on the couch." I mumble sleepily.

"Shut up and go back to sleep." I feel as well as hear his deep voice rumble.

"Whatever." I answer.

Axel snorts in response. I just cuddle into

him further.

I feel him place me down in his bed and I immediately cuddle into the pillow.

"Mmm, mufushu." I mumble.

"What?" Axel asks.

I can't make my brain function enough to form actual words, so I just nod my head.

I feel Axel sweep my hair from my face. I feel his warm gentle lips as he places a kiss on my forehead.

"Night Patience."

I awake the next morning feeling like I've had the best nights sleep of my life. I stretch out and smile to myself. Here I am, currently without a home, but I feel relaxed and happy. I should be stressed after all of the shit that went down yesterday. It's amazing what one night away from it all can do for you.

I get up and use the bathroom and then go in search of some coffee.

As I walk into the living area I see Axel sprawled out on the couch, his face peaceful in sleep. I smile. The blanket rides low on his hips, exposing his ripped body. While he's asleep I shamelessly sweep my eyes over his delicious body. My eyes go to where the blanket lays. I look back to check that Axel is still asleep and slowly lift the blanket to have a peak. Just as I'm leaning forward to look, Axel reaches out and grabs me. I don't know how he does it, but he manages to flip me so I'm under him. He leans over me, his eyes sleepy.

"You like trying to look at a guy's cock while they're asleep?" Axel asks.

My face burns bright red in embarrassment that I've been caught red handed trying to take a peak at his cock.

"Um, you weren't asleep, were you?" I stupidly ask.

Axel's lips twitch, fighting a smile. He shakes his head.

"No, I wasn't." He answers.

We both stare at each other in silence for a moment. I can feel his hard erection pressed up against me. I shift my hips slightly for friction. Axel's jaw tenses. I can see the desire in his eyes too.

Without warning he thrusts his hips, making me gasp, making me want more.

I move my hips, needing more friction, needing more of him.

All of a sudden Axel grabs my wrists and pins them above my head and stops the movement altogether.

"Stop, this can't happen. Fuck, I want you

so bad my cock is going to hate me for this. I just can't give you what you need. Not just that, you don't need another relationship or complication right now." Axel states.

Embarrassed I look away.

"Don't. Don't do that. Believe what I say. I could fuck you right now, I want to, I really fucking do."

He sounds tormented so I look up at him and the sadness is back behind his eyes.

"I'm fucked up and I'm no good for you. You're fucked up and at this moment in time, you're no good for me either."

My eyes soften and I pull a hand free and reach up and cup his face.

"In a world that's full of people, the fucked up will always find the fucked up. So maybe when we're a little less fucked up, we could, um, well, do this without stopping." I say smiling.

Axel surprises me with a full blown beautiful smile. My breath is completely blown away.

"That's the first time I've ever seen you smile properly." I whisper.

His smile immediately fades and I wish I could take those words back.

"I can't honestly remember the last time I had a reason to smile or felt like smiling." Axel answers.

My heart breaks hearing that. He looks to the side of the couch, his mind obviously going elsewhere.

"Well, I shall do my best to make you smile again. So friends?" I hold my hand out to shake. Axel gives me a small smile this time and shakes my hand.

"Now let me make you some of the best pancakes you'll ever taste. You want to go, um, you know, sort yourself out while I make them up?" I gesture to his erection.

Axel snorts back his laugh and jumps up, wrapping the blanket around his waist. He pulls me up to my feet and walks off to the bedroom.

"Give me ten minutes to have a shower and take care of this." He shouts over his shoulder.

"Eww god damn it Axel!" I yell back.

All I hear is his deep laughter. I can't deny, the thought of him in that shower relieving himself makes me clench my thighs together.

Damn it! Why couldn't I have met Axel a year ago? Or even in about a years time?

He's right though, I've got my shit to sort out. He clearly has his own stuff going on. Damn, I wish I could just be his casual fuck buddy but I know I would want more than that. The attraction I feel towards him is powerful right now so god knows how I will feel if we actually sleep together. That's a scary thought. It didn't feel anything like this with Austin.

I snap myself out of my deep thoughts about Axel and start making breakfast.

As I'm mixing up the batter for the pancakes there's a loud knock on the door. I look in the direction of the bedroom and can still hear the shower running so I make my way to the door and swing it open.

"Well, you took long enou-." Rose stops immediately when she sees it's me.

"Uh, hi. Axel is in the shower. I'm just making breakfast if you want to come in and join us?" I ask feeling anxious.

Rose eyes are alight. She nods.

"Oh yes, we would love too." She smiles widely.

"We?" I ask.

She points over her shoulder and I watch Blake help a heavily pregnant Lily out of the truck. Daisy and Carter following behind. Shit! At least Rip isn't here, he's a little to close to my folks. I wouldn't put it past him to call them and tell them to come over.

"Hey Firecracker." I hear rumbled from the other side of the open door. Standing there smoking is Rip.

"Fuck." I blurt.

He smirks and I roll my eyes.

"You gonna call my folks and tell them where I am?" I ask.

Rip just smiles and shakes his head.

"No." He answers.

I sigh, relieved.

"Not yet anyway." He states stamping out his cigarette and walking past me inside.

"Oh god, where is the bloody bathroom? I swear this kid is having a dance off on my bladder." Lily groans, walking past me. I point her in the right direction. She's not even fazed that I'm here.

"Oh wow, it's Patty right?" I turn back around to greet Daisy.

I nod and smile.

She pulls me in for a hug.

"So happy you guys found each other." She says squeezing my arm and walking past me.

Blake and Carter come in next carrying bags of groceries. Both of them just give me a chin lift.

I take a steadying breath and close the door, plastering a bright smile across my face.

"I'm just mixing up some pancakes. I will, um, just make some more batter. Coffee is in the jug. Help yourselves." I smile.

Rose and Daisy are on the kitchen stools watching me. I feel like I'm in a zoo and everyone is fascinated, watching every move I make.

"Well that's better, Jesus Christ how am I supposed to fit my fat arse on these stools?" Lily says, trying to master her big bump and hop onto the stool.

"Watch it fatty! This place is rented. The way your arse is getting you'll have to have that stool surgically removed." Rose snorts.

"Oh piss off! I remember when you were pregnant with Caden you were as big as a whale. I was ready to start calling you Moby Dick and spear you with my harpoon." Lily bites back.

I choke on my coffee, holding back the laughter. All three sisters burst out in hysterics. Christ! They are bat shit crazy but clearly love each other a lot.

"What the fuck?!" Is barked from the other side of the room.

Axel stands there in faded jeans and a fitted black t-shirt with his hair still wet from his shower. His eyes come to mine and I just smile and shrug. He rewards me with a smile and in that moment I want to run to him, wrap my legs around his waist, and beg him to make love to me.

"Holy fuck! I think the woman in the next

building just got pregnant from the sexual tension in here." Rose blurts.

I snap out of my daze and feel my cheeks heat in embarrassment.

"So why the hell on earth have you all decided to turn up to my place at nine in the bloody morning?" Axel questions.

"Well excuse us for being concerned! Rose said she had tracked you down so we wanted to see you. Mum and Dad don't know where you are yet, but I will be begging you to tell them soon because Mum is out of her mind worrying about you." Lily says, giving Axel a tight hug.

His eyes warm looking at his sister. He touches her belly and smiles.

Damn! My mother fucking ovaries!

Daisy walks up to him next and sniffles. She wipes her tears as he pulls her into a hug. I know he's the baby of the family, but he clearly takes care of them and watches over them, like a big brother should do.

There's more sniffles coming from Lily and Rose as they join in the hug. All three of his sisters have their arms wrapped around him.

"We got you, you know that right? Don't deal with this on your own." Lily says as she steps back, wiping her tears.

"I'm fine, I'm not on my own." His eyes flick

to me.

That statement and that look has me feeling like I've been hit by a bus. Sweet lord, this man is not making it easy on me. It's barely been an hour since we agreed to sort our shit out first.

I look up to see all eyes on me. I give them a small sheepish smile and shrug.

"Yeah, we can see that you're not on your own." Rose states.

Rose and Daisy are helping me in the kitchen cooking breakfast. I make the pancakes and waffles while they make the eggs and the bacon. Lily perches on a stool, watching us and chatting.

"So, okay, I have to ask as the big sister..." Rose gets interrupted.

"Hey! We're all his big sisters." Lily informs her.

"Fine, as we're all his big sisters, we have to know what is going on between you two. I hate to say this but he's going through some really tough shit at the moment that we don't even know about, and, well... what I'm saying is just don't add to it. Don't bring your shit to his door." Rose states firmly.

I nod and give her a tight smile.

"I understand, I do. Nothing is going on.

We're just friends. He's just putting me up until I can get somewhere else. I only turned up at his door last night."

They look a little surprised by my answer.

"What?" I ask.

"Well, it's just that the way you look at Ax and the way he looks at you. yet you say you're just friends? Those looks were not 'friends' looks. They were 'I'm gonna fuck you right now looks'." Lily points out.

"Lily!" Daisy chastises her.

"What? It's true. You saw the way they were looking at each other. I may be a hormonal whale, but I'm not blind." Lily adds.

All three of them look at me, waiting for a response. I thought I'd already given a response. I guess not.

"Err, well, I am attracted to him and I think he is attracted to me, but we agreed that we have enough going on in our own lives to not dive into anything. I mean I literally left Austin last night. So I ain't ready to just roll around with anyone else." I answer honestly.

They all just smile back at me.

"All in?" Rose turns to them and asks.

Lily and Daisy both nod eagerly, diving into the bags and pulling out their purses.

"Err, all in?" I ask confused.

They ignore me and carry on.

"I'm guessing tomorrow at midday." Daisy hands over twenty dollars.

"Ha! Don't be silly! Clearly Patty is called Firecracker for a reason, she'll give him hell first and make him beg for her. Yup, I'm going for tomorrow at 8pm." Lily puts in her twenty dollars.

"You're betting on me doing what exactly?" I ask.

Again I'm ignored.

"So you just said that she's going to make him sweat and make him beg for her, yet you only bet for eight hours later?" Daisy asks.

"Well yeah. I said she'll make him beg for it, but you saw how she looked at him! I'm guessing she doesn't have a lot of will power when it comes to Ax." Lily answers.

"Well you're both wrong. Because they will both give in on Wednesday. I'm thinking not until the evening, say around 7pm?" Rose adds in her twenty dollars.

"For the love of hell! Will one of y'all tell me what's going on?" I ask, frustrated.

Rose places her hand on mine and gives it a squeeze.

"Okay sorry, we got carried away. It's just

something we do. We've always done it since we were kids, except it was betting for sweets then. So we've just bet for when you and Ax will get it on. Not just in a sex way because well, eww, that gross and he's our brother, but in like a get together type way." Rose explains.

"Can I place a bet?" I ask.

All three of them look surprised that I've asked.

"You kinda have an insider advantage on this one. It's not exactly fair." Lily points out.

"Okay but I can't make your brother cave in. I can only go by when I think I'm ready for it to happen." I add.

"Fine, what are you going for?" Rose asks.

"At least six months from now." I answer.

All three of them burst out, full on belly laughing. It gets to the point where I'm concerned that Lily is laughing so hard it's causing the baby harm, her belly is moving so much.

"Oh Patty! You're so far off it's hilarious. I think you're going to fit right in with this crazy family." Daisy giggles.

CHAPTER NINE

Axel

To say I was shocked walking out of the shower and seeing nearly all of my family there is an understatement. I mean, just add my parents and it's a full blown family fucking gathering.

Seeing Patience surrounded by my sisters and very clearly being questioned to death and not being fazed by it at all was weird. Any other person would more than likely be cowering and would most definitely feel intimidated.

I guess that's what it's like being brought up in an MC, you must get used to constantly being around large groups of intimidating p\

"So how you doin' Ax?" Blake asks,
seat on the couch.

I look away from the girls and face the guys. I
shrug.

"This ain't no therapy group, don't worry.
Just remember what I told you, you ain't the
first or the last to be going through what you're
going through right now. We've seen it before.
So as brothers do, we're checking up on you and
making sure you're doing okay. We've watched
too many men pretend to be fine and lose their
battle. The Satan's doors are always open." Rip
states.

"You starting a new recruitment for men
now? Is this what you do? Look for ex-military
guys with PTSD, suck them in, and then use them
for their skills?" I ask, pissed off.

Rip spins and has me pinned to the wall with
his hand around my neck.

"Woah! Rip! What are you doing?" Rose
shouts and comes running over.

Blake and Carter don't even move, in fact, I
think I see them both fighting a smile.

I can feel myself getting angry.

"Get the fuck off of me Rip." I growl.

"Shut up boy! That's what I'm calling you, a
boy, because you're behaving like a fuckin' child.

Listen to my words of warning, it will get to a point where everyone is tired of your shit, tired of you constantly snapping and taking your shit out on people. You're fucking lucky that you have a family that give a shit about you. You're lucky I fuckin' love your sister because if it wasn't for her you'd be feeling my blade right now for disrespecting me!"

"Feeling your blade? I hope that's not a fucking euphemism? Bet you say that to all your boys." I goad, smiling.

"Ax!" Rose yells in warning.

Rip's face changes. It changes and I understand what makes people afraid of him, but I'm not afraid of him. I know what I'm doing. One swift move of his blade across my neck and the nightmares would be over. The haunting flashbacks, the torment I live with every day, it would all be fucking over.

Rip smiles.

"Nice try fucker. I ain't about to kill my old lady's brother and I ain't that fuckin' stupid to not realise when someone is damn well trying to play me! Now I know you'd love for me to end your life right now but you don't want that, not really." Rip states.

He leans in and speaks quietly so that only I can hear him.

"I see it, we all fuckin' see it. She is your

damn salvation, your fuckin' dark angel. You'd stop anyone from hurting her. Hell, right now I'm betting that you think that you'd be the one hurting her. Your head may be fucked and believe me, women like to fuck with it a bit more, but in a damn good way. They fuck with us in a way that means we'll do and fight anything that'll take them away. With her by your side you will fight your PTSD, and you'll want to do it because of her." Rip says, leaning back. He's smiling wide.

He knows. He sees it already, he fucking sees it. Loosening his grip on my neck he holds out his hand. I look from his face to his hand and shake my head. I grip his hand and he pulls me to him and slaps my back.

"Yeah, now you know what I'm fuckin' talking about!" Rip bellows with laughter.

"I'm sorry, did I black out for a second? What the hell was that all about?!" Rose questions.

Rip pulls her into his arms.

"Ain't nothing but two brothers airing shit that needed to be aired." Rip says smiling.

Rose rolls her eyes at him.

"I swear you have more emotional outbursts than a teenage girl during her period. Bloody men!" Rose moans.

"Shut up woman." Rip tells her.

Rose gasps and is about to lay a load of shit on him but he quickly takes her mouth, kissing her quiet.

I walk away, leaving them to it, and step outside for some peace.

I lean against the fence and close my eyes. I pinch the bridge of my nose, trying to get a hold of my emotions, raging inside me. I wanted nothing more than for Rip to end it all there and then. I didn't care. I just want peace.

I hear footsteps approach and look up. Patience stops just in front of me.

She doesn't say anything, she just looks at me. I don't try and hide the emotions behind my eyes; I let her see it all.

Without a word she walks straight to me, takes hold of my face in her hands, and kisses me. I immediately respond by kissing her back and holding her body close to mine. I walk until her back is pressed against the wall.

She nips my lip which makes me moan. I trail kisses down her neck and nip hard. She lets out a gasp and moans when I lick my tongue over where I bit. I feel her moans go straight to my cock. I'm using everything in my power not to fuck her up against the wall.

"Well bugger me! We were all wrong! They're practically already shagging. Daisy, you're the winner with the closest time." Rose shouts from the window of my apartment.

Moment broken I break the kiss, pulling my head back slightly to look at her. Patience is staring up at me, her eyes hooded, her cheeks with a slight blush, and her lips swollen from my kiss.

"Fuck me." I sigh, running my finger through her hair and tucking it behind her ear.

"Is that a statement or a question?" She asks.

"Both." I answer honestly.

Her eyes are alight. She liked that answer. I groan, wishing my family were anywhere but my apartment.

"You know this is fucking crazy right?" I ask.

Smiling patience nods.

"Totally fucking crazy."

"I'm so messed up Patience. I don't want to hurt you and mess your life up more. But god! I can't fucking keep away from you. I want nothing more than to bury myself deep inside you right now. It's taking all of my self-control to not kick my family out." I state.

I watch as she runs her tongue across her bottom lip. I lean down and take her mouth again.

I slow the kiss.

"Stop distracting me with that perfect

mouth of yours." I whisper across her lips.

"I meant what I said. I don't want to mess your life up more." I repeat.

"I know, but there's something between us and I want to see what happens. I can't stop thinking about you. Messed up attracts messed up, right? So let's get fucking messy." Patience says with a smile and a wink.

I throw my head back laughing.

"Seriously, you're a damn good man and I know I'm safe with you. I feel like my life, our lives, will get better together. Maybe we're meant to help each other heal and make each other happy?" Patience suggests.

I smile and kiss her again. I can't help myself, she's like a drug.

"Y'all gonna stop making out like damn teenagers and have some breakfast or what?" Rip yells down.

I look up to see him smiling. I give him a smile and lift my chin. He nods.

"Come on, let's face this shit. God, they're going to be relentless." I moan, pulling patience to my side.

The guys all wolf whistle as we walk inside. My sisters grin like Cheshire cats.

Patience laughs, I kiss the top of her head and then whisper in her ear.

"When they're gone, you're mine." I wink.

She sucks in a shuddering breath and I smile, knowing what effect that had on her.

Damn! I know I shouldn't be starting any-thing with her, but her smell, her smile, her touch. I can't keep away. Something in me is pulling me to her, something in me needs her. I just pray that me needing her, wanting her, doesn't break her more. I want to be the one that heals her, that fixes her, not the one that destroys her. I guess that's a risk we're both taking. It's a risk I know deep down in my fucking soul will be beyond worth it.

CHAPTER TEN

Patience

I can't explain the swirls of emotions that are rolling around in my stomach right now. I feel like a teenager again: excited, nervous, and horny.

I'm so thankful that his family are good people because it makes the waiting to be alone with Axel easier to deal with.

My cell starts ringing from my bag and without looking I answer.

"Hello?"

"Where the fuck are you?" Austin asks, sounding pissed off and rough.

"Err, look Austin, after last night I'm done. I'm done with your shit. I'm done with being treated like trash."

"I'm not done with you. I say when we are fuckin' done!" Austin yells down the phone.

I feel myself getting extremely pissed off. I don't hold anything back.

"Fuck you! I could have been fucking raped last night! You were happy to let that creep have me just so you could get your drugs! Do not call me again! Do not come near me again or I will call in the Satan's." I threaten and disconnect, not giving him the chance to reply.

I feel heat on my back. I spin around and come face to chest with Axel.

"You were nearly raped last night?" Axel asks, his face cold and his jaw locked.

"I, err, well, it didn't get that far...I..." I pause as I notice Blake, Carter, and Rip moving in behind him. All of them have their arms crossed over their chests. They have the same look as Axel, like they all want to kill someone.

"Look, I dealt with it. It's fine. I can take care of myself, you know that Rip. And I did! It was just my creepy neighbour." I try to appease them.

"Fuck off. Don't start the 'I can take care of myself' shit Firecracker. We all know you can, but that don't mean that family can't help. We're here to look out for you when you need and we can give you some extra damn help! That's it, I'm done lying to your folks. I'm calling them right now. I promised if there was any trouble I would call them. Well this fuckin' counts!" Rip barks and storms outside.

I sigh and pinch the bridge of my nose. This is why I distanced myself from the Satan's. I love their loyalty, but it's my life and my business. If I was a guy I wouldn't be treated this way.

"Great! Now my parents are involved and no doubt half the damn club will show up." I sigh.

Axel grabs my chin, forcing me to look at him.

"Stop being a brat Patience. You being attacked, nearly raped last night, it's a big deal whether you dealt with it or not. Think of it like this, if it was Maddie, would you want to be there to take care of her? You'd want to be there for her, and I'm going to guess you'd want to kill the bastard too?" Axel asks.

I close my eyes because god damn it, he's right. I hate that he's right. The thought of anyone hurting my baby girl makes me sick to my stomach.

"Fine, okay. I guess you're right." I mumble.

Axel smiles.

"Baby I'm always right." He smirks.

I snort back my laughter and roll my eyes.

Axel leans down and take my mouth, kissing me softly and gently.

We look at each other and no words are needed. I know, and he knows: we have each other. We are going to be messed up together.

It's not long before I hear the rumbling of not one bike engine but several.

"Sweet Jesus." I groan.

There's a loud bang on the door and Axel opens it. My ma storms right past him and right for me.

"Patty, what in the hell?! You get nearly god damn raped and you don't tell anyone, you don't even ring your parents, your family?! What do you do? You come here to Axel's even though you hardly know him." She fumes.

"Did she tell you?" She spins round to ask Axel. He shakes his head in response.

"It was no big deal Ma, I kicked his ass. No clothes were removed. It's all good." I try to re-assure her.

The pain in her eyes hurts me and I know what's she is going to say. I silently beg her not to.

"After what you went through last time I think that just maybe, just god damn maybe, it's something that should be taken fuckin' seriously Patty!" She yells.

I get to my feet, having had enough being yelled at.

"It is what it is. That's in the past! It doesn't affect me now and I don't understand why it should effect you!" I yell back.

"Are you serious right now? You were raped. You were raped by a club member! That is something that's always going to affect me. I am your god damn mother! You are my daughter! I failed you then and I will not fail you now!" She screams. Tears sting her eyes.

I can feel everyone's eyes fixed on me. I grit my teeth and clench my fists at my side.

"It happened to me, not you. Me! I've come a long way since then and I'm trying to forget it. Why the fuck can't you?! Why does everything that happens to me have to go back to that time? I will remind you that it's also fucking personal and you've just screamed it in front of everyone! Anything else you want to share with them while we're here airing our shit? Do you also want to tell them that the sick fuck that raped me is Maddie's father?! Hhmm?" I scream, tears streaming down my face.

I walk towards the door, needing to get as far

away from here as possible. Before I walk out of the door I spin around and face her.

"This! This is why I've distanced myself from you, from the club. It's my life, my business, not everyone else's. Don't come after me. Leave me the fuck alone!"

Axel grabs my arm, halting me. There's sadness, pity, in his eyes. This is exactly what I didn't want. I shrug him off and storm out.

My pa smiles when he sees me but as soon as he gets a look at my face his smile falls. He grabs me.

"What's happened?" He asks.

"Ma, you, the club, my private life being aired! I need space, I need to get away." I seethe.

He looks at me, pulls me to him, and hugs me tight. He kisses the top of my head.

I can't help but wrap my arms around him and cry into his chest. Why are fathers so good at soothing? It's like they have these magic arms that take it all away. The safety of their hold is like no other.

"It's okay darlin'. Your mom means well, she just worries about you, that's all. I know you're a strong independent woman because god damn, that what I raised you to be. But you need to listen to your Pa on this one. Being strong and independent don't mean you can't lean on others when it's too much for those strong shoulders to bare." He soothes.

I sniffle and nod.

"Now you gonna come on in with me and sort this shit out?" He asks.

I sigh and nod.

"Fine. I suppose they all know what happened to me in there and I'm gonna have to face them at some point." I relent.

"That's my girl. Now when we get in there you're gonna give you're ma a hug and apologise, and she will do the same. You're both as bad as each other. You two really are a pain in my ass." He grumbles as we walk in.

As we enter the rumble of chatter ceases and all eyes come to us. Axel walks directly to me, takes my hand, and pulls me into his arms. The move shocks me but I bury my face into his broad chest and close my eyes.

"Someone want to update me on what the fuck is going on here?!" Pa barks, pointing to me and Axel.

"Oh, them! Well, they official started sort of seeing each other all of what, maybe two hours ago? But they've been pining for each other longer than that." Rose yells across the room.

"You failed to mention that outside darlin'." Pa points out.

"Sorry Pa. It's…it's…well…um." I stammer.

"Sir, the bottom line is that I like your daughter a lot and she likes me. There is something between us and we're seeing how it goes. I promise you, I will never hurt your daughter. I won't let no other fucker hurt her either." Axel States firmly.

Pa just looks him up and down and nods.

"Fair enough boy. Treat her right and we ain't got no problem." Pa reaches out and shakes Axel's hand.

"Baby girl." Ma whispers from behind me. I turn in Axel's arms and look at my ma, her tear stained eyes look back at me.

"I'm so sorry…I just…Well when I heard, it took me back to that day. I thought I'd failed you again." She apologises.

I step out of Axel's hold and pull my Ma in for a tight hug.

"I'm sorry too Ma." I sniffle.

"Love you baby girl." She sobs.

"Love you Ma." I croak.

"Oh sweet Jesus! You girls are gonna be the death of me. Where's the damn beer?" Pa grumbles, walking further into the apartment.

"It's ten AM!" Lily shouts.

"Well it's fucking five PM somewhere sweetheart. All of this shit before lunch means I deserve a damn beer!" Pa booms across the room.

"Already got you covered man." Mammoth hands my dad a beer.

I turn and see the rest of the guys leaning against the kitchen worktops drinking beers.

"Mammoth, Khan, Rubble." I nod.

"Good to see you Firecracker. It's good to see you haven't changed." Khan winks.

I flip him off and he fakes a wounded heart.

"Where's Maddie?" I ask.

"She's with Wes. He's bringing her along in a little bit." Ma says smiling.

I smile and my heart warms immediately at the thought of seeing my cupcake. I've not been the best mom, but I'm trying my best. She didn't ask to be brought into the world the way she was and I can honestly say I never regretted having her. She was the light after a very dark time; she still is. On the days when things are too much, just the thought of her brightens my day.

"Can I talk to you for a moment?" Axel asks from behind me.

I snap out of my daze and nod. He grabs my hand and pulls me outside to talk.

He pulls me to him and wraps his arms tightly around me. It takes me a moment to ease into him.

"Listen, I think the last couple of hours have proven how incredibly messed up we both are. I mean shit! We've not even been on a fucking date." Axel sighs.

I watch as his jaw tenses and he looks off into the distance, looking torn, troubled, or angry. I can't tell which. I brace for whatever he's about to say. The truth is, for whatever reason it may be, I'm scared that he will end us before we've even started. It's insane. We've made out, we've talked, but mainly we've just argued. I barely know him, and he barely knows me. But in the short time I've known him, something inside me tells me this is it, that he is it.

"I really fucking like you, but..."

I interrupt Axel before he can finish.

"But it's too much and you think we should cool it off." I finish for him.

"What? No. Why, do you?" Axel surprises me.

I smile and shake my head.

"Good. What I'm trying to say is that, well, obviously we're both seriously fucked up. It may not seem it but just having you around is helping me. Unless you decide otherwise I'm just reaffirming that as fucking messed up as it all is, I want to take you on that date. I want us to have some normal shit in our lives. So just incase you were thinking of backing off, don't. I don't fucking want you to." Axel states as he tucks my hair behind my ear and cups my face.

"I wouldn't have it any other way." I smile.

Axel smiles before crashing his mouth down on mine, his lips caressing, and his tongue stroking and teasing mine. I moan and Axel lets a deep groan out from his throat.

"Oh for fuck sake you're at it again?! Jeez I'll be a bloody auntie again before I know it!" Rose yells.

We stop and start laughing, watching Rose walk back inside flipping us off.

I bite my lip, smiling up at Axel. He runs his thumb across my lip, his eyes following the movement.

"Umm Axel?" I ask.

His eyes come to mine.

"Yeah baby." He answers, and god do I like hearing him calling me that.

"Can we keep this between us? I want to keep this from Maddie for a little while? Because, well, I don't want her getting confused or upset. If this doesn't work out, say in like a couple of weeks, I don't want her to get attached to you for her to lose you." I explain.

Axel smiles and kisses me briefly.

"Of course. You're her mother and you have to put her first. Just so you know though, this isn't going to be over in a couple of weeks, so you might want to get that thought out of your head." Axel adds before kissing me again.

I hope he never stops kissing me.

CHAPTER ELEVEN

Axel

I swear to Christ it's like the past twenty-four hours have gone by in a complete fucking blur. One minute I'm on my own wanting nothing but solace and even contemplating taking my own life, and now here I fucking am with my pain in the arse sisters and what feels like half of Texas, including Maddie. She is so fucking cute, it's no wonder she steals everyone's hearts, she might even be warming up my dead one.

"Hey! Axel! I'm talking to you!" Maddie taps me on the arm.

I shake my head and smile down at her. She's currently sitting on my lap and telling me who her favourite princesses are and which ones she would like for her birthday.

"Sorry princess, my mind wondered off for a moment there. What were you saying?" I ask.

Maddie smiles back up at me.

"I said, who is your faveworte pwincess?" She asks.

"Well I only know one." I answer.

Maddie stares at me, clearly shocked that I only know one princess, especially after she's just listed at least 10.

"Who?" She asks impatiently.

"Well, this princess is the best of the best. I mean, the others just don't compare. All of the other princesses want to be just like her. She's beautiful inside and out, she has a very caring heart, and, well, I haven't heard her sing, but I can imagine her voice is beautiful." I state.

Maddie's little face is in awe. She's captivated, waiting and wanting to know who this princess is.

"Who is she? Pwease Axel tell me." she begs.

I laugh and smile. I lift Maddie off of my lap so she's standing. I get up and stand in front of her. I look up and notice Patience watching me, her eyes soft and a smile on her lips.

I bow down and take a knee in front of Maddie.

"Your highness, you are the most perfect

princess there is." I say.

Maddie lets out a loud squeal and then bursts out laughing. I'm nearly knocked over as she jumps at me, wrapping her little arms around my neck.

"Oh Axel, you are a funny guy. I'm not a real pwincess." She giggles.

I pull back a bit and look at her little face.

"Maddie, just because you're not royalty, that doesn't mean you're not a princess. You are more beautiful than any other princess, you are as caring as any princess, you are a princess of the highest standard. Never let anyone tell you otherwise." I state.

Her smile beams across her face. She hugs me tight and kisses me on the cheek before jumping down and running off to her mum.

"Mama! Did you hear what Axel said? He said I was a real pwincess!" She says with so much excitement I think she might burst.

Patience's eyes meet mine. No words are exchange but her look says it loud and clear: thank you.

"Well played with that one man! To get my approval you need my daughter's and granddaughter's approval too. I think it's safe to say you just got that. Although that doesn't mean I won't kick your ass if time calls for it! It just means you're cool for now." Big Papa says, coming to stand next to me.

"Okay, bit soon for that speech don't you think? It hasn't even been a day. We haven't even gone on a date."

He laughs and claps me on my shoulder.

"Listen here, I ain't stupid and I ain't blind. You must be though if you don't see it. Hell, just take it, and one day when you've got kids of your own you'll get it. When you see it like we all do, you'll get it. I thought you Brits were supposed to be smart?" Big Papa hollers, holding his side and laughing.

I just look at him in confusion. What the hell is this guy on about? I shrug.

The front door is slammed open and in storm Mum and Dad.

"Oh shit." I mumble.

All three of my sisters laugh. I give them an evil look.

Mum walks right up to me with her hands on her hips. She looks furious.

"Do you have any idea how bloody worried I've been?! I rang the army! They told me you'd gone AWOL, pissing AWOL! I knew that was a load of shite because you adore the army! We were all careful not to say anything to you at the wedding. We could see something was going on, so we all took a step back to give you time. Time! Bloody time! You hide not ten bloody minutes away! Then your sisters tell me you're safe and well but we need to leave you alone. Then suddenly I get a call to come over and see you AND you're with Patience?! Do you hate me? Is that it? Do you hate your mother?" Mum screeches.

I pinch the bridge of my nose and take a deep breath.

"Mum, I don't hate you, I just needed time on my own. If you'd known where I was you wouldn't have given me that. Also, Patience and I aren't together! We haven't even gone out yet. We haven't had a chance because you're all bloody here. I'm sorry I hurt you Mum, but I needed time." I answer sincerely.

Mum's eyes soften.

"You're okay though?" She asks, sniffling.

Damn it! I can't handle seeing my mum cry. I pull her into my arms.

"Yeah, I'm getting there." I sigh and kiss the top of her head.

"Good, but cut me out again and you'll leave me no choice, I shall be forced to move in with you. Now, where's Patience, let me give her a hug and warn her what she's letting herself in for." Mum pats my face and walks over to Patience.

I shake my head and laugh.

Dad walks up to me, pulls me into a hug, and pats my back.

"I'm glad you're doing alright son but pull a stunt like that again and I'll kick your arse. Your mum has been worried sick about you. She's made my life hell these past few weeks! Don't fucking do it again." Dad warns.

I smile, knowing it's his way of dealing with his emotions, giving me a bollocking for making him worry.

I look around the room and notice the guys are in a close huddle and a few quiet words are being exchanged. Gone are the smiles and relaxed faces. They look tense and ready for blood.

I walk over to them and stand behind Blake.

"What's going on?" I ask.

They break and turn to me. No one says anything, they just look to Rip.

"Club business." Is all he says.

"Right, so why are these guys talking about it when they ain't brothers? Stop bullshitting me, you're in my home. Judging by the look on all of your faces I can see something is going down. I'm going to hazard a fucking guess that it's something that could affect my sisters. So I will ask again, what the fuck is going on?!" I demand.

I see Blake, Khan, and the others cough back their smiles and laughter. I don't pay them any attention, my eyes are solely focused on Rip. I've pissed him off, I can see that. I feel my lips twitch, fighting back a smile. Rip notices and his eyes almost turn to sheer ice.

"Easy brother, he's family." Khan whispers in his ear.

Rips jaw is set so tight I'm surprised it's not cracking.

He steps forward coming nose to nose with me but I don't back down.

"Listen here G.I. Joe, you may be all big and badass playing war but this is one war you do not want to start. Are we fuckin' clear?!" Rip growls.

I don't flinch or say anything. I don't react at all.

"Now the sooner you learn this the better. What goes on in my club is mine and my brothers business, who I fuckin' tell is down to me. You want to know what is going on? I'm offering you a place in the club. But listen to me, what I say goes. Let me explain it in a way that you'll understand. I am your sergeant major, I am your captain, your colonel, your mother fuckin' General. I am the President of the Satan's Outlaws. You will fall in line and respect what I say." Rip yells.

Again, I don't react. I can see that it's taking all of his restraint not to hand me my arse right now.

The whole room has gone silent.

"I want in, but on one condition." I demand.

"You've got this wrong; you ain't the one making the conditions." Rip smiles back.

"Hear me out. I want in. I understand I can't be patched straight in, but there is no fucking way I'm being your club's bitch to get that patch. You need my skills. You don't need me mopping up the bar. You know that. I'll respect your orders, your choices, but I will give you my opinion regardless of whether you ask for it or not. That's it, that's all there is too it." I state.

Rip eyes are alight. He wanted this, he's wanted me to be a part of the club since we met. He knew my skills. This mother fucker just played me.

Rip smiles when he sees the realisation flicker across my face.

"Yeah fucker, I agree to your conditions. Welcome to hell mother fucker!" He yells, pulling me to him and slapping me on the back.

The guys all laugh and cheer.

"Don't fuckin' try that shit again. I will gut you, family or not." Rip whispers in my ear.

I nod, knowing what he's saying is the truth. It doesn't scare me. Hell, it doesn't worry me. I questioned him and called him out in front of his men, I'd be more concerned if he didn't threaten me.

"Now that all the family drama is done with, we have a celebration cookout at the club later. We gotta welcome the newest member of the Satan's Outlaws!" Khan yells.

"Oh Jesus." Says Rose.

"I may as well just dye my hair grey." Mum says.

"I call church in an hour at the club. Axel, be there. The rest of the brothers need to vote you in." Rip informs me.

I nod and he leaves along with everyone else to go and get the food and everything ready for the cookout.

Maddie has her arms wrapped around Patience's neck and is showering her with kisses. Patience says goodbye and that she will see her later.

I leave them to it and start to clear up the dishes.

Patience walks next to me and leans her hip against the counter.

"What is it?" I ask.

"Why did you do that?" She asks.

"Do what?" I reply.

"Join the Satan's." She answers.

I put the plate back into the soapy water and grab a towel. Drying off my hands I go to her and lift her so she's sitting on the counter. I stand in between her legs.

"Why, are you not happy I joined the Satan's?" I ask.

She sighs and shakes her head.

"No, not really. I mean shit! I moved away from the Satan's for a reason. They were, are, controlling. I wanted to be free from that. My whole life has been about the club, everything, I wanted out. I wanted freedom." Patience sighs, looking down.

I reach up and cup her face, making her look at me,

"You are free. You're not a little kid anymore. Just because I've joined doesn't mean it has to take over your life too. Okay? I promise. Plus I really like the image of you pressed up against me on the back of my bike." I say.

Patience snorts.

"I think you're forgetting I'm my own biker bitch. As soon as I have the money I'll have my own Harley."

I sweep her hair off her neck and trail kisses.

"Hhmm. I will happily ride on the back of your bike with you nestled between my legs." I say in between kisses.

She pulls back and looks at me.

"What?" I ask.

"You'd do that?" She asks.

I shrug and nod, not really understanding why she's bothered by it.

"You know no biker would be seen riding on their woman's bike. The women ride on the back of their man's bike. That's the way it is."

"I'm not your normal biker. So now we have this cook out thing to go to tonight, and I know we haven't really had alone time, but if I take you in my bed now and fuck you, taste you, we won't be leaving for a really fucking long time."

The look in Patience's eyes has me using all of my efforts not to take her right here, right now.

"Baby, don't look at me like that." I beg.

She smiles and pulls my mouth onto hers. I love the taste of her and the feel of her mouth on mine. I lose what hold I had and grab her behind, pulling her flush with me so she can feel exactly what she's doing to me. She lets out a gasp.

"Feel what you do to me baby." I whisper as I nip and kiss along her neck and collar bone.

Patience leans back and gives me more access. I trail kisses down across her bust. I lift her top off of her, leaving her in her red lace bra. I step back and just look at her. Her jet black hair is hanging wildly down over her shoulders, her bright lust filled green eyes watching me. I run my finger under her bra strap. My other hand reaches round and unclasps her bra. I slowly pull the straps over her shoulders and down her arms, freeing her fucking beautiful breasts.

"Fuck baby." I rasp.

Patience tugs on my t-shirt and pulls me to her. My mouth crashes down on hers. My hands are everywhere. I cannot get enough of the feel of her soft body. I take her nipple in my mouth, teasing her with my tongue. She watches me with hooded eyes. I don't take my eyes off of her as my hand glides into her panties.

I slowly run my finger over her clit, still teasing her nipple in my mouth. I slide my finger inside. Her eyes roll back and she lets out a sexy moan. I move over her G spot and slowly add another finger, stroking her, stretching her, feeling her build. I kiss and nip up her neck and take her mouth. I tease her with my tongue and bite her lip, making her gasp.

"Look at me baby, give me those beautiful green eyes." I demand.

She opens her eyes, they're full of desire.

"Good. Keep them open." I order.

Keeping up the movement with my fingers circling her G spot, I move so my thumb is on her clit, adding to her pleasure. She moans, closing her eyes.

"Eyes open baby." I remind her.

Her eyes flutter open. I keep circling, feeling her build and tighten on my fingers. I smile, knowing she is close to the edge.

"Come for me baby. Let me feel you." I order just as I bend down and take her nipple in my mouth. She cries out and clamps around my fingers.

"Oh fuck Axel! Shit!" Patience cries out.

Her hips buck erratically and I slow my movements as she comes down from her orgasm.

Patience opens her eyes. I remove my hand from her panties and place my fingers in my mouth, sucking the taste of her off of them. I moan.

"Hmm, fucking delicious." I state. Her eyes grow hungry again and I smile.

Patience leans forward and goes to undo my jeans. I grab her hand, stopping her.

"No, not now. I told you we have the cookout. If it wasn't important to everyone else and Maddie wasn't going to be there waiting for you, I'd say fuck it, but we can't. So baby, I will wait." I say, tucking her hair behind her ear.

"Damn it, you're right. But we are good for

after the cookout, right?" She asks.

I laugh and nod.

"Fucking counting on it."

I step back and pull her off of the counter and into my arms. I kiss her then step back and slap her arse.

"Now go and get dressed. We're going shopping for a bike." I smile.

She walks off, flipping me the bird as she goes.

Fuck me! I'm in trouble. I've not even been inside her and she's got me fucking whipped.

CHAPTER TWELVE

Patience

I can't wipe the smile from my face as I shower. I don't know what it is that feels so different with Axel. It's crazy fast yet it doesn't feel wrong, it just fits. Normally I'd be running for the hills right now, especially after Austin, but I know that Axel isn't like Austin in any way. The fact that my Pa didn't want to kill him at first sight is saying something.

I chuck on a pair of cut off jean shorts which come to just below my ass, and pair them with a plain black tank top. I sit on the edge of the bed put on my black strapped wedged sandals. I walk over to my bag and pull out my black lace choker and put on my silver bangles. I grab my biker jacket and head out to the living area.

Axel is sitting at the breakfast bar scrolling through his phone. I cough to get his attention. His head whips up in my direction and his eyes do a sweep of my body. His eyes become hungry and I watch as he runs his tongue along his bottom lip. Fuck he's hot. I walk towards him, putting an extra sway in my hips. When I'm just a foot away Axel reaches out and grabs me, pulling me too him. He crashes his mouth on mine, kissing me fiercely. He stops and we are both breathing heavily.

"You look fucking amazing baby." He compliments.

I smile.

"I guessed you liked the outfit. Come on, let's get you a bike." I say excitedly.

I cannot wait to be back on a bike. I miss the freedom you get from riding on the open road. I miss the feeling of the wind in my hair. Even though we're not shopping for a bike for me, I'm just excited to be on the back of Axel's.

I drive us to Denvy's Custom Motorcycles. It's the only place I trust, he's been selling the Satan's Outlaws' custom bikes since before I was born.

I pull up and put the truck in park.

"This place?" Axel asks, looking at the big

warehouse with just a sign on the front.

I smile.

"Come on. Just wait until you see what Denvy has." I say as I jump down from the truck.

We walk inside, Axel's hand on the small of my back.

I see a few of the guys working on some bikes. They greet me as we walk past them but eye up Axel.

I walk to the office door and knock.

"Yeah!" Denvy shouts.

I walk in and there's Denvy a sixty year old guy with a shaved head, silver goatee, and tattoos coming up from his neck and covering his bald head. He's pretty much covered head to toe in tattoos.

He's a big guy, fit, and still works out regularly. He certainly doesn't look sixty.

He gets up smiling and walks towards me and pulls me in for a hug.

"Well, well Firecracker! What do I owe the pleasure of seeing your beautiful face today?" He asks.

"Well Denvy, I was wondering if you could hook my friend here up with one of your bikes?" I ask.

Denvy's eyes cut to Axel and sweep him, assessing him.

"Hey, he's cool. He's joining Satan's. Also, he's the Rocke sisters' brother." I add, knowing full well that almost everyone around here has heard of them. They've caused quite a stir. Axel raises his eyebrow in question.

"Your sisters made quite an impression on the town and, well, the surrounding towns." I inform him.

He shakes his head and smiles.

"Why doesn't that fucking surprise me." He answers.

"Well then son, if those are your sisters, and you're becoming a brother, let's get you a fucking bike. Can't be a damn biker without a bike!" Denvy leads the way.

He walks us out the back and into another large warehouse. He unlock the door and gestures for us to step inside. It's pitch black.

"Welcome to fucking paradise." Denvy says, flicking on the lights.

Once my eyes adjust I smile. There are rows upon rows of beautiful bikes. I look to Axel and my smile grows.

His face is in awe. His eyes flicker from bike to bike.

"Told you this was the place to go." I add.

"You weren't fucking kidding. This place is amazing!" Axel says smiling.

"Well don't just stand there, go look around. Find the right girl for you. If you can't find her, come to my office and we can talk about making you a custom." Denvy says, leaning against the wall.

I walk with Axel up and down the rows, admiring the paint work and the detailing. Axel comes to a stop in front of a bike. It's a custom Harley fat boy, matt black with polished chrome pipes. It's simple but badass. It's so Axel.

"This is her. This is the one." Axel points out.

"She's perfect." I agree.

He calls over Denvy, who nods his head in agreement. He knew before we even came in. It's like he has a special power. He knows from looking at the buyer which bike they will pick, which bike is perfect for them.

"So let's get you a helmet and you can go on a test ride. You taking Darago out for a spin?" Denvy asks. I grin wide and nod.

"Darago?" Axel asks.

"Darago is Firecracker's bike. It chose her." Denvy adds.

"You have a bike?" Axel questions.

"Ah well, I'm about five thousand dollars off

of her being mine officially. Denvy here keeps her safe for me until the day comes when she'll be fully mine. You want to see her?" I ask excited to show him.

Axel smiles warmly and nods. I take his hand and lead him to her.

"Ta dah!" I say when we reach her.

I run my hand over the air brushed fuel tank. It's detailed with a marble flame effect in a plum and sort of red mix. She has a beautiful chrome engine and accessories. I sigh with happiness, knowing that one day she'll be mine. The only modification I want is either a seat on the back with belt or a side car for Maddie.

"Isn't she a beauty?" Denvy asks Axel.

"She sure is." Axel answers, but he's not looking at the bike, he's looking at me.

"Alright you loved up fuckers. Let's you get you out on a test drive before I get fucking pregnant." Denvy roars over his shoulder.

We both laugh and follow him.

We are both on our bikes, engines rumbling.

"You sure you know how to ride a bike? I don't want you to feel less of a man when I out ride you." I tease.

Axel doesn't say anything, he just smiles and pulls off, flipping me the bird over his shoulder. I burst out laughing but I'm quick to catch him up.

Soon we're riding side by side. The sun warms my face and the breeze whips around me. I can't wipe the smile from my face. This is home. This is heaven. Pure freedom.

I look to Axel who looks just as at peace as I feel. He was made to be on a bike. He looks hot as hell riding a bike; I knew he would.

After twenty minutes we are pulling back into Denvy's.

I park up and hop off my bike and walk straight up to Axel before he's even switched the engine off. I grab his shirt and pull hard to bring his mouth down onto mine.

I kiss him passionately, pouring out what twenty minutes of riding with him has done to me. Axel moans, pulling my body closer to his. He takes control of the kiss.

"I see you like the bike then?" Denvy coughs next to us.

We stop kissing immediately and laugh. I rest my face in Axel's chest, embarrassed.

"Sorry Denvy." I mumble through my laughter.

"Err, yeah Denvy. I'll take her." Axel laughs.

"That's great son. Now if you two can hold off from getting all hot and heavy for a while, let's go to my office and sort out the paperwork."

He says wiping his oil stained hands on a rag.

While Axel is sorting the paperwork out I grab a cloth and rub down Darago.

A while later Axel comes out with the papers in his hand.

"All good?" I ask.

"Yeah, I have one question though." Axel says pulling me into his arms.

"Okay shoot, what do you want to know?"

"Okay. One, why haven't you asked your folks for help with the bike? They seem like they would help you out in a second. And two, Darago?" He asks, tucking my hair behind my ear.

"Okay to answer question one, I will never ask for help unless I'm desperate. As much as I want her, she's a luxury, not a necessity. I know she's mine and I will appreciate her even more when I've paid for her by myself. Two, Darago is the warrior goddess associated with volcanoes. Her fiery nature was appeased by giving her annual sacrificial offerings. Denvy came up with it. He said it suited the bike and me." I say smiling.

"You are one stubborn woman, but I admire that. Now tell me what sort of offerings am I supposed to give the warrior goddess?" He asks as he leans in, kissing along my neck.

"Hhmm, I'm sure I'll think of something. Now come on, you ride your bike and I'll drive the truck. We have a cookout to get to." I pat his chest.

Axel salutes and kisses me briefly before walking to his new bike and sitting on her. He starts her up. The loud rumble of the engine roars as he revs it. I don't know what it is but seeing him on that bike makes me just want to jump him right here right now. Axel catches me staring. He has a big grin across his face. I shake my head, snap out of it, and flip him off which makes him laugh. I jump in the truck and follow him to the clubhouse.

As we approach the large metal gates I can already smell the food cooking and hear the loud music playing. I smile to myself. I always loved cookouts. It has been a long while since I've been to one.

I park the truck up next to Axel. I jump out and Maddie comes running at me full throttle.

"Mama!!!" She screams, smiling.

I open my arms wide and catch her. Holding her tight I spin her around. Her giggle warms my heart and I shower her with kisses and blow a big raspberry on her cheek, She grabs my face in her hands and does the same to me, although it's a lot wetter.

"I miss you so much Mama." She says giving me endless kisses.

"I miss you more Cupcake." I reply honestly.

I turn to Axel who's watching Maddie and I intently. His eyes are soft and he's smiling.

"Oh Axel!" Maddie squeals and literally throws herself from my arms to Axel, who makes quick work of catching her.

"I'm sooo happy you came too. I can show you my pwincess castle. Pops made it for me." she says excitedly.

"I'd love that! Lead the way." Axel gestures.

Maddie jumps down and runs ahead.

"This way!" She shouts over her shoulder.

Axel grabs my hand and I immediately pull away. He stops and frowns questioningly.

"Not in front of Maddie, remember? I'm already a fuck up when it comes to being her mom. I make it a rule not to introduce any guy I'm seeing until I know it'll last." I say apologetically.

Deep down I hope that Axel will be a round for a long time. Axel nods.

"Sure thing, you're her mom, it's your choice. Maybe you want to revise that rule though. You know, since Austin was allowed to be introduced to her and look how that turned out. Real daddy material." Axel bites back at me.

I stop, taken aback by his sharp remark. He was understanding back at the house. I feel my blood boil as my anger builds. I check to make sure Maddie isn't looking.

I step toe to toe with him.

"Well, you've just proven to me why my rule works. It shows me exactly what a person is like. For your information, I didn't want Maddie to meet Austin. He set it up on purpose. I suggest you keep the fuck away from me right now." I seethe.

I don't wait for a response, I storm off around the corner to the cookout, leaving Axel.

When I approach everyone Mammoth sees me first.

"Whoa! Hell Firecracker, you look like you need a drink." He hands me a bottle of beer. I take it gladly.

"Good to see you haven't changed a bit but try not to make sparks fly tonight." Mammoth warns jokingly. I smile and nudge him with my elbow.

Axel comes to stand next to me. He leans in and whispers in my ear.

"Can I talk to you in private?" He asks.

I shake my head and continue to ignore him and drink my beer.

"Stubborn fucking woman." He murmurs under his breath.

I walk off to see my ma.

I try to mask my anger and count to ten to relax but I'm not sure it's working.

I hug my ma and she looks at me questioningly. I shake my head, warning her not to go there. She knows. Your ma can always tell when something is not right. You don't even need to say a word, they just know.

"Yo! Axel, brothers, church now!" Khan yells.

I watch as all of the brothers leave to go to church. Axel looks back at me but I turn my back.

He hit a nerve. I've made enough mistakes being Maddie's ma, I don't need a reminder, especially from someone I thought cared about us.

CHAPTER THIRTEEN

Axel

I follow the guys into church feeling pissed off. I'm pissed at myself for making that stupid fucking comment. I didn't mean it to come out like that. It crushed me how she pulled her hand out of mine when she mentioned keeping us quiet from Maddie. I couldn't help but feel pissed off at the fact that fucking low life was allowed into Maddie's life and I'm not. I know I'm being childish and selfish, and ultimately I know she's right. I just need to remind myself that we're still new, so new it has barely been a day. I do know one thing; I'm not going anywhere. I know that she's it for me.

Joe always said he couldn't wait until I met the right girl because he couldn't wait to tear me to shreds about it like I did to him.

He met his wife young and it all moved really quickly with them too. I told him to slow it down and not to rush into it. I asked if he was sure he knew what he was doing. He said he'd never felt surer of anything in his damn life. I didn't understand that then. Hell, I really didn't understand it when after being together for only four weeks he proposed to her. I get it now. I completely understand how he felt and where he was coming from.

"Bet you're fucking loving every second of this aren't you, you prick." I murmur to myself.

We make our way in the room they call church. It's a large room with a large table and chairs. Rip is sitting at the head with, to my surprise, a gavel.

"Brothers, we are called to church in an unusual situation. Axel here wants to join the Satan's Outlaws. Let me make the situation clear for y'all that don't fuckin' know. Axel, if you vote him in, will not be following the normal prospect route. That's not just because he's my old lady's brother, but because he has some skills we could really fuckin' use, especially at the moment. However, I'm not saying he'll get a free pass. He will still have to earn his cut, his road name, his mother fucking respect, just like the others. He will simply be doing it in a different way." Rip states while pausing to light a cigarette.

"Thought you'd given up?" Rubble asks, smirking.

"Fuck off." Rip barks.

The guys all laugh and shake their heads. I snort back my laughter.

"That's one fuckin' test for you Ax, keeping shit to yourself. Don't tell your sisters." Khan points out.

I hold my hands up in surrender.

"Hey man, you're forgetting one thing, I've lived with them. I know exactly what they can be like, especially Rose. I wouldn't poke that bear, believe me!" I answer.

The guys all nod and laugh. Yeah, they definitely know what Rose can be like.

"So, as I was saying, we will review his standing in a few months. That depends on what you do to prove your loyalty to the club, of course. Now one rule that stands with all new members is that you're on a need to know basis. You don't get to sit in on church, you don't get to hear the plan, our business, nothing. Not unless we tell you otherwise. You'll be told what you're needed for and when. Clear?" Rip asks.

"Clear." I answer.

"Any of you fuckers got a problem with Ax?" Rip asks.

Thankfully all of the guys shake their heads.

"Right, that's it then. Now let's go and get some beer and food." Rip bangs the gavel and the guys start to leave.

I start to stand.

"Sit the fuck down!" Rip barks.

Mammoth's hands clasp my shoulder, forcing me back into my chair.

"What the fuck?" I ask.

Khan walks to the door and closes it behind the others.

Rubble is still seated opposite me. Rip is still smoking his cigarette.

"Now I've put my ass on the line for you in front of my men. I've vouched for you. If you let me down, you let the club down. You even think of being greedy and taking money for information, and believe me, you will be offered, you'll stop fuckin' breathing. We have enough fuckin' enemies out there." Rip threatens.

I roll my eyes at him which seems to piss him off.

"Is that it? You've already given me a little talking to about how you'd kill me. Blah fucking blah! I've faced death so many fucking times, this is nothing to me. I ain't no snitch, even after the shit I've gone through I've still kept my mouth shut. Don't you worry, my mouth will continue to stay that way." I bite back.

"I know that, brother, just checking. It ain't me who wants to have a chat right now. I was just warming you up." Rip smirks standing.

"Big Papa!" Rip calls out.

"Fuck." I moan.

Mammoth and the other throw their heads back and laugh. Big Papa walks in.

"Thanks Pres. Now Ax, I'm sure you're wondering why I asked my brother here to hold you back?" He asks, perching on the table next to me.

"No, actually I'm not. I'm guessing it's to do with me seeing your daughter." I answer honestly.

"Damn, you're a bright kid." Big Papa says sarcastically.

"Now shut the fuck up and listen. My baby girl has gone through a hell of a lot of shit in her life already. She's been to hell and back. I see the way she looks at you and I see the way you look at her. Now if you were any other fucker I'd have my knife to your throat while having this little talk, but out of respect for your folks I'm not doing that. I like them; they're good people. I'm also cutting you a break because it's been too long since my daughter came to the club, too long since she actually visited and spent time with her family, and I have you to thank for that." Big Papa pauses and waits for my response.

"Okay." I nod.

"Now here's the thing about that mother fuckin' low life Austin, I don't think for one second he's just gonna be disappearing. He's in some deep shit with the Cartel. We've been watching him. The idiot actually thinks they're his friends, but they aren't stupid. They were using him as a way of getting to us through Patty. She has no idea about any of this and that's the way it's gonna stay. The last thing I want is her worrying. I'm not going to risk losing her again. Now that she ain't with the scum, she's safe. I'm thankful she's with you because you know how to kill a man. As her father, that gives me some relief." Big Papa states.

I immediately sit straighter and feel my muscles tense when I hear that Patience was in danger and she still could be.

"What do you want me to do?" I ask.

"You need to keep an eye out if Austin comes crawling back, especially if he shows with any of those Mexican friends of his. You not wearing a cut works in our favour. Keep her close and keep her safe. I'm trusting you and I don't fuckin' like trusting anyone when it comes to my little girl.

Now remember, this doesn't go past this door. Do this and I won't cut your dick off." Big Papa laughs as do the rest of the guys.

"Very fucking funny. Consider her safe. I've got good security at the warehouse so she's safe there too. You know she's going to kick all of our arses when she finds out about this." I warn.

The guys all nod.

"Yeah, but I'd rather that then something happen to her." Big Papa states.

"Damn straight." Mammoth agrees.

"Right, this is all lovely and heart-warming, but I'm fuckin' starving and I need a beer. You guys can carry on sharing your feelings, but I'm gonna go get my food." Khan says, patting his belly as he leaves.

We follow him out to the compound. I spot Patience laughing with a prospect. He's playfully dancing with her and making his fucking move. My blood rages.

"Good luck with that one brother." Rubble laughs, slapping me on the back.

I walk directly to them, pull Patience from his hold, and throw her over my shoulder.

"Hey! What the fuck man?!" He asks, pissed off.

I spin around. Pulling back my fist I hit him hard so hard I hear his nose crack. He falls to the floor.

"What the fuck Axel! Put me down!" Patience screams, hitting my back.

I ignore her and leave the guys laughing while helping the lad up off of the floor. I keep walking until I find an empty room in the main building. I slam the door shut and place her on her feet.

Patience immediately pushes me with all of her might.

"What the fuck do you think you're playing at?" She fumes.

Her eyes are alight with fire burning behind them. Fuck she's hot!

I walk her back until her body is pinned up against the wall. She doesn't say anything. Her angry eyes just watch me, waiting.

"I'm sorry." I say quietly.

She looks shocked at my words.

"I'm sorry for saying that shit to you earlier. My ego was hurt by the fact that you allowed him into her life and not me, but I understand. I get it. I'm sorry I was a dick." I apologise further. Her eyes soften a little.

"And are you going to apologise for that little outburst too?" She asks.

"Fuck no. That shit head deserved it, flirting

with my woman. I'd do it again in a heartbeat." I affirm.

She looks pissed off again. She goes to move but I don't let her.

"Axel, move. Let me go!" She protests.

I grab her chin firmly and make her look at me. I'm careful not to hurt her.

"You're mine Patience, you can't argue about it. You feel it, you're mine." I say before crashing my mouth onto hers. The kiss is rough, it's hungry. I moan deep in my throat as she bites my lip. I kiss down her neck and bite hard then run my tongue over it. She moans. She places her hands under my t-shirt and scrapes her nails down my back.

"Fuck baby." I rasp.

I cup her arse and lift her up. She wraps her legs around my waist, grinding down on my hard length. She moans.

"Fuck baby! You need to stop or I'm going to come in my damn jeans." I say as I kiss her neck.

Suddenly there's a loud bang on the door.

"Hey motherfuckers! You better not be fucking in my goddamn room!" Rubble shouts from behind the door.

We both freeze and then burst out laughing.

"Shit." I sigh, resting my head in the crook of

her neck.

"Um, you want to let me down now?" Patience asks giggling.

"The answer is no. I fucking don't, but I really don't have a choice, do I?" I ask. I lift my head and look at her beautiful flushed face. Her eyes are still burning with desire. I tuck her hair behind her ear and cup her face in my hand. I kiss her softly.

"I fuckin' mean it y'all! Get the hell out of my goddamn room!" Rubble yells again.

Sighing I kiss her forehead and place her down on her feet.

"Come on baby, there's always tonight." I say grabbing her hand.

I swing the door open to see a pissed off Rubble.

"Sorry man, I didn't know. We didn't fuck, you have my word." I say as I drag an embarrassed Patience behind me.

We head back to the party. As soon as we are in sight of others I let go of her hand. She gives me a soft look of thanks and I return it with a wink.

Fuck! I'm suffering some serious blue balls. I cannot wait to get her back home in my bed. Shit, I need to stop thinking like that or I'll get hard again.

With the cookout in full swing I walk around to the parking lot to show the rest of the guys my new ride.

"So what do you think?" I ask.

"Fuckin' sweet ride man. You go to Denvy's?" Khan asks as he walks around the bike.

I nod.

"Yeah, Patience took me there. She said it was the best place to go."

The guys smile.

"She show you Darago?" Big Papa asks.

Surprised they know about her bike, I nod.

"I didn't think you guys knew about it. She said that it was hers and that she was paying it off so I just assumed that you guys didn't know about it. I thought it was her secret."

All of the guys laugh.

"She's had that bike made and ready for her since she was fifteen. We've always used Denvy's; he has a long history with the club so we don't go anywhere else. He does us good deals on bikes and in return he gets our protection. Anyway, Patty's always been a firecracker, even when she was just a toddler she would have no fear in telling us all what to do. You could never make her do anything that she didn't want to do. God help anyone that messed with her family! I remember a six year old kid pushed Wes over and kicked dirt in his eyes. Can't remember why but Patty marched right on over to the kid and kicked him right in his balls and threatened him." Blake laughs.

"Well I could've handled him on my own, she didn't have to get involved. Damn kids kept on teasing me saying I had a pocket ninja protectin' my ass! I had to go kick another kid's ass just to prove I could handle myself." Wes grumbles.

I snort back my laughter, imagining a cute dark haired girl with that fiery spark kneeing some poor kid in the nuts.

"Patty always showed us her love for bikes. Denvy saw it early on and, well, my girl knew what she wanted and drew him a picture. She asked if he could make her a bike like it when she turned sixteen. He did just that, minus the glitter flames coming out the pipes." Big Papa smiles.

"Why didn't she get it at eighteen? Why wait all this time? She mentioned she likes to pay her own way, but I don't get it. I know you're the type of father that would have brought it regardless of what she wanted to do, just to see her happy. Am I right?" I ask.

The guys all exchange a look.

"Damn straight I would have. It's because of what went down, what she went through, it changed her life. It caused a fuckin' dark cloud over her, a fuckin' dark storm that nearly destroyed us all. But then came the light, the only good to come from it, and that was Maddie. Her world was turned upside down, her priorities changed, and Maddie became the focus of her life, not Darago." Big Papa sighs.

I grit my teeth at the reminder of what she's been through. I'm just glad the son of a bitch is dead because if he weren't I know I'd be hunting his arse down.

"Strong fucking woman." I state.

The guys all nod and grunt in agreement.

Raven walks up to Big Papa. She smiles and wraps her arms around him and kisses him.

"You good, woman?" Big Papa asks, smiling down at her.

"I'm good big guy. Y'all coming to get some food?" Raven asks.

The guys all nod and start making their way back for food.

Raven walks up to me and squeezes my arm.

"Thank you. You brought my girl back home. Jace and I are deeply grateful, you know that, right?" Raven asks.

"Jace?" I smile.

"Whoops, sorry, big guy." Raven smiles and

winks at Big Papa.

"God damn it woman! Yeah my name is Jace, but you call me big Papa and that's it. Only my woman gets to use that name." Big Papa grumbles, pulling Raven along to get some food. She laughs as he whispers into her ear.

CHAPTER FOURTEEN

Patience

I'm carrying my tired baby girl to my Ma's truck; it's late and she's ready for her bed.

"You sure you're okay having her tonight Ma?" I ask feeling guilty. I want her with me but I don't even have my own place for us yet. It's not fair on her.

I kiss the top of her head as she snuggles in and yawns.

"Love you Mama." She says sleepily.

"Love you too Cupcake. I'll see you in the morning and you and I are going to spend the day together. Okay?" I ask.

She lifts her head off my shoulder, smiles,

and nods.

"Yes! Will Axel be there?" She asks.

"Well, I thought maybe just some you and me time tomorrow?" I suggest.

She's scrunches up her little face.

"That's nice Mama, but I weally want to see Axel too. He is so much fun and he told me that I'm the best pwincess ever!" She beams.

Ma snorts back her laughter.

"Give your Mama a kiss goodnight now. We've got to get you tucked up in bed. The sooner you fall asleep the sooner it will be morning and you can see your Mama and Axel." Ma promises. Maddie smiles at me the entire time.

Maddie grabs my face in her little hands, gives me a big wet kiss, and then practically throws herself from my arms to Ma.

"Night Mama! I love you. Quick, go to sleep so morning will be here super super quick!" She yells excitedly from her seat.

I laugh and blow her a kiss.

Ma shuts the door and pulls me in for a hug.

"Love you baby girl." She says with emotion.

"Love you too Ma." I say squeezing her tight.

I watch as they drive off. Maddie waves and

blows kisses. She's gone from falling asleep to being wide awake and hyper in a second.

I feel a pair of strong arms circle around my waist. I lean my head back and look up at Axel. His face is soft. He tucks my hair behind my ear and kisses me softly.

"I can go out for a few hours tomorrow to give you and Maddie space and time alone together if you want." He says softly between kisses.

"You were watching?" I ask.

"Yeah I was. I couldn't take my eyes off of you. The way you were with Maddie was beautiful." He whispers across my lips.

I turn in his arms and pull his mouth down to mine, kissing him with all of the feelings and emotions bursting inside of me.

It gets hot and heavy quickly.

Axel stops.

"You ready to go home baby?" His voice is gravelly.

I know what he's really asking, and I don't even need to think about it. I smile, biting my lip, and nod.

Within a second Axel has grabbed my hand and is dragging me to his bike. He hands me his helmet.

"What about the truck?" I ask.

"Pick it up tomorrow. You ride with me." Axel states, starting up his bike. I don't argue. I quickly put on the helmet and jump on the back of his bike. I wrap my arms around his waist as we speed off out the parking lot.

On the ride back I purposefully splay my hands across his hard toned stomach, feeling his muscles tense when I slowly stroke my fingers back and forth. I move my hands slowly so they are under his t-shirt. I feel him suck in a breath. I nip and bite across his back.

"Fuck, baby. You are not making this an easy ride." He yells over his shoulder.

I laugh, enjoying teasing him.

I press my chest into his back and continue to slowly move my hands, stroking his stomach.

Axel groans in his throat.

"Shit! Hold the fuck on." Axel shouts out.

He pulls on the throttle and the bike speeds faster, making me grip tighter. I laugh, loving the effect I have on him and enjoying the thrill of the ride. We eventually pull up and Axel parks up the bike. I jump off only to have Axel yanking off my helmet and throwing it across the ground.

"Axel!" I complain.

I don't get a chance to say anymore. His

hand cups my face and he crashes his mouth on mine. Neither of us can hold back anymore. Our tongues collide and our lips move quickly, hungrily.

Axel moves quickly, unbuttoning my shorts, and picks me up almost in one smooth movement.

"Wow, that was smooth." I pant teasingly.

"I have many many more smooth moves to show you. The night is still young." Axel smiles and winks as he carries me inside.

Once inside he places me on my feet. Switching on the light he lifts off his t-shirts and discards it on the couch. The whole time his eyes are me as he walks slowly towards me, for each step he moves forward I take one step back, heading for the bedroom. Smiling I bite my lip and lift my top over my head and chuck it onto the floor. His eyes darken. I keep moving back and he keeps moving forward. He starts unbuttoning his jeans. I stop. Placing my hands on my shorts I slowly slide them down and kick them off. I'm standing in front of him in nothing but my red lace bra and matching thong. I watch as he runs his tongue slowly across his bottom lip.

"Hungry?" I ask.

"Baby you have no idea how hungry I am." Axel says smiling.

I clench my thighs together at his words.

Axel kicks off his boots as I continue to walk back. Our eyes are connected. I stop just before the bedroom door and turn slightly, giving him a view of my behind. He clenches his jaw, lets out a low growl, and pounces. I let out a squeal and a giggle. I start to run. I don't make it far; he grabs my waist and pulls me so my back is against his front. I'm panting at the feel of his hot hard body pressed against mine. He leans down and nips my ear.

"Feel that baby, feel what you do to me. Let me feel what I do to you." He whispers as his hand slowly travels down into my thong. His finger runs along my entrance.

"Hhmm, just what I thought, you're fucking soaked." He rasps.

He removes his hand. He brings his finger to his mouth and sucks, letting out a low moan.

I swear I've never felt so turned on in my life. I feel like I'm going to combust.

Quickly he moves me to the bed. I lie face down. He grabs my hips and pulls them up so my ass is in the air. He makes quick work removing my thong and I feel his mouth on me.

"Oh God!" I cry out.

His tongue moves, circling my clit over and over. My legs start shaking, my orgasm building. He hums, not easing or stopping.

"Oh fuck Axel I'm gonna come!" I scream.

He doesn't answer. He just continues licking, sucking, and circling my clit until it's all too much. My orgasm hits me hard. I can no longer hold myself up. Axel's arm goes around my waist, holding me in place. He slows his movement and runs his tongue slowly across my entrance which makes me shiver.

He unclasps my bra, throws it across the room, and lets go of my waist so I'm laying flat on the bed. I hear him stand and remove the last of his clothing.

His hands start at my ankles and continue all the way up to the curve of my behind. He gently bites my cheek.

"Told you I was hungry."

He is still moving his hands slowly up my back, his mouth trailing kisses. I feel his body over mine as his mouth kisses my shoulders. He sweeps my hair to one side and kisses my neck. I lift my behind, feeling his hard length pressed against me. I moan, moving my hips, teasing him.

His hands reach around and cup my breasts. He pinches my nipples which makes me gasp.

"You want my cock?" He whispers.

I feel him grind against me. I nod.

He reaches back so he's straddling over my

legs. I feel him position himself at my entrance. I wriggle against him, needing him inside me.

"It's yours Baby, take it." He growls out.

With that he thrusts inside me, filling me. He pauses for a moment.

"Fuck! You feel so fucking good."

He grabs both of my wrists and places them above my head, holding them with one hand. He moves slowly in and out of me, making me whimper and circling his hips. He hits that spot.

"Axel please." I beg, trying to raise my hips. I need more.

Releasing my hands he leans on his side, pulling me with him, and spooning me from behind. He thrusts harder with one hand cupping my breast. The other hand moves to my clit.

"Oh my god!" I cry.

He picks up his pace, thrusting harder and harder, over and over. I can't take it anymore; my climax crashes over me. I arch my back as it hits. Not letting up, Axel still continues pounding into me.

"Fuck baby." He groans.

I feel Axel's body tense as he slams deep inside of me. He lets out a deep groan as he finds his release.

We are both panting and trying to control

our breath. I'm wrapped in Axel's arms. I feel it hit me. I feel, well, feelings I've never felt before. The feelings overwhelm me and I don't know how to handle them. I panic.

Axel is trailing kisses along my shoulder. We are still connected. I make quick work of pulling away and jump out of bed, grabbing the sheet with me and wrapping it around me.

"Patience, what the fuck?" Axel asks, clearly dumbfounded.

I look at him sprawled out, beautifully naked. I allow my eyes to brush over every hard inch of him. I shake my head to get myself to snap to out of it. I turn and head to the bathroom, desperate to get out of here.

"Baby?" He calls after me.

"I'm sorry, I can't, I just can't." I say as I slam the bathroom door shut behind me. I move to the sink and run the tap, splashing cold water over my face. It's all too much. I can't handle it.

Axel knocks at the door, making me jump.

"Baby, open the door." He says.

"Busy! I'll be out in a minute." I reply.

"I said open the damn door." He demands.

I feel myself getting angry at his tone.

"I said I'm busy. Now god damn wait!" I yell back.

Axel's knock is louder this time.

"Patience open the fucking door!" He yells.

That's it. Raging I walk to the door and swing it open.

"I said I was..." I don't get to finish. Axel bends down, picks me up, and throws me over his shoulder.

"What the hell do you think you're doing?" I yell.

He throws me down onto the bed and places himself on top of me, pinning me so I can't kick him in the balls. He smirks at me as I still try.

"I knew that would get you to open the door, Firecracker." He smiles,

He played me and used my short temper against me! I frown and feel myself getting even more pissed.

"Now I'm going to ask you again, what was that all about? We've just had fucking amazing sex, mind blowing sex! That was the best I've ever fucking had. I know it was the same for you too, so I don't get why you would run so fucking fast, especially when my fucking cock was still buried deep inside of you. What's going on inside that head of yours?" Axel asks, stroking my hair off of my face.

I close my eyes and take a deep breath.

"It's too much." I whisper.

"What? What's too much?" He questions.

I take a minute to try and gather the words. It's not something I normally do, I like to keep things locked up tight.

"Us. This. It's all so fast. It's hit me like a freight train. I feel like I can't breathe. I don't do this, I don't feel. I don't do feelings, and I definitely don't ever rely on anyone but myself." I blurt out.

I watch Axel frown. He looks slightly pissed for a moment but soon turns to a smile.

It's my turn to frown in confusion.

"You have feelings for me?" He asks.

Annoyed at being mocked I shove at his chest.

"Don't fuckin' mock me." I growl angrily, still shoving at his hard chest.

"Okay, okay, calm down. Baby, you're just scared." Axel points out.

I freeze at his words.

"It's okay, I've never felt this before either. If it makes you feel any better, I'm scared shitless too! I have no idea what I'm doing and this is all crazy fast. But I know one thing for sure, I know you damn well feel it too. It feels right. It might be scary as shit but it feels good, damn good. I ain't letting you run away. You're the first good thing to come into my life, I'll be damned if I let you go just because you feel a little scared." He states, still stroking my hair.

"I don't know how to deal with it."

"Just don't think. Let's just enjoy us." Axel answers.

He kisses along my neck which gives me goose bumps.

"You don't play fair." I whisper, arching my neck to give him more access. I feel him smile against my skin.

"With you baby, I will always play dirty." He says as he nips my ear.

He was right, he really does play dirty. I've never felt so relaxed and exhausted from my orgasms. Not many guys have given me mind blowing orgasm like Axel did that night.

I lay in the darkness and watch the moonlight hitting his face, watching him sleep. He looks so peaceful. I lift my hand to stroke his face. As I touch his face his eyes spring open and he grabs my wrist painfully and twists my arm behind my back, making me cry out in pain.

"Axel! What are you doing?" I scream.

His eyes are wild and frantic. It's like he's not

here, he's somewhere else.

"Axel! You're hurting me." I shout.

I try to buck and kick him off me but he just tightens his grip on my wrists.

"Axel!" I scream louder this time.

He freezes and it's like he's finally woken up.

"Axel?" I ask.

His eyes come to mine and I see the panic take over. He lets go of my wrists like they've burnt him. He jumps away from me and sits on the end of the bed, placing his face in his hands.

I watch him, rubbing my wrist. I'm scared, not just for me but for him.

CHAPTER FIFTEEN

Axel

I grip my head. All of my muscles are tense; they feel like they're going to rip. I was back there again. I had another flashback. Except I wasn't really there, I'm here, and I hurt her. I've scared her.

I feel the bed shift. Her warm soft body comes behind mine. She wraps her arms around me and kisses my back.

"It's okay Axel. I'm okay." She soothes.

I shake my head.

"No, no, it's not fucking okay." I state and turn and grab her hands, looking at her wrists. There are red marks that I caused. I run my thumb gently over them.

"Axel, look at me." She orders.

I look up at her, there is sympathy and worry in her eyes.

She moves so she's straddling my lap and cups my face.

"Axel, it's not your fault. You weren't even aware of what you were doing. You were somewhere else. I was someone else to you. I've got you and I will help you in any way I can. I will help you fight these demons that plague you. We're just two messed up people, remember? I'm not going anywhere." She affirms.

I look into her emerald eyes. They drown me, consume me, swallow me.

I don't say anything. I hold her wrists gently in my hands and I kiss each of them over where I hurt her. I cup her face in my hands and bring her mouth to mine.

I kiss her slowly, tentatively, sweeping my tongue over hers. She lifts herself slightly and slowly slides herself down on my cock, taking me inch by inch. I groan, feeling her tighten around me. She moves slowly rocking her hips, raising up and down so painfully slowly. I hold her close, her body flush with mine. I kiss and nip along her neck as she circles her hips and grinds herself down on me, over and over, bringing me closer to the edge.

"You need to come soon baby, I'm not sure how much longer I can hold off." I groan as she smiles against my neck. She's fucking killing me.

I take her nipple in my mouth and suck. She arches her back, still riding my cock. Picking up rhythm she moves faster. I can feel her starting to tighten around my cock.

"Fuck! That's it, come for me." I growl, gripping her hips and thrusting my hips up to meet hers.

She cries out and I feel her walls squeeze around me as she climaxes. I thrust up deep inside her and feel my muscles tense as my orgasm explodes.

I bury my face in the crook of her neck as the pleasure takes over my body.

We stay like this for a while, getting our breath back, but also not wanting to move, to lose our connection.

"I'm so fucking sorry." I say with my face still buried in her neck.

She runs her hands through my hair soothingly. I lift my head and look into her emerald eyes.

"Enough with the apologising. It's not your fault." She states sincerely. I can see she means it and is not just saying it to appease me.

She goes to move off of me but I stop her

and grab her hips, keeping her in place. I shuffle back onto the bed, making sure we don't lose that connection. She doesn't say anything, she just wraps her legs around me and holds on. I lay down and she lays her head down on my chest. I run my fingers through her silken black hair. I feel her breathing settle as she drifts off to sleep. I lay awake, too worried to fall asleep, too worried I'll hurt her again.

Eventually my body can't stay awake anymore and I drift off to sleep with Patience sprawled across my body, still connected.

I feel movement. I slowly wake to find Patience trying to slowly get up. I quickly roll her so she's beneath me. She lets out a surprised yelp.

I smile and kiss her.

"Morning baby." I say across her lips.

She smiles back, still slightly sleepy. She looks so fucking beautiful.

"Fuck. You're just as beautiful first thing in the morning." I say.

She rolls her eyes at me, clearly thinking I'm full of shit.

She hooks her leg up over my hip, holding me close.

"So you're a smooth talker in the mornings too?" She teases.

"Baby, you'll never catch a break from this smooth mouth." I wink.

She laughs.

Just seeing her this unguarded, this carefree, is making me hard. I move my hips slowly, still connected. I watch as her lips part and her eyes darken with desire.

"Yeah, fucking beautiful." I state as I lean down and take her mouth.

A couple of hours pass and we are both up and dressed, getting ourselves breakfast. Patience's hair is wrapped up in some kind of towel tower that only women seem to know how to do. I take a sip of my coffee and watch as she fries up some bacon and eggs.

I still wasn't ready to let go of her after we made love in the bed so I carried her into the shower. Just remembering the feel of her soapy wet body against mine has me fucking hard. I shake my head to make myself snap out of it.

She looks up at me and smiles.

"What are you thinking about?" She asks.

I put my cup down and walk towards her. Standing behind her I wrap my arms around her waist and kiss her neck.

"I'm just remembering you screaming my name and how fucking hot your soapy wet body was." I answer honestly.

She bites her lip and a slight blush touches her cheeks.

"Hhmm." She nods, not saying anything. I know it's because my words have an effect on her. I laugh.

My phone starts ringing, I walk over and answer it.

"Hello."

"You need to come down the club today, got an update." Khan states.

"Okay, be down there in about an hour. That good?" I ask.

"Sure. You sound happy this mornin', you get yourself some pussy action?!" Khan says and wolf whistles.

"Fuck off Khan." I say, shaking my head. I disconnect the call.

I walk back to the kitchen area and sit at the bar. Patience hands me a plate.

"What time have you got to pick up Maddie?" I ask.

"Ma rang and said that she has a hair appointment at twelve, so I'll grab her a bit before that." She answers in between mouthful of food.

"Okay. I've got to be down the club in the hour so you can pick up the truck and go from there. Is that good? Then I'll meet you back home." I ask.

She smiles and nods.

I lean over and kiss her. Even when she's eating bacon and eggs, she's still so fucking hot.

We finish up our breakfast and head out to the club. When we arrive I kiss Patience goodbye and she leaves to get Maddie. I walk to Rip's office and knock.

"Yeah?"

I walk in to see Rip, Khan, Mammoth, and Wheels.

"Bout fuckin' time!" Khan shouts, laughing.

I flip him off and take a seat.

"So what's this about?" I ask.

"We had our guy look into the Cartel. Turns out Luis has another kid no-one knew about." Rip states.

"So?" I shrug.

"Well that kid lives in this damn town. They changed their name and identity and moved here, and they are now an adult. They could've been feeding him info, feeding it to the Cartel." Rip states, lighting a cigarette.

"Do you know who his kid is?" I ask.

Rip shakes his head.

"No I fuckin' don't but believe me, I will find the fucker and I will gut them from ear to fuckin' ear!" He fumes.

"Surely there's a paper trace? Birth certificate?" I ask.

"No fuckin' paper trace. Kid was born and taken away somewhere. Not adopted. It was pre-arranged, they were kept away from the Cartel life. We have sources and they are narrowing in on whoever it was that raised the kid. Rubble is hacking bank accounts as we speak." Mammoth adds.

I nod.

"So who else knows about this?" I ask.

"Us, my Pa, Blake, and Wes. No one else, not right now. I don't want word getting out that we're looking. If we find the Bastard kid, not only do we have levy, but we have a way in. We can take down the Cartel from the inside and watch them fuckin' crumble." Rip spits.

There's a loud commotion coming from outside the door. The guys all look at each other and reach for their guns, Rip grabs his blade. We all move slowly, armed and ready. As we turn into the bar we see Lily doubled over, holding her stomach. Her head comes up and she shoots us what I can only describe as a look so evil even Satan would shit himself.

"What the fucking hell are you lot doing?! I'm in god damn labour and you're all pointing your cocking guns at me?!" She screeches.

We all put away our weapons. Khan and Mammoth make a break for it.

"Good luck Flower!" They both yell over their shoulders as they make a run for it.

"Fucking pussies!" Lily shouts after them.

"Ow! Shit, shit, shit! Jesus arsehole licking wanker!" She pants, holding her stomach.

We burst out laughing, which is a mistake. The death glare comes at us again.

"For fuck's sake! Will one of you ring Blake? Or at the very least get me to the bloody hospital! Morons! Bloody Morons!" She shouts over her shoulder as she waddles slowly to the parking lot.

"You take her to the hospital, we'll track down Blake and the rest of the family and meet you there." Rip orders.

"Hold the fuck on! I am not sitting in the truck with that!" I state, pointing to my sister who is now in a squatting position next to the truck, panting like a bull.

"Firstly, she is your goddamn sister! Secondly I'm the president of this club so you do what I fuckin' say." Rip smirks.

I sigh.

"Fine, but you better make sure Blake hurries the fuck up because I am not staying in the delivery room with her." I yell as I jog to the truck and help Lily into the back seat.

I put my foot down and speed off.

I catch Lily gripping onto the door for dear life.

"Will you drive more bloody carefully. I do not want to have this baby in the back of this truck!" She yells.

"Sorry skin and blister. I'll be more careful." I apologise.

I head for the freeway.

"Take a left! Quick! This exit!" She screams.

I swerve the truck across three lanes, nearly hitting several cars.

"Ahhhhhh!" Lily screams in the back.

I make it across and breathe a huge sigh of relief.

"We're good, now which way?" I ask.

"Are you fucking kidding me?! You don't even know where you're going?! You just nearly killed us and now you're telling me you don't know your way to the fucking hospital?! Why would you drive me if you don't…aaahhh fuck!" She cries out.

She starts doing some weird breathing shit.

"Saved by the contraction." I mumble under my breath.

"I heard that!" She pants.

"Straight for two miles, then a left, a right, and the second left." She pants.

"Right, got it," I say.

I end up taking the first left instead of the second left and I'm lost.

"Oh shit, uhh, Axel!!" she screams.

"What?" I yell back.

"My waters have gone. My fucking waters have gone! It's like the bloody Nile back here!" She yells, panicking.

"Okay. You still have loads of time, right?" I ask, panicked myself.

"Oooooooooo! Mother of Judas priest! Suck me fucking sideways till Christmas!" She screams. I can't help but snort in laughter.

I see a sign for the hospital.

"Oh thank fucking Christ." I sigh.

I swerve into the hospital parking lot honking the horn. I slam the breaks on and screech to a halt.

Blake is are already here. Blake yanks open the back passenger door and helps Lily out and into a wheelchair.

"Where the wankering wiggles have you mother of effing pearl been?!" She screams at him.

"I'm sorry darlin', I'm here now. Come on, let's get you inside." He says calmly.

"I'm glad someone's fucking calm, my nerves are shot to shit! I swear the gates of hell will be smooth sailing compared to driving my sister here." Rip laughs. He takes the truck keys and chucks them at the prospect.

"Go park the truck and meet us inside." He orders.

We walk inside and everyone is there: Mum, Dad, Rose, Daisy and the rest of the club members.

"How in the fuck did you all get here before us?" I ask.

"We drove the correct way son." Dad laughs.

"Fuck." I sigh.

CHAPTER SIXTEEN

Patience

"Aunt Lily is having a baby!" Maddie sings excitedly in the back of the truck.

I smile.

"Yeah, she is Cupcake." I pull on to the freeway and head to the hospital to meet everyone. We're a little behind because I took Maddie to get a new princess dress as a treat. She's currently wearing it with her little crown, fake plastic rings on her fingers, and her plastic dress up high heels.

As we are driving a long I notice a black sedan type car behind us. I frown and change lanes, ready to come off of the freeway. The car follows. I shake my head, I'm sure I'm just being paranoid. I decide to put my mind at rest and go the long way around to the hospital.

Every turn I make, the sedan makes to. My heart starts beating faster in my chest. I keep calm and am careful not to increase my speed so the car doesn't suspect anything. I pull into the hospital parking lot, turning quickly in front of an oncoming car to give me time to try and hide the truck in the busy parking lot. I spot a prospect getting out of a truck and there's a space next to it. I quickly pull in and jump out, grabbing my bag and Maddie.

"Hey!" I yell, looking all around me for the black sedan. The prospect turns and smiles.

"Hey, come on, I'll show y'all where they all are." He gestures.

I give him a tight smile and keep looking over my shoulder. I don't take a breath until we're in the safety of the hospital.

As soon as we walk in Maddie lets go of my hand and runs as fast as her legs will take to Axel. She leaps straight into his arms. I freeze, watching them. My heart feels like it's about to explode in my chest.

"It gets you right in here, doesn't it?"

I jump, not realising anyone was standing beside me. I look to see Penny smiling widely.

"It gets you full pelt right in the heart. For

me, it's not just seeing a beautiful moment, it's seeing my son happy again. It's been so long since I've seen him like this." She says, giving my arm a squeeze. She walks over to Ben.

I look back and watch Maddie twirl, showing Axel her new dress. I take a deep breath, smile, and walk over to them.

"And Mama got me some new heels too. Look! Aren't they just the pwettiest?" Maddie beams.

Axel's eyes come to mine.

"Yeah, they're beautiful." Axel states, his eyes never leaving mine.

I clear my throat and smile.

"Hey Mama, I was just showing Axel my new outfit. He loves it! Ooo look! There's Nana and Pop! NANA!" Maddie shouts and runs off excitedly.

I smile and watch her show off her new dress to my folks, and anyone else that will listen. Axel takes a step towards me, closing the distance. I look up at him. He reaches out and tucks a strand of hair behind my ear.

"All I want to do right now is kiss you." Axel states.

I bite my bottom lip and smile.

"I want that too." I whisper.

Axel looks over to Maddie, takes my hand, and pulls me around the corner where he pins me against the wall. He wastes no time in kissing me and my whole body comes alive at the feel of his lips on mine.

He slows the kiss and rests his forehead on mine. He runs his thumb across my bottom lip.

"Fuck, I needed that." Axel states.

"Me too." I reply.

We stay like this for a moment longer.

"Come on baby. We need to get back before everyone starts a search party." Axel kisses the top of my head and grabs my hand. We make it about a step before we both freeze.

Maddie is standing there, staring at us. I look up and see my Ma standing behind her. I know she did this on purpose and I will deal with her later, but right now I'm concerned about Maddie.

"Umm Cupcake...I...err...um..." I stumble over my words.

"Axel, you were kissing Mama." Maddie states.

"Yeah." Axel affirms.

"So do you love Mama?" she asks.

"Err um." Axel turns to me, panic in his eyes.

"Cupcake, well, the thing is...adults..."

Ma cuts me off.

"Maddie, your Mama and Axel are boyfriend and girlfriend. They have only just got into a relationship, and in time, their love will grow." Ma states.

Maddie nods, thinking the words over with no expression on her face.

"Cupcake? Are you okay with me and Axel being together? I ask nervously.

Maddie stands there, her eyes flicking back and forth between Axel and I, her finger tapping her chin like she's trying to solve a math problem. She walks forward so she is directly in front of us.

"Axel, do you pwomise never to make Mama cry?" Maddie asks.

My heart swells even more. Bless her, she's making sure I'm going to be okay.

Axel smiles.

"I promise the only tears your Mama will cry will be happy ones." He states.

Maddie nods, accepting his answer.

"And do you pwomise never to leave?" Maddie asks.

"Cupcake I don't…" I try to interrupt but Axel squeezes my hand gently.

He gets down on his knee in front of Maddie.

"What I promise, princess, is that I don't plan on ever leaving. Sometimes things don't work out how grown ups want them to or thought they would. I'm telling you now that if that was to happen, and princess I really don't think it will, but if it did, I won't go far. I promise I will always be around for you. Is that okay?" He asks.

I swallow back my tears; he's killing me. The urge to bolt is high but the only thing stopping me is Maddie.

"Yeah, that's a good enough pwomise." Maddie says smiling. She jumps into him arms and hugs him tight.

"Holy fuck." Ma sniffs behind me. I turn to look at her and smile as a tear escapes and runs down my face. I take a deep breath to try and stop any more tears from falling.

Axel stands with Maddie in his arms. I smile and bite my lip, desperate to control my emotions.

"He's good Mama. Nana said you know who the weally good princes are because they will never make you cry sad tears. They will only make you cry happy ones. Prince Axel is a good prince Mama, he pwomised me." She smiles widely.

The tears I've been fighting to keep in finally fall. My sweet cupcake fills my heart with her sweet soul.

Axel reaches over and wipes my tears away. I lean into his hand and smile.

Maddie leans forward and kisses my cheek.

"See Mama, happy tears." She states happily.

"Well there goes my make-up." Ma complains behind us.

We laugh and Maddie jumps down.

"Wait till I tell Caden!!" She runs off around the corner.

Ma follows her, giving us a moment alone. Axel pulls me into his arms and kisses me softly.

"You good?" Axel asks.

I smile and nod.

"Too good." I answer honestly.

He cups my face and kisses me again.

"That's all you'll ever feel from now on, too damn good." He says firmly.

It has been nearly three hours since we arrived and we're all still in the waiting room waiting for any news on Lily and Blake's baby. Khan hasn't stopped chatting up the nurses. I think he has at least three dates this weekend now. Maddie and Caden were playing happily until Maddie started getting tired. She cuddled into Caden and fell asleep. Penny has been on edge and bouncing around anxiously. The rest of us are all just waiting.

"Wes, who are you texting?" Daisy asks him.

He looks up from his cell and the smile that was on his face is now gone.

"No one important." He states, putting his phone in his pocket.

"No one my ass. Men only smile like that when they're looking at their phones when it's a bitch or porn." Khan states, sitting down.

"I ain't watching fuckin' porn." Wes says angrily.

"Ah, so it's some bitch then?" Khan asks smiling.

"No. It's nothing so just drop it, alright." Wes snaps.

The room goes quiet and looks are exchanged.

"Definitely a bitch." Khan mumbles.

With that Wes is out of his chair and has Khan by the throat up against the wall. Khan just smiles.

"She ain't some bitch!" Wes grits through his teeth.

Rip walks over like there's nothing wrong.

"Wes, back the fuck down. Go and call off. Don't fuckin' let Blake see this shit." Rip orders.

Wes nods, lets go of Khan's neck, and storms off out of the room.

Khan laughs and coughs for breathe.

"It's always a bitch that has you by your balls; they make you act like that." Khan affirms.

"Shut the fuck up Khan or I will strangle you myself. Just fuckin' wait until some bitch has you by the balls." Rip warns.

"HA yeah Pres, that ain't happening. I'm a player. The only thing I'm interested in is getting my dick sucked or getting buried in some pussy. I'm not having no bitch control me; I'm a wild animal that can't be caged." Khan boasts.

We all burst out laughing.

"Khan sit down and stop talking shit." Rose laughs.

"You'll find yourself a young lady who will make you see the world differently. Mark my words. You'll be pussy whipped so quickly and you won't even see it." Penny states.

Hearing Penny say pussy whipped makes us all laugh that bit more.

Blake shows up at the door looking stressed.

Penny jumps up from her seat.

"Well?" She asks.

Blake shakes his head.

"Rose and Patty, Lily wants to see you. Now." Blake demands.

I frown and look at Rose, wondering why on earth she wants to see me.

"Are you sure she isn't confused, being on the gas and air?" I ask.

"Oh she knows exactly what she wants. If you two could hurry the fuck up and get in there, that would be great. She's gonna have me by the balls if you don't." Blake states with his hands on his hips.

I raise my hands in surrender, as does Rose. We follow him to the delivery room. Blake opens the door and we walk in.

Lily is toking on the gas until she spots us.

"Hey Bitches!" She shouts.

I hold back my laughter but Rose doesn't hold hers back.

We stand either side of her bed.

"What is it you want skin and blister?" Rose asks.

Lily takes another long toke on the gas.

"Ah shit! This stuff is goo-ood! I'm totally taking it home with me. I want your honest opinions. Is this little gremlin going to hurt, you know, coming out?" She asks panicked.

I look to Rose who looks to me and shrugs.

"Err Lil', don't you think it's a bit late in the day to be asking that?" Rose asks.

Lily tokes some more on the gas and shakes her head.

"I've avoided all of the videos. I cut that part out in the books. I know if I ask Mum or Raven they'll give me the nicey nicey story. I just know it's going to hurt me like a mother fucker, isn't it? It's going to be like being fisted by the Hulk, isn't it?! Oh fuck! Here comes another shitting contraction!" Lily pants

She cries out and tokes on the gas. Blake tries to comfort her but she just hits him away.

"Don't touch me! You did this to me by sticking your magnificent dick in me." She seethes.

Rose laughs.

Eventually the contraction eases.

"Um Lily, I don't know how to say this but you want honesty so here it is, it really fuckin' hurts. It kills. I swear it feels like someone is using a blow torch down there." I state.

"Oh shit oh fuck! I knew we should've paid for a C-section!" She panics.

I grab her hand.

"Lily, it hurts now but as soon as your baby is born you will feel out of this world. There is no better feeling than holding your baby in your arms for the first time. It's worth the pain, believe me." I say.

She looks at me and then at Rose.

"Is that true or is she just being nice?" Lily asks.

"It's true. You're going to hurt for a while after but it's nothing you can't handle. Now stop your bitching and whining and push the damn baby out!" Rose orders.

"Oh go fuck yourself and piss oooofff! Fuck me!" Lily screams.

We walk away and leave them to it and all we hear is Lily's ranting.

"Sweet mother ducking fucking twat! Bollocking bastard twatwaffle!" She screams.

Rose and I burst out laughing.

"Where does she even learn words like that? I ask.

"Ahh, well we used to spend a lot of time on urban dictionary after a few drinks. Our language after became very colourful." Rose giggles.

I sit down next to Axel while Rose fills everyone in on why Lily wanted to speak to us.

"All okay?" Axel asks.

I nod.

"Yeah, your sister really has a dirty mouth." I point out.

"Can't argue with you there." Axel laughs.

CHAPTER SEVENTEEN

Axel

It has been five hours now. Patience and Raven just took a tired and hungry Maddie and Caden off to get some food.

Some of the guys have gone off to the hospital canteen and Mum and Dad have drifted off to sleep. Daisy is on her laptop doing work for her woman's shelter while huddled in close to Carter. Rose and Rip took off. I don't know where they went but judging by Rose's giggles and the look Rip was giving her, I'm guessing it wasn't for food.

Sitting here alone with my thoughts my mind can't help but trace back to last night, to what I did to Patience. What if I had really hurt her? The chances are Maddie will be staying with us too now. I want her to stay with us, but I just can't risk letting anything happen to her or Patience. Why can't I just forget? Why won't the past let me live? I need to find a way to deal with this and keep it under control because I will never risk hurting Patience or Maddie. Deep down I know I'm going to have to bite the bullet and talk to someone. The medication alone isn't enough.

On top of sorting myself out I'm always thinking about Miguel. I spend most of my day wondering how he is doing and if there are any improvements. I made a promise to his mother and I will honour that promise; he will always be taken care of.

I'm snapped out of my thoughts when Maddie and Caden come running in.

"Hey uncle Ax! Listen to this, I made up this awesome and amazing story. It's going to make me millions when I'm older. Want to hear it?" Caden asks excitedly.

"It's a weird story. There aren't even any pwincesses in it." Maddie huffs, sitting on the chair next to me.

"Go on dude, tell me all about it." I say to Caden.

"Well you got these zombies. They're not

like normal zombies, they can control their bodies and move so much better than normal boring zombies. They ride these dinosaurs and…"

I interrupt.

"How are there Dinosaurs?" I ask.

"Because it's set in the Mesozoic era. Duh!" Caden says, rolling his eyes.

"Of course it is, do continue." I gesture to him.

"So anyway these zombies are riding the dinosaurs into an end of the world battle to save all of zombie kind!" Caden says excitedly.

I laugh.

"That sounds really cool, but who are they fighting if it's an end of the world battle?" I ask.

"The men from the future that have travelled back in time to kill and wipe out all the zombies. You see uncle Ax, the Zombies evolve over like a million years. They become super smart and totally rule the world and even take over other planets. So that's why these bad dudes come back from the future to stop them taking over their planet. The zombies are total badasses, I mean, they ride dinosaurs. You can't get more badass than that!" Caden finishes proudly.

"Well I think it will be a huge blockbuster

movie. Did you just come up with that now?" I ask.

"Yeah, I make stories up all the time in my head. The real world is boring. I need to think of stories to make it more exciting and so I don't get bored." He states.

I give him a high five.

"Who wants some candy from the vending machine?" Dad asks.

"ME!" Both Caden and Maddie shout, running off after Dad.

"We had that the entire time we were out. That boy has an imagination like no other." Raven says placing down bags of fast food.

My stomach rumbles at the smell. Patience hands me a bag.

"Here, keep your noisy stomach quiet."

I grab her wrist and pull her to me and kiss her.

"Thanks baby." I say across her lips.

I let her go and she dishes out the food for everyone.

We all sit laughing, chatting, and enjoying the food when Blake walks in holding a tiny bundle wrapped in a pink blanket.

"Everyone, I'd like you to meet Ivy Rose Daisy Stone." Blake introduces proudly.

Everyone erupts in cheers. Rose and Rip walk back in.

"Aww she's adorable, what's her name?" Rose asks, cooing over her.

"Ivy Rose Daisy Stone." Blake repeats.

"You used both of our names?" Daisy asks, coming to stand beside Rose.

"Yeah. Well Lily said she sure as shit ain't goin' through that ever again and she wanted to make sure both of your names were in there." Blake laughs.

"Oh she is simply perfect! Totally perfect. Isn't she Ben?" Mum sobs.

"She sure is Penn." Dad smiles proudly.

"Well good luck raising a daughter man. If she ends up even half as hot as your wife you're gonna be threatening every guy she meets." Khan chuckles.

"Ain't no fucker coming near my baby girl. She won't ever be getting married." Blake states.

I snort back my laughter.

"Blake, if she has half an ounce of my sister's determination, you haven't got a hope in hell. Good luck man."

"Ain't that the bloody truth." Dad agrees.

There's a loud commotion coming from down the corridor.

"Got damn it Evelynn! Why did you get the giant baby balloon? It's a pain in the ass! The damn thing kept hitting me in the back of the head the whole damn journey here!" Suellen complains, her hair static from the helium balloon.

"Oh quit your damn bitchin', it's cute. Lily will love it." Evelynn argues back.

"That thing is not cute. It looks like it came straight from the gates of hell. Damn well looks like the baby version of sloth from the Goonies. That thing needs some damn holy water and prayers." Suellen snorts.

"It's not my fault you shut the damn truck door on its head!" Evelynn argues back.

They are both so engrossed in their own argument that they don't realise we're all watching them.

"Ladies." Rip greets, smiling.

Both of their heads swing up and they look a little embarrassed for a second before they spot Blake holding the baby.

"Oh my look at her! She is just the cutest little thing I ever did see!" Evelynn coos.

"She's as cute as a pie supper!" Suellen adds.

"Right, I'm gonna take Ivy here back to her Mama. You guys can come and see her properly in a while. Penny, Ben, Aunt Trudy, Max, you want to follow me?" Blake starts walking then pauses and turns.

"Where did Wes go?" Blake asks.

"He took off for some food. I will get him back." Rip answers.

We all exchange a look, knowing he didn't take off for food.

Blake gives a brief nod and carries on.

Rip pulls out his phone and calls Wes straight away. It goes to voicemail.

"You need to get you head out of your damn ass. The baby has been born. Get back here now. You have a niece." Rip says angrily down the phone.

"Khan, Mammoth, Rubble, go and ride around. Try and find his fuckin' ass." Rip orders.

They don't hesitate. They head off to try and find him.

"What's going on with Wes?" I ask Rose.

"No one knows. He's not been himself for a while. Daisy, you're close to Wes, has he mentioned anything to you?" Rose asks.

"No, nothing. I can try and talk to him if you think it would help?" Daisy asks.

"Worth a shot I suppose." Rose shrugs.

We sit down and wait to go in and see Lily and Ivy.

A little while later Rose, Daisy, and I are allowed to go in and visit.

We walk in and Lily smiles. She's holding little Ivy in her arms. I give her a kiss on top of her head and smile proudly down at her. I'm so proud of everything she has overcome. She really has found her happy ending.

"How's your wizard sleeve?" Rose asks.

"Fucking sore. Thanks for asking." Lily says rolling her eyes.

I mock gag.

"Can we not talk about your bits please? You're my sister, I don't need to be hearing that shit." I groan.

"Oh stop whining like a little girl and give me my niece." Rose says holding her arms out.

She holds Ivy in her arms and smiles down at her.

There's a tap on the door and Rip sticks his head in.

"Alright if we come in?" He asks.

"Of course!" Lily answers.

Rip and Carter come in.

Rip kisses Lily on the head.

"Congratulations flower."

Rose sits down in the rocking chair and

starts talking to Ivy.

"You're the cutest little thing in the whole wide world! Just remember I'm the cool auntie. Your aunt Daisy is the soft, kind, loving one. I'm the one that will give you your first beer, and if you fancy a boy I won't tell your folks. If you want to go out to a party I will drive you there and pick you up. I will kick anyone's arse if they mess with you. If you need anything, you come to your aunt Rose." She says as she kisses Ivy's little nose.

She hands Ivy to Daisy who rocks her gently and sings to her.

Rip pulls Rose into his arms.

"Sweetheart, when we get home, I'm fuckin' you and we're making a baby." He states.

"Whoa! Hold on there biker boy, yes to the fucking but no to the baby." Rose says adamantly.

"I will get you to change your mind." Rip states, kissing her neck.

"Seriously, you want to keep that shit in the bedroom and away from me? I don't want to hear it Rose." I moan.

She just laughs and pats me on the chest.

"I'm going to go and get Caden." She says walking out of the room.

Daisy walks up to me with Ivy in her arms

and hands her to me.

"Here you go Uncle Axel, meet Ivy.".

I hold Ivy in my arms, scared that if I even move slightly I will break her. She's so tiny.

"Oh Axel! Can I see her?" I hear Maddie ask. I turn round and see Caden and Maddie come into the room followed by Rose and Patience.

I kneel down and let Maddie and Caden see Ivy.

"She's so small." Caden says.

"I'm going to show her all of my pwincess stuff. She will love it!" Maddie's states excitedly.

"I guess that's another girl I'm going to have to protect around here. Jeez, when are one of you going to have a boy? I'm going to need some help around here you know!" Caden states seriously, but we all laugh.

I look up at Patience. Her eyes are soft. God, she looks fucking beautiful. I slowly stand and walk to her. I don't say anything, I just take her mouth with mine and kiss her softly.

I pull back a little and give her a wink. She smiles and blushes slightly. I hand Ivy back to Lily.

"Aww, you guys are so sweet together." Lily sobs.

I look at her.

"Why are you crying?" I ask.

"Because my damn bloody hormones are all over the place! If you had just given birth you'd know that!" She says in a huff.

"Okay, that's our cue to leave. Love you skin and blister. We will send the others in to see you in a sec." Rose says as we all head to the door.

"Wait!" Lily shouts.

We all turn.

"Where's Wes?" She asks.

"He will be here soon, I promise." Rip answers.

She nods and smiles okay.

Once we step outside Rip pulls Carter and I to one side.

"I'm going to find Wes. You two stay here. Keep Lily and Blake occupied until I can get his ass back here. I don't know…" Rip pauses as Max approaches.

"You still not found him?" He asks.

"Nope." Rip answers.

Max sighs and shakes his head.

"You know Blake is gonna kill him?"

We all nod, knowing that Blake is going to be pissed that Wes just took off when today is so important to him.

Rip puts his cell to his ear.

"Wes?!" Rip yells.

We all look to Rip in surprise.

"Yeah, where the fuck are you? Blake is asking for you. Lily has had the baby he wants his damn brother here. You just took the fuck off without a word!" He fumes down the phone.

"Right well just get your ass here now! I can't keep covering for you." Rip hangs up.

"So where is he?" I ask.

"He wouldn't say. He just said that he was on an errand and he's now on his way. I'm gonna call the brothers and tell them to head on back." Rip states, walking away to call them.

A little while later Wes walks in. His lip is split and his eye is busted.

"What the fuck happened to you?" Wheels asks.

"Nothing, I just got into a fight with some dick. It's no big deal. Which is there room?" Wes asks.

"Two-hundred and sixty-eight." Daisy answers.

Wes looks at Daisy, gives her a small smile, and turns and leaves.

We all exchange a look, each of us clueless as to what Wes is dealing with or why he's being so secretive. If my experience is anything to go by, when someone keeps something secret, it usually isn't something small. It's usually something big, something that will cause a ripple effect amongst everyone.

CHAPTER EIGHTEEN

Patience

I'm cuddled up with Maddie. She fell asleep on me about thirty minutes ago. My leg has gone dead and my arm is cramping but I daren't move for fear of waking her. I know these moments won't last forever; there will come a day when she will be too old to sit on my lap and cuddle with me. I will happily put up with a dead leg and cramp in my arm for a cuddle like this.

"Honey do you want me to take her back to ours and put her to bed?" Ma asks.

I shake my head and kiss Maddie's head.

"I'm fine Ma, I like having her cuddled with me." I whisper, being careful not to wake her.

"I know, but it's late and I think Rose and

Daisy are talking about going out for a few drinks to wet Ivy's head." Ma smiles.

I frown in confusion.

"Aren't Blake and the guys supposed to do that? Or at least wait for Lily to join us?" I question.

"I am not waiting around for Lily! She is breast feeding! We won't get out for months. I need a drink, and so does Daisy. Lily did the same when Caden was born. It's like a little tradition we've started. You're part of the family which means you're part of the tradition too. Let's go get shitfaced!" Rose hoots.

I laugh and relent.

"Fine, you good with this Ma?" I ask.

"Honey, don't be silly! I love spending every minute with my grand baby. Now go and have fun with the girls." Ma states, taking Maddie. She doesn't even stir.

I stand and groan as pins and needles run through my leg from having Maddie sitting on me.

Axel walks to me and smiles. He drops to his knees and carefully massages my leg, easing the pain.

"So you're going out with my sisters?" He asks.

"Yup."

"Have a good night baby. If you need picking up, call me. Okay?" Axel says.

He stands and kisses me.

"Okay." I say softly across his lips.

"Ax put her down. You're wasting tequila time. You ready for this Patty? Ready for the initiation into the Rocke family?" Rose asks.

"Oh shit, I will make sure I have a bucket ready for you to puke your guts up into." Axel states.

"I will be fine. I grew up with bikers, remember?" I remind him. I reach up and kiss his cheek.

Rose and Daisy link arms with me and we leave, making our way to a bar Daisy chose. I would be lying if I weren't a little apprehensive; I don't want to make a fool out of myself, they are Axel's sisters after all.

We sit outside on a really nice, well lit decking with white string lights everywhere and candles on every table. It's a really nice bar. Everyone seems nicely dressed with the girls in high heels and little black dresses and the guys in suits or designer shirts and jeans. They are all clearly wearing designer clothing. This place is definitely not somewhere I would normally go. I look down at what I'm wearing: my cut off and ripped black denim shorts that come to just below my ass, my white Rolling Stones tank top that's fairly low cut, my silver bangles and chains, paired with my red strapped wedged sandals. I paired my outfit with my long black hair and my make-up. My cropped biker jacket is on the back of my chair. I stick out like a sore thumb.

"More Margaritas?" Rose asks, already pouring into my glass before I can answer.

"I guess so!" I answer, laughing.

I catch a few stares from bitchy women and I also catch appreciative looks from some of the guys.

"Ignore them." Daisy says.

I look at her. She fits in here in her cute yet sexy summer dress.

"Yeah, ignore the snobby pricks." Rose adds.

Rose might be blunt and have no filter, but she can also fit right into a place like this. She's wearing a simple figure hugging royal blue bodycon V-neck t-shirt dress that comes to her knees.

Both of them gorgeous and they are getting just as many appreciative looks from the guys here. They either don't see it or choose to ignore it.

We clink our glasses and drink our margaritas. Rose starts telling us a joke but pauses when an expensive sports car pulls up alongside the bar. We watch as a guy with slicked back styled hair, dressed in an expensive suit and designer shades, gets out of the car. He smiles and his perfect smile and bleached teeth nearly blind me.

I cringe, roll my eyes, and carry on drinking. He swaggers, cockily smiling, and takes off his shades. His eyes land on mine.

"Oh god." I groan as he walks to our table.

"Well good evening ladies. I hope my staff are treating you well." He states boastfully, like we should be in awe that he owns the bar and has staff.

"Yes thank you. They've been lovely." Daisy answers politely.

"Excellent." He smiles.

He calls over the waiter by clicking his fingers.

"Give these ladies anything they want, no charge. They are my guests." He orders. The waiter nods and scurries off.

"Please enjoy your evening on me ladies." He smiles and winks arrogantly.

I roll my eyes and snort back my laughter while downing the rest of my drink. His eyes flicker to mine. He goes to speak but Daisy jumps in.

"Thank you, so very kind of you." She smiles

sweetly.

He gives Daisy a charming smile, nods, and walks off.

"Well, free drinks ladies! I'll drink to that! Hey boy! Another round of margaritas!" Rose bellows.

"Damn arrogant rich boy. He's probably got a tiny dick." I mumble.

Both Rose and Daisy laugh.

"How did you come to that conclusion? He was a very good looking guy. He's not my type but he was like an upper class Zac Efron." Daisy points out.

"I'll tell you how I know this. Men that feel the need to own a fast sports car, rev their engine to announce their arrival, and flash their wealth around in people's faces usually either have a small dick or like speed for a reason. He needs it just to give the ladies some kind of thrill. I'm guessing his car isn't the only thing that can go from zero to sixty in seconds! There's only one type of speed a girl wants and it ain't in the bedroom." I point out.

Rose and Daisy are doubled over laughing.

Their laughter soon dies down and their smiles fall from their faces.

"What? It's true!" I giggle.

"Uhh, Patty." Rose points behind me.

I turn and see the guy standing behind me looking pissed. I can't help but notice he actually looks more handsome pissed off.

He leans over, his aftershave filling the air. I'd be lying if I said he didn't smell amazing. He leans in closer and I can feel his breath across my face and I can smell the expensive scotch on his breath.

"Oh my darling, I live for speed. Speed makes me hard. Watching my woman writhe and climax in minutes just from my touch."

I draw in a shuddery breath, his words and scent turning me on. But I'll be damned if I will ever let him know that.

"Well it's good to know your strengths and weaknesses. At least your woman can get off somehow. It'll make up for your tiny dick, maybe lessen the disappointment for her." I bite back.

Rose snorts and Daisy gasps. He smiles widely.

"My darling, I'd be more than happy to give you a demonstration of my, as you say, strengths. Then you'll see and fucking feel that there is nothing weak about me." He states smoothly.

I feel my face blush and I swallow. My mouth suddenly feels dry.

He doesn't say anymore. He just walks away.

"Shit, I think I just had an orgasm." Rose says bluntly.

"That was pretty hot, I have to agree." Daisy giggles, drinking her drink.

"Who does that guy think he is?" I ask feeling a little flustered.

"Oh come on! You were totally turned on! It's okay, we won't tell Ax. Just as long as you don't tell Rip or Carter we also found it hot, because we sure as shit don't need that headache." Rose states.

"Deal." I agree.

We clink our glasses and down the rest of our drinks. Rose calls for the waiter to bring us another pitcher of Margaritas. The night carries on with a lot of laughter and a lot more drinks. I'm feeling okay, just a little tipsy, unfortunately the same cannot be said for Daisy.

"Oh how I looovvveee yooou Patty!" She sings and stumbles down the steps. Rose and I burst out laughing.

Daisy spins in a circle, holding out her arms like she's in the sound of music.

Rose pulls out her cell and makes a call.

"Yoo-hoo biker boy, we're ready for our ride home! And if you're a good boy maybe I will give you a ride in return." Rose says, her eyes twitching in a weird way.

"You alright? What's wrong with your eyes?" I ask.

"I'm winking." Rose states.

I burst out laughing.

"Oh thank god. I thought you were having a fit or something."

"The beautiful night sky-yyy twinkling so brriiight!" Daisy sings, swaying on her feet.

"Okie dokie. We shall see you in a spit spot what!" Rose hangs up.

"How come you're not more pissed up like us?" Rose asks and points to Daisy who is currently on the floor trying to make snow angels in the dirt.

"I told you, I was raised by bikers. I grew up surrounded by bikers so I learnt to hold my liquor at a young age," I state, "anyway, I am a little buzzed." I add.

"Oh hello! Nice to meet you and who are you?" We hear Daisy ask. We both turn and look. I freeze.

"Austin."

"As in, your ex Austin?" Rose asks.

I nod.

I walk towards Daisy and help her off of the floor. Putting her behind me I take a step back from Austin.

"What are you doing here?" I ask.

"Well come on now, that ain't no way to greet your man is it?" He sneers.

"You aren't my man." I spit back.

"Oh I think I am, see, you owe me. I own you, which makes you mine and me your man." He sneers.

I hand Daisy to Rose who is on her cell. I turn back around to face Austin.

"I owe you damn well nothing. I am not yours. I want nothing to do with you. You're fuckin' dead to me so take your pathetic tiny dick to some dirty whore who will have you." I spit.

Austin moves quickly, taking me by surprise. He swings out and slaps me hard across the face, knocking me to the ground. I grab hold of my cheek. It feels like it has split open.

"You son of a bitch!" Rose yells, coming to help me.

I hold out my hand, telling her to stay back.

"You feel better? Feel better for hitting me? That was your one and only shot. Now I'm telling you to fuck off before the Satan's get here. As soon as they find out you hit me, you're a dead man. Take this as you're warning and leave. Leave town and don't ever fucking come back." I say.

Austin smirks.

"I ain't scared of your pathetic biker family. I have friends that could kill everyone of them. Now bitch, get your ass in my damn car." Austin demands.

I laugh and shake my head.

"I'd rather die than get in your car and go with you." I snap.

Austin smiles and holds up a gun, aiming it right at my head. I freeze.

"That can be arranged." He sneers.

"Oh shit, this isn't good. No no nooo!" Daisy sings behind me. If I didn't have a gun to my head I would probably laugh.

I hold my hands up and slowly walk towards Austin. It's the only thing I can do. I just hope the Satan's hurry up.

"I don't fucking think so." A deep voice yells from behind me.

I turn and see the guy who owns the bar aiming a gun at Austin.

"Who the fuck are you?" Austin asks.

"I'm the guy that's going to shoot you between the fucking eyes if you don't fuck off right now." He threatens.

I look back at Austin and I see fear flitter across his eyes. He grabs hold of me, using me as a shield with his gun pressed against my head. He takes slow steps back to his car, dragging me along with him.

"This isn't over sweetness, not for you, and not for the Satan's." He whispers in my ear.

I feel a hard hit on the back of my head, and everything goes black.

CHAPTER NINTEEN

Patience

My eyes flutter open. I groan as the worst headache takes hold; it feels like a stampede of a hundred elephants has trampled on my head.

"Shhhh, it's okay, you're safe." A deep soft voice soothes.

The owner of the bar is leaning over me. He holds some ice to my cheek and I wince. With his other hand he sweeps my hair from my face and gently strokes my cheek. I notice he has unusual eyes. They're hazel with flecks of green running through them.

"Where am I?" I ask.

He smiles.

"Don't worry, I carried you into my office at the bar. Your friends are just outside. How are you feeling?" He asks concerned.

"Like I've been hit in the head." I answer. I move to sit up too quickly. I immediately regret it as the room spins slightly.

He reaches out, holds me, and pulls me to him. My head rests on his chest.

"I got you."

"Who are you?" I ask looking up at him.

He strokes my face and smiles.

"Tate." He answers.

"Tate." I repeat.

He smiles wider and nods. He is stunning man.

"You're pretty." I state.

He laughs.

"Pretty isn't what guys liked to be called, but I'll take it as a compliment. You on the other hand are one of the most beautiful women I've ever seen." He says, still stroking my face.

We stare at each other. His eyes flicker to my mouth and he moves slowly, bringing his mouth to mine. His lips barely graze over mine and then the door is flung open. Axel is standing in the doorway looking pissed.

"Oh shit." I mumble.

"You want to explain why the fuck you were about to kiss my woman?" Axel seethes.

"Your woman?" Tate asks, looking at me. I nod.

"Well if she is your woman you need to take better fucking care of her. If she was mine I wouldn't let her out of my sight for a second." Tate bites back.

He carefully stands, laying me back down on the couch, and goes to stand toe to toe with Axel. I try to stand and push myself in between them but I'm very wobbly.

"That's enough." I say. I turn to Axel to get his attention.

"Axel, look at me." He turns his gaze to mine.

"Nothing happened, okay? He was comforting me, that's all." I affirm.

"With his mouth?" Axel asks.

Fair point.

"Okay, fine. He went to kiss me. I promise though nothing else happened. I was caught up in the moment and it shouldn't have happened. I know that's no excuse, I'm sorry." I plead.

Axel looks at me and then to Tate. Tate

must have said or done something because Axel lunges for him and in doing so knocks me out of the way. I fall to the ground with a thud.

"Ow! Mother fucker." I say, rubbing my hip and trying to slowly get up.

"For fuck sake! Axel get the fuck off of him. Jesus Christ. You okay Firecracker?" Rip asks.

Axel and Tate both get up and look my way. Axel comes over and helps me up.

He cups my face gently, being careful not to hurt me.

"I'm sorry baby, are you okay?" He asks.

I nod.

Axel leans in and kisses me carefully.

"Let's get you home." He says across my lips,

I nod and he takes my hand and starts leading me out. I stop and turn to face Tate.

"Thank you." I smile.

"Anytime my darling." He winks while wiping the blood off of his lip. Axel must've split it.

"Holy shit! As I live and breath! It's Little Tate Alexander!" My Pa yells as he walks through the door, stopping us in our tracks.

I frown and turn to Pa.

"How do you know Tate?" I ask.

He turns to me and the smile falls from his

face.

"Which motherfucker do that to you?! I'm gonna hunt him down and gut him."

"Pa I'll be fine. How do you know each other?" I ask.

"You know I'm hurt you don't remember me, but I guess it was many years ago." Tate smiles.

"You must remember! Although, when were you taken away boy? What were you, seven or eight?" Pa asks.

"Yes sir, it was just after my eighth birthday. Patty would've only been five at the time." He adds.

"Will someone just tell me what's going on?" I ask.

"Tate here used to live next door to us when you were little. His shithead mother was a crack addict and she brought some right low lives into her home. Your Ma and I used to have Tate over as much as possible to give the boy an escape. We couldn't bear the thought of what he was witnessing. That all stopped when the child protective services took him away. Well, it's good to see you son! I shall tell the woman. It's damn good to know you're doing alright." Pa shakes Tate's hand.

"Holy shit T? You're T?" I ask, shocked.

Tate smiles and nods.

I let go of Axel's hand and walk up to Tate. I smile wide and hug him tight.

I remember the little boy next door would come and play with me, he would read to me and protect me from the bullies in our street. I also remember the bruises on his arms, the shouting, and the screaming that would come from his house.

"I'm glad you're good. How did you know it was me?" I ask.

"Your eyes and smile. I could never forget those." He states.

"Ooooooooooo! This is just sooo cute. It's just like something out of a musical." Daisy shouts from the doorway. Then she starts twirling and singing.

"Fucking Christ." Axel mumbles, pinching the bridge of his nose.

"Right, this has been fucking weird, I ain't gonna lie, but I have a drunk wife outside who is begging for my cock. Firecracker, we will talk tomorrow and hunt the fucker down. Stay with Axel. Don't go anywhere without him." Rip orders.

"Oh biker boy!" Rose shouts from outside.

Rip just smiles and winks, leaving the room.

"I did not need to hear that shit." Axel complains.

"Who is taking Disney sing along home?" Axel shouts after Rip.

"Carter is just pulling up." Rip shouts over his shoulder.

"Ooo it's the love of my life! Dance with meeee!" Daisy squeals.

"Come on sweetheart, let's get you home." Carter chuckles.

Axel surprises me. He walks up to Tate and holds out his hand.

"Thanks for being there for her tonight, and sorry about the lip."

Tate smiles and shakes Axel's hand.

"Forget about it."

We leave and Axel helps me into his truck. My eyes feel heavy. I'm exhausted and drained from the nights events. Just before I fall asleep I hear Axel.

"Try and stay awake baby."

I completely ignore him and drift off into a deep sleep.

"Baby wake up." Axels whispers.

"No." I answer.

I hear him laugh.

"Good enough for me."

I feel his arms come around me as he lifts me from the truck. I snuggle into him.

I feel him lay me down on the bed and tuck me in.

He kisses my forehead and sits with me.

"I will wake you up every hour baby. You might have a concussion, I'm just going to get you some water and painkillers." He says as he leaves. I drift back off into a deep sleep.

He wakes me every hour, and every time I want to punch him. I growl at him, curse, and throw a full on tantrum. I'm not good without sleep.

I awake to the sun beaming through the windows. I squint and groan; my head is throbbing. I sit up and take the painkillers. I realise Axel isn't next to me. I frown and look up, seeing him in the armchair asleep with his head resting in his hand.

My heart swells. He must be exhausted. He stayed awake all night to wake me every hour. I get out of bed and walk to him.

"Axel." I say while stroking his face.

His eyes flutter open. He just reaches out and pulls me onto his lap. He snuggles his face into my neck.

"Sleep baby." He says, his voice all gravelly.

I smile.

"Then let's get to bed." I say, kissing him on his head.

I stand and Axel sleepily comes with me. As soon as we reach the bed Axel pulls me into him arms.

"I need you close." Is all he says before he drifts off.

I smile and snuggle into him. I feel myself drift off to sleep.

CHAPTER TWENTY

Axel

There is a loud banging on the door.

"Tell them to shut the hell up." Patience groans next to me.

I lean over her and kiss her head.

"I will see who it is, go back to sleep." I kiss her again and get up. I pull on my jeans and head to answer the door. The pounding on the door continues.

"Alright, alright! Calm the fuck down!" I yell.

I open the door and don't even get a chance to say anything before Raven barges past me, followed by my mother.

"What the hell?" I ask.

Big Papa and my dad follow.

"Sorry son. I held her off from coming here for as long as I could. She would've been here at the god damn crack of dawn if I hadn't stopped her." Big Papa says.

I look at the clock.

"It's nine in the morning!"

Big Papa holds up his hands in surrender.

"Don't be angry son. She just wants to make sure that her little girl is okay, that's all." Mum says, unloading bags in the kitchen.

"What's in the bags Mum?" I ask.

"Breakfast of course! Now where's your frying pan?" Mum looks around the kitchen, opening cupboards as she goes.

I look at Dad who quickly buries his head in the newspaper.

"Ma! What are you doing here?" We hear shouted from the bedroom.

"I'm making coffee, anyone want one?" I ask.

"Does a bear shit in the woods? Don't ask stupid questions son." Dad says without even looking up from his newspaper.

I laugh and shake my head. Dad lives off of coffee.

Raven comes back out of the bedroom and joins us.

"She'll be out in a minute, she's just getting dressed." Raven smiles and Big Papa pulls her into him.

"Where's Maddie?" I ask, handing everyone their coffee.

"She's with Khan and Mammoth at the moment." Raven states.

I raise my eyebrow in question.

"Khan and Mammoth?" I question.

"Oh you're worrying for the wrong reasons; Maddie has them wrapped around her little finger. Last time Khan baby sat he ended up with a full make over. He look so pretty with pink lipstick and glitter all over him. Then there's the time Mammoth looked after her! Well, she made him do a whole dance routine to Beyoncé's 'all the single ladies'." Raven says.

I laugh and shake my head. That little girl really can wrap anyone around her little finger.

A few moments later Patience comes out of the bedroom. She walks straight to me and I pull her into my arms and kiss her.

"You good?" I ask, stroking her bruised face.

"I'm good." She smiles.

"Oh my! Sweetie look at your face! Ben will

you look at her face! What an utter wanker!" My mum cries.

"Mum." I warn.

"What? What are we doing about it? Are we going after the bastard? I'd like to get my hands on him." Mum states while whisking furiously.

"Penn, let the club take care of it." Dad states.

"What? You don't think I could take him? You know how I get when I'm angry Ben, and believe me, I still have enough anger built up from the last arseholes. I reckon I could kick some serious behind." Mum says, pointing the whisk at Dad.

"For fuck sake." I groan.

"Penny, don't you worry yourself, we will get the fucker. That man's got a marker on him now and we will make him pay." Big Papa affirms.

"Good." Mum agrees.

"So how are Lily and Little Ivy doing?" Patience asks, changing the subject.

"Oh well we haven't been up to the hospital yet but I spoke to Blake this morning and both of them are doing well. Blake had a huge argument with the hospital manager because he refused to go home. He wasn't leaving his woman or newborn baby daughter. He said if they even tried to remove him he would bring the full force of the club and the media to the hospital." Mum chuckles.

"The man is going to age, mark my words. He has a daughter, and not just any daughter, she has the Rocke blood in her. God help the man." Dad grumbles, still reading through the paper.

"You've got that right. I was the only one who didn't give you any problems, right Dad?" I ask.

"Ha! You're joking! What about that time we got called to the headteachers office because you decided to beat the shit out of that James kid?!" Dad asks, raising his eyebrow.

"He was picking on Daisy!" I argue.

"He was two school years above you and Rose had already threatened him. It was the first time a second year student had ever beaten the shit out of a fourth year student! Ax was, what, thirteen at the time, and the lad was fifteen!" Dad boasts proudly.

"Ben! That is not something to be proud of!" Mum chastises.

"Fuck, if that were my boy I'd be proud, protecting his sister like that. You'll definitely fit in well with the Satan's." Big Papa states.

"I hate to say it Penn but you should be a little proud him sticking up for her like that."

Raven adds.

"Well obviously I was but I was never going to tell him that. It just made it hard from then on. He had the reputation then. It didn't stop there though did it Ax? How many other times did you have to protect your sisters?" Mum asks.

"With your beautiful girls I'm guessing a lot." Raven states.

"Yeah, it happened once or twice." I shrug.

Patience laughs.

"Well I think it's a good thing you were there to look after them, even though you are the baby of the family." She says, reaching up and kissing my cheek.

There's a knock on the door and Dad gets up to open it.

Rip and Rose walk in. Rose is looking a little pale.

"Well, don't you look healthy!" Mum yells loudly on purpose.

"Quieten down woman. It is not too early for me to put you in a home." Rose groans, laying down on the couch.

"Well Patience was with you last night and she isn't as hungover as you are! See, she's sensible and knows her limits." Mum points out.

"Actually Penny, I drank exactly the same as

Rose and Daisy last night, I can just handle my alcohol better."

"Where are Daisy and Carter? Are they coming over too? If so I will have to make more batter." Mum asks.

"I spoke to Carter and Daisy has her head down the toilet." Rip chuckles.

"Oh." Mum says smiling and shaking her head.

"Where is Caden?" I ask.

"We dropped him off with Mammoth and Khan. You should've seen them! Maddie had been at the face paints and she'd braided Mammoth's beard." Rip laughs.

We all laugh. God help them now Caden is there as well.

My phone starts ringing. I frown and walk over to it and see the caller ID.

"I've just got to take this a second." I state and walk to the bedroom. I don't miss the sideways glances everyone is giving each other.

I shut the door behind me and answer the phone.

"Hello?"

"Hello Mr Rocke. I am sorry to contact you but you said to call if we thought it was important and, well, I think this is important.

Miguel has stopped eating, He won't eat any-thing. We've tried chocolate, sweets, cake, any-thing that any other child would want straight away. I think he needs to see you, I am extremely concerned. Please Mr Rocke, I know you wanted to stay silent in all of this because you wanted him to be adopted into a family, but the longer he isn't adopted, the longer he suffers. He's in pain. He's unhappy. You are the closest thing he has to his mother and he needs that right now." She pleads.

I sit on the bed and hold my head in my hands.

"Fuck!" I shout.

I take a deep breath to calm myself. I can't leave him like that; I made a promise to his mother. I don't have much choice. At least if I bring him here he has my mum and the others to support him.

"I'm sorry. Okay fine. I will be down today to pick him up. It'll take me a few hours to get to you. Have the relevant paperwork ready." I in-form her.

"Oh my Mr Rocke! Thank you so much, you have no idea how much this will mean to him. Will you be adopting or fostering?" She asks.

"Fostering. I will see you later." I disconnect the call.

It amazes me what money can do. The right

amount of money can fast track paperwork and falsify records. I don't care how much it costs, as long as it gets Miguel here. Now I need to break the news to Patience and my family. Shit, this is going to be fun. I haven't told anyone about what happened and now in a matter of minutes I'm having to share what's been plaguing me. It's time to let it out, not just for me, but for Miguel. I don't know if I feel ready for it yet but I am not fucking leaving Miguel to suffer.

I walk back into the main room. All laughter dies when they see the expression on my face.

It is now or fucking never. I clench my fists tight and take a deep breath. Every muscle in my body is coiled tight and I can feel a cold sheen of sweat across my back. My heart starts racing in my chest and I can hear my blood rushing. It's like going back there, it's letting it out. It's damn well nearly causing me a panic attack.

"Axel, are you okay?" Patience asks, coming to me.

I look down to her. I look into her emerald eyes. I immediately feel my heart rate slow and a calmness starts to take over. I take a deep breath and nod, pulling her into my arms.

"I will be." I answer honestly.

"Mum, Dad, Everyone, sit down. There's something I need to tell you guys."

I've just told them what went down, about Miguel, about everything. My mum broke down and now my Dad is comforting her. The whole time Patience held my hand, stroking her thumb in a soothing motion. I know I wouldn't have been able to do it without her.

I look to Rip. He gives me a chin lift and a knowing smile. I nod and smile back. Yeah, he was right. She's my angel, my salvation.

"So, what are you waiting for son? Go get Miguel. That boy needs you." Dad states.

"What about Mum?" I ask.

Mum wipes her tears stained eyes and smiles a sad smile.

"Oh honey, I will be just fine. That little boy needs you. Now go and get him. We will set everything up here for him ready for when you get back." Mum sniffles.

I stand and kiss Mum on her head. I grab Patience's truck keys and head for the door.

"Wait, I'm coming with you." Patience shouts, grabbing some bottles of water and her jacket. She turns to her mum and pauses.

"Yes, go with him. We have Maddie; she'll be fine. Go." Raven orders.

Patience grabs my hand and we jump in the truck.

On the drive I hold Patience's hand in mine and kiss her palm. I never want to let her go. I need to touch her in some way; I can't explain it. Her presence, her touch, it calms me. Feeling her quietens the war within me.

"You sure you're okay with this?" I ask.

She smiles and nods.

"Of course. Miguel needs you. He needs all of us right now. Just like you need me. That's all there is too it." She states.

I lean over and kiss her briefly.

"I will say this, I think we're breaking all sorts of records with what's happened to us in such a short damn time." I state.

"Maybe we're supposed to have it all happen now and then it'll be smooth sailing from here on out." She suggests.

"I'm down with that." I wink.

The rest of the way there all I can think about is if Miguel will remember me. What if he won't come with me? What if I can't look after him? I have no idea how to look after a child. Sure, Caden's my nephew, but I've always just been the fun uncle. This is going to be different, completely different.

I pull the truck to a stop outside the orphanage: The Oak House Children's Home.

"Ready?" Patience asks.

"I guess I'll have to be." I state, looking up at the big house.

"You coming inside?" I ask.

"I don't think this is good for the kids to see." She says, pointing to her face.

I suppose she has a point. I nod, kiss her, then jump out of the truck.

Before I go inside I turn back around and look at Patience. She gives me an encouraging smile.

I swing open the door and I'm greeted by a sweet looking woman with glasses sitting behind a desk. She smiles as I approach.

"I'm here for Miguel." I state nervously.

"Mr Rocke! Well I say, it's nice to finally put a face the voice." She says warmly.

I immediately recognise her voice from our phone conversations.

"Likewise. Is he ready?" I ask.

She smiles and nods.

She hands me some forms to sign and some official looking documents.

"Here are the documents you'll need to use for schooling. You can use the same ones if you decide to officially adopt. These make him a legal citizen, no one will question them. Keep them safe." She hands me a brown envelope.

I nod and follow her down the hall into a large living room. Sitting on a window seat and staring out of the window is Miguel. He looks smaller than when I last saw him.

"Miguel, Mr Rocke is here to take you home with him, okay sweetie? You're going to have such a wonderful life. Please my child, be happy." She pleads.

Miguel doesn't turn to look at me or even acknowledge us.

I walk towards him and perch myself on the window seat next to him.

"Miguel, I don't know if you remember me or if you understand me right now, but I saved you that day. Your mother asked me to take care of you and I'm here to do just that. I couldn't do that before because, well, I wasn't well enough, but now I am. Please little man. I promise if you just give me a chance, if you give yourself a chance, you'll see that you can be happy again."

His big brown eyes come to mine and I feel like I've been punched in the gut. There is so much pain and emptiness behind those eyes. There is no way a three year old should have anything like that there. He looks out of the window once more before crawling onto my lap and wrapping his hands around my neck. I hear the woman gasp. Miguel doesn't say anything, he just holds on to me. I wrap my arms around him and hug him tight, a wave of emotion hitting me. It takes me back to when his mother placed him in my arms. I swallow back the lump in my throat and stand.

"Mr Rocke, I cannot tell you what seeing Miguel like this does to me. I believe the two of you being together will be the glue that will fix both of you." She beams.

I nod and we leave. I wave to her in the window as I sit Miguel in Maddie's car seat.

Patience turns around and smiles at Miguel. He just stares back at her.

"Hi Miguel, I'm Patience." She says softly then turns back around, giving him space.

Miguel falls asleep and when we finally pull up at home I lift him out. His eyes spring open and his face goes from peaceful to frantic.

"Hey buddy, it's okay. It's me, Axel." I reassure him.

He stops and those deep painful wounded eyes meet mine. He practically jumps in my arms, holding on tight.

"I've got you. You're safe." I try to comfort him.

Patience goes in ahead of me and Miguel to brace the family.

When I walk in everyone that was here this morning is still here.

Mum is holding back her tears. I look around and see that some toys and teddies have been left out for Miguel.

"We've set up a temporary bed in your room until he settles in. There's casserole in the slow cooker and I went shopping and picked up some bits: child's medicine, a thermometer, soap and tooth paste, that sort of thing. I also made sure you had a fully stocked fridge and cupboards so you won't have to go anywhere for the next few days." Mum states.

"Thanks Mum."

Patience walks up to me.

"Listen, I'm going to stay a couple of nights at my folks to give you and Miguel some time. I need to spend some time with Maddie as well." She smiles.

My heart lurches at the thought of her not being here with me. I just want to be there to look out for her after what happened last night, but I know she's right.

"You promise to stay with your dad at all times? You promise you won't go out on your own?" I ask.

She smiles and crosses over her heart.

"I promise." She swears.

I lean forward and kiss her.

"I will call you." I whisper across her lips.

They all hug and say their goodbyes. The whole time Miguel clings on to me, too shy to speak or even look at them.

"Okay little buddy, it's just you and me now. Let me show you around." I state.

His head slowly lifts and he looks at me. Then he looks around, taking everything in.

"Let's get you some food."

I sit him down on the bar stool and dish up some casserole. I pull up the stool next to him with my bowl and start eating. He looks at me then back to his bowl. I pretend to ignore him but inside I'm screaming at him to eat.

I catch him licking his lips and then his little finger dips into the bowl and then into his mouth.

"Hmmm, this is good." I say, more to myself than to him.

He slowly picks up the spoon, takes some casserole, and starts eating. I smile, still acting calm when in reality I want to jump for joy.

"Do you know what Miguel? I think we're going to be just fine."

CHAPTER TWENTY-ONE

Axel

I put Miguel to bed about an hour ago. I read him a bedtime story that used to be Caden's favourite. He just looked up at me not saying anything, there was no emotion on his face.

I'm sitting on the sofa having a much needed Jameson in silence, worried that if I have the TV on it'll wake Miguel, or I won't hear him. Scrolling through the contacts on my phone my thumb hovers over Patience's name. No, I can't call her now, it's late and she's probably asleep. I scroll further and hit call.

"What's up?" Rip answers.

"Hey man, I know things went a little arse up

earlier, so I wanted to ring in and check on what the situation is with that prick Austin?"

"Give me a sec." Rip states.

I hear Rose in the background asking where he's going and to bring her back the tub of ice-cream.

"You're so pussy whipped by my sister." I laugh.

"I ain't ashamed to admit that brother. She fucking owns me." Rip grunts.

"So, about Austin?" I ask.

"Okay, so this stays in the club. I haven't said a word to Rose and I expect you to keep this from Firecracker." He pauses.

"You have my word."

"So we've been watching and following Austin for a while now. The guys he hangs with are part of the Cartel, which I think Firecracker knows. At first we thought they were just low runners but Rubble followed Austin late last night and he saw some big time players of the Cartel there. I think they're using Austin as a way into us. I think that's why Austin is so desperate to have Firecracker. He doesn't really give a shit about her. He will tap any ass he can, but they are behind him pulling the strings. They've made it clear that they're interested in Firecracker and the little shithead will do anything to impress his new powerful friends." Rip states.

"Fuck." I sigh.

"Yeah, you got that right. We have to play this extra careful. We can't let on that we know their intentions. We can't let Firecracker out of our sight. Austin is a pussy cat compared to these guys. I don't want anyone but the brothers knowing. If Raven or Rose find out, christ, they will attempt to beat his ass and end up getting themselves killed in the process. We have to act like everything is normal, like everything is damn good. They are fucking watching and waiting for their moment, and that will be to use Firecracker as leverage and a way in." Rip finishes.

"You have my word, I won't say anything. Just let me know when the next step is and what you need. I'm ready." I grit, wanting blood.

"Sure will. How's the kid?" Rip asks.

"I got him to eat and he's asleep now. I'm not sure what to do. It's like he's dead inside." I state.

"Just keep doing what you're doing. Once he sees what normal life is like he will come around I'm sure." Rip answers.

"Yeah, maybe." I shrug.

"Listen brother, with what you told us went down, what you went through, you must be messed up from that shit. With what that boy went through, it ain't no wonder that he's messed up too. Give him time man. Give yourself time too. You're a Satan now and we have your back." Rip states and disconnects.

I finish my drink and then decide to get to sleep since I don't know if Miguel is going to wake me up in the night or at the butt ass crack of dawn. I best get some shut eye while I can.

I awake through the night hearing shuffling around. I lean over and switch on the bedside light. I catch Miguel standing by his bed, holding his sheet in his hand.

"Hey buddy, what's up?" I say getting up out of bed.

His eyes flick down to his sheet then back to me. As I get closer I notice that his sheet has a wet patch on it. His pyjamas are wet too.

"Hey, it doesn't matter. Let's get you cleaned up and give you some fresh sheets." I take the sheet from him and hold out my hand to take him to the bathroom. It takes him a moment but eventually he puts his little hand in mine.

I take him to the bathroom, clean him up, and put him in fresh pyjamas. Thank god I baby-sat Caden when he was this little; it means I've dealt with this sort of thing before.

I clear up his bed and give him fresh sheets. I gesture for him to get into bed but he doesn't move, he just hugs his teddy tight.

"What's the matter mate?" I ask.

He looks to me and then to my bed.

"Ah, you want to sleep in my bed with me?" I ask.

He doesn't say anything or show any emotion. He just takes himself to my bed and curls up.

I sigh and climb into bed on the opposite side to him. He looks up at me with his big brown eyes, hugging his teddy tight.

"Goodnight Miguel." I say smiling and lay down on my back, not wanting to turn my back on him or completely face him either. It's a very surreal situation for a guy to be in.

I'm not sure how long I waited before I fell asleep.

The next couple of days continued like the first. Miguel still wasn't saying anything. He didn't play with his toys and he didn't smile. The only thing I was grateful for was that he was eating. It was still early days I suppose, and he was taking small steps.

I wake to someone softly calling my name: Patience.

I open my eyes and see her smiling down at me.

"Hey, what are you doing here?" I ask groggily.

"You gave me a spare key, remember? I thought Maddie and I would come on over and help you guys with breakfast. Oh, and I missed you." She whispers.

"Why are you whispering?" I ask.

She smiles and nods her head. I look down and cuddled onto me is Miguel with his little arm draped over my chest. I smile.

I catch Patience taking a photo on her phone.

"Hey!" I shout.

She laughs.

"Shhhh you'll wake him."

I hear Maddie skip in.

"Hey sleepy heads. Get up, I'm starving!" She yells.

"Maddie shh! Miguel is asleep." Patience points out.

"Not anymore." Maddie points to Miguel.

Miguel is sitting up. His hair is messy. I watch as his sleepy eyes take in Maddie and Patience.

"Morning buddy."

I sit up next to him. He looks to me and then

back to them.

"Um, you remember Patience from the car ride, right? This is her daughter Maddie." I introduce them.

"Pwincess Maddie." Maddie pipes up.

"Sorry. Princess Maddie." I smile.

Miguel just looks at each of us. He is clearly uncertain about what to do.

"Come on Miguel. Mama brought us chocolate for our pancakes, come see!" Maddie says excitedly.

Miguel doesn't say anything, he just shimmies off of the bed and follows Maddie.

I sit here utterly stunned.

"I can't believe he just got up and followed her. He listened to her and followed." I state, amazed.

Patience smiles.

I reach out and grab her hand, pulling her onto the bed. I flip her onto her back.

"You are a goddamn angel! You know that?" I say while kissing her neck.

"I didn't do a thing, that was little miss attitude." She points out.

"Yeah well little miss attitude came from you so in my eyes, you're an angel. Oh and she's a princess, of course."

I kiss her, long and slow.

"Easy there solider. We can't take this any further. We both have little children now, remember." Patience states.

"Fine, come on then before I decide to take you in the shower and fuck you there." I say, biting her neck.

I stand, taking her with me.

We walk into the living area and I see Maddie and Miguel sitting together watching cartoons. I can't wipe the smile off of my face. Seeing him behaving like a normal child gives me hope that he will be okay.

Patience and I make breakfast. Well I make the coffee and Patience makes the pancakes. I can't cook for shit.

I stand to eat my pancakes and both Maddie and Miguel eat at the bar. Miguel doesn't leave a crumb.

After breakfast I jump in the shower while Patience watches Miguel for me.

I come out to see that she's helped Miguel get dressed and he's sitting and drawing with Maddie.

I smile and walk over to him.

"What you drawing bud?" I ask.

He stops drawing and I take a look at his picture. I draw in a breath.

It's a picture of a woman: his mother.

"Your mother?"

Miguel doesn't say anything. I place my hand on his shoulder in comfort.

"It's a good picture. Don't worry, we won't forget her. I think I'll put this on the fridge if that's okay? Just until we can get a frame for it."

I place the picture on the fridge and turn to see Miguel staring at it. Jesus, this kid is going to kill me.

Patience and Maddie stay until lunch and then leave to give Miguel and I some time together. I read him stories and we watch cartoons. While watching a cartoon Miguel falls asleep on the couch. I cover him with a blanket and let him sleep.

I send a quick text to Rose.

Me : *Hey sis, how long do I let Miguel nap for?*

Rose: *whatever you do, don't let him sleep for too long or he won't sleep tonight, but also don't wake him unless you want to release Satan. :)*

Me: *Wtf?! So I don't wake him but wake him?*

Rose : *Ha-ha yeah. Kids are crazy little bastards. You'll be fine. We will pop over later with Caden, might help him a little. X*

Me: *Yeah great. Come for dinner and bring pizzas and beer.*

It turns out my sister was right; Miguel was a nightmare to wake up. He even groaned a little, but I wasn't cross, I was just happy he was showing some emotion.

I took him out to the local park but he didn't play like the other kids, he just sat with me on the bench and watched all of the kids run around and play.

I gave in and drove us home which was good because just as we arrived Rip, Rose, and Caden turned up along with Carter and Daisy.

I carry Miguel inside, his arms holding me tight. He's clearly unsure of the new people he's meeting.

I introduce him to them all but he keeps quiet and doesn't say a word.

We all sit down and the kids sit in front of the TV eating their pizza and watching cartoons.

"He's a cute kid." Rose states.

"Yeah he is." I agree.

"He needs professional help Ax." Daisy adds.

"He tried that back at the home and it didn't work."

"We have some of the best doctors at the shelter. I can sit in with him. I can try and help him. It's worth a shot Ax. What he saw will come to the surface at some point in his life. Please just say you'll consider it." Daisy begs.

I nod.

"She's right man. I've met the staff at the centre and it's nothing like a children's home or a doctor's surgery, this could be just what he needs." Carter points out.

I know they're right, to think I would be able to fix him on my own is ludicrous. I can give him comfort but I can't help fix what has already broken in him.

CHAPTER TWENTY-TWO

Patience

Seeing how much Axel cares for Miguel is overwhelming. Finding out about what Axel went through, what caused his PTSD, broke my heart. The fact that little Miguel witnessed it all as well, I can't even imagine what he's going through.

I'm driving back to my parents after picking up takeout for us. Ma is back at home waiting with Maddie and Pa should be home any minute. I smile to myself, I can't remember the last time I spent time with my folks like this. It's nice and it's definitely doing Maddie and I some good.

I hit the call button on the hands free and call my parents' house to let them know I'm on my way.

"Hello." Pa answers.

"Hey Pa, I'm on my way back with our Chinese, tell Ma to get the plates out ready." I state.

"You're out on your goddamn own?!" Pa shouts.

I frown, confused.

"Yeah but only to get Chinese and I'm safe in the truck. It's fine. I'll be back in about five minutes." I say, trying to appease him. I know he worries a lot sometimes.

"I don't give a damn. You get your ass back here, it's not safe for you to be out on your own Patty." He sighs.

"Oh stop overre-" I am about to finish my sentence but stop suddenly as the truck behind shunts me.

"What the hell?!" I yell.

The truck speeds up and slams into the back of my truck again, jolting me forward. I struggle to control the truck so it doesn't spin out.

"Patty? What the fuck is going on?!" Pa yells.

"Some guy is ramming my truck from behind!" I shout.

"Fuck! Listen to me Patty, put your damn foot down. Drive fast and drive smart. I'm gonna stay here with you until you're home safe."

"Ahhh shit! The mother fucker did it again.

He's trying to run me off the road!" I yell frantically.

"Where are you now?" Pa asks.

"Umm I'm just turning down Wilson's Avenue." I state.

"Good. At the end turn right on Beech street then left on Mercer. There's a small dirt cut through that runs through the back of the houses, it'll bring you out at the end of our street." Pa instructs.

"Yeah Pa, I remember." I say, swerving around cars.

I'm driving so fast that my back tyres screech as I turn the corner. My backend fish tails and I nearly lose control of the truck. I look up in the mirror and see that the truck is still behind me, trying to keep up with me. The one advantage I have over whoever is driving is that I know these streets like the back of my hand. I put my foot down through the dirt track and turn and swerve onto my parents road. I can see my dad with his gun out. He's aiming at the truck behind me. I pull up onto the drive and slam on the breaks. I hear the gunshots go off. Then there's the sound of screeching tyres and a loud crash.

I'm shaking. Dad swings open the door and drags me from the truck and to the house.

"Get inside. Stay with your Ma and Maddie. Don't come out until I say." He orders then shoves me inside and slams the door.

Ma runs up to me and pulls me into her arms. Maddie comes running to me as well, her little arms going around my legs.

"Thank god you're okay. The Satan's are on their way." Ma reassures.

I pick Maddie up and hold her close. We hear more guns shots and they make us jump. I move to the window and look out. I can see some guys running off down the street but I can't see Pa.

"Sit down here, okay? Here's my phone; ring uncle Rip. Don't come out." I say to Maddie. She nods and presses the call button on my cell.

I go to Dad's gun cabinet and pull out his shot gun. Loading the gun up I head to the front door.

"What are you doing?! Stay inside!" Ma yells.

"Pa is on his own and I'm not leaving him out there. He needs help until the guys get here." I say, slamming the door behind me. I move quickly around the end of the driveway. I see Pa crouched down holding his shoulder. Shit.

I quickly run to him and crouch down next to him.

"Fuck! When will you learn to do as you're damn told and stay in the goddamn house!" Pa fumes.

"Shut up old man. You've been shot, there is no way I'm waiting inside and leaving you on your own out here. Here, let me wrap this." I state, taking off my jacket. I tie it tight over the wound on his shoulder and he hisses in pain.

"Stay there and don't move your arm." I order.

I start creeping around the truck and look over the top. Gun shots are fired at me. I duck quickly.

I slowly look again and see a guy reloading his gun. I take aim and shoot, hitting the guy straight in the top of his shoulder. He goes down. I smile and make my way to him. He is on the floor and the gun he dropped is a few feet away from him. He isn't moving. Keeping my gun aimed at him I walk to where the gun is and kick it away. I kick him to see if he's conscious. He rolls onto his back, his eyes closed.

I breathe a sigh of relief; he's out cold. I look down the road and see the guys coming on their bikes. I wave them down. This is a my mistake. In a split second the guy has grabbed my ankles and pulled my feet out from under me. I land on the ground with a thud and before I can do anything, he's on top of me with a knife to my throat.

"La puta." He sneers.

I spit in his face.

"Fuck you. If you're gonna kill me, just do it."

He smiles.

"No te voy a matar todavia." (*I'm not going to kill you yet.*)

"Let go of the fuckin' girl." Is growled behind him.

I turn and see all of the guys with their guns aimed at him.

He smiles widely.

"Satan's."

He doesn't move. He still has me pinned to the floor with the knife against my throat.

"Muero por honor. La Guerra viene por ti." (*War is coming for you*) He says right before he move his knife and slits his own throat. His blood splatters my face and his lifeless body falls on top of me. I freak out, screaming at the guys to get him off of me.

Rip is quick to grab me, holding me close so I calm me down.

"Shhhh it's okay Firecracker, you're good. You're safe." He soothes.

"Guys, get this shit cleared up. Call Jared and get him down here. He's the only officer I trust to deal with it. Rubble, go to the house and get Raven to take Maddie to her room; she doesn't need to see this shit. Mammoth, go pick up Big Papa get him inside. Khan, call Rose and get her ass here fuckin' now. Tell her to bring the medical equipment." Rip orders.

We head inside and Ma loses it.

"What the fuck were you both thinking?! Do you honestly think I could handle losing you both?! Do you?!"

"Woman, get your ass over here." Pa orders.

She walks to him, her arms folded, looking pissed off. She looks like she wants to kill him and hug him all at the same time.

Pa pulls her onto his lap and he crashes his mouth on hers, kissing her passionately.

"I ain't going nowhere and I'm sure as shit never letting anything happen to our girl. I'm fine, it's just a graze. Patty is good too, she's a strong girl and she knows what she's doing." Pa reassures her.

I stand at the sink washing my hands and face, the water running red with the guys blood. I don't think about it. I block it out. If I think about the fact that I'm washing some dead guy's blood off of me I will freak out. I need to be strong right now, my little girl is probably petrified. I need to get cleaned up so I can go to her.

"I'm going for a shower, getting cleaned up, then seeing to Maddie. When I know she is okay, we are all sitting down and having a fucking chat! You knew something was and is going down and you chose not to tell me. Well now I want to know everything. I'm not a kid, if it's something that affects me and my daughter, I have a right to know everything." I state and storm out of the room.

I shower and change, hoping that the space and time I spend doing so will calm me down a little.

I come out of the shower and go straight to Maddie. I find her curled up on the bed cuddling her dolly and watching Cinderella.

"Cupcake?" I whisper.

Her little tear stain face turns to me. Her bottom lip is wobbling. She jumps into my arms and sobs, holding me tight. I rock her, comforting her trying to calm her down.

"Shhhh, it's all okay. Mama is okay and so is Papa." I repeat over and over.

Eventually she lifts her head and wipes her eyes.

"Mama, are bad men gone?" She asks.

"Yeah Cupcake, the bad men are gone. You know I would never let anyone hurt you and Papa wouldn't either." I promise.

"I know. I wasn't scared for me, I was scared for you and Papa. I didn't want the bad guys hurting you. I love you Mama. I don't want to end up like Miguel with no Mama." She sobs.

My heart breaks and I hold her tighter to me. Hearing her say that breaks me in two.

"You can't get rid of me Cupcake. I'll be with you until I'm old and grey." I say, kissing the top of her head.

After a while I carry Maddie into the kitchen. Rose is here just finishing patching up Pa. Maddie runs right up to him and jumps onto his lap, hugging him tight.

I open the fridge, pull out a beer, and watch Pa comfort Maddie. He looks up at me and I give him my best 'I'm still pissed off with you' look. He just flashes me a smile. I roll my eyes at him.

There's a knock at the door and Officer Jared walks in. He's the same age as me. We went to school together. He knows about the club and he helps them out a lot with messy situations.

"Hey Patty, how you holding up?" Jared asks.

"Fine Jared, just fine. Have you taken the neighbours statements?" I ask.

He nods.

"Yeah, you're all good. Luckily for you Mrs Peterson down the street wrote a minute by minute account of what happened." He laughs.

"Good old Mrs Peterson, always there to catch people out and document everything, just like high school. She could never skip a day. She'd be on that phone to our parents within five seconds." I laugh.

"Yeah, Mrs Peterson always was the only person able to keep us on the straight and narrow." Jared laughs.

The front door is practically kicked open and Axel comes storming in. His face is thunderous. His eyes connect with mine as he takes long powerful stride to me. I bite my lip.

He doesn't say anything, he just takes me in his arms and crashes his mouth to mine, kissing me with fierce passion. He stops and we are both out of breath.

"I've never been so fucking scared in my life. I thought something happened to you. Fuck! I'm so glad you're okay." Axel breathes.

"Good to see you're with someone that cares for you Patty." Jared says.

Axel lifts his head.

"Who's this guy?" He asks.

"Axel this is officer Jared, we grew up together. Jared, this is my boyfriend Axel."

Jared holds his hand out in greeting and Axel shakes it, but he's still assessing Jared to see if he's a threat or not.

"So how long have you guys been together?" Jared asks.

I laugh.

"Um, like, what are we on now, fifteen days?" I ask Axel.

He smiles brightly.

"Yeah about that. It's hard to know because a lot of shit has happened." Axel states.

"Wow, the way you guys are I thought it had been a few months at least." Jared says, stunned.

"Yeah, it's intense. But for some reason it just works." I state, smiling up at Axel.

"Happy for you Patty. I'll call you in the next few days because I need your statement. Right now I'm gonna go sort this shit out. No doubt the local press are here, fucking vultures. I'll catch you guys later." Jared says, waving over his shoulder.

"Where's Miguel?" I ask.

"Daisy and Carter offered to stay and watch him. He's good. Daisy has a way with kids." Axel smiles.

Maddie goes with Mammoth into the back yard to play. As soon as the door closes, I let go.

"Someone tell me what the fucking hell is going on?!" I yell.

Rip looks to Pa and to Axel. I spin round to face Axel.

"You knew too?!" I fume.

"Yeah." Axel admits.

"Spill now!" I demand to the whole room.

Rip steps forward and updates me on everything that's been going on.

"Why in the fuck did you keep it from me too?!" Rose yells.

"Don't you start with me sweetheart. It's club business, you know that." Rip sighs, pinching the bridge of his nose.

"This is why I distanced myself from the club. This is why I stayed away! I've been back in your lives for a couple of weeks and now look what's happened. Don't even get me started on the goddamn 'it's club business' bullshit!" I yell. I'm absolutely furious with them all.

I storm outside into the back yard and sit on the porch swing. Maddie waves and smiles at me as Mammoth chases her around the garden. I blow her a kiss.

"Here."

I turn to see Rose offering me a bottle of beer. I take it and Rose sits down next to me.

"Cheers." We clink bottles and I take a long pull, enjoying the refreshing liquid.

"Thanks I needed this." I smile.

"Well if I had it my way, this would be a bottle of tequila." Rose admits.

"Can I say something? Do you promise you

won't get pissed off at me and bite my head off?" Rose asks.

I look at Rose who has her pinkie finger out-stretched. I laugh.

"Really? A pinkie promise? I hadn't realised we were in kindergarten." I snort.

"Hey, don't diss the pinkie promise! Everyone knows it's an iron clad promise." Rose grins.

I stick out my pinkie and we link fingers.

"Say 'I promise to listen to the beautiful and intelligent Rose and not lose my shit and yell or hit out at her'." She smirks.

"I promise to listen to the beautiful and intelligent Rose and not lose my shit and yell or hit out at her." I repeat back.

"Good. Now, I like to think I speak the truth. Sometimes it may be blunt or harsh but I promise it comes from a place of love." Rose states and takes a swig of her beer.

I wait for her to continue.

"Okay, so don't get me wrong, it pisses me off to no end that Rip keeps shit from me. It drives me absolutely insane that I get treated like the little wifey who is too delicate to know anything in case she breaks. I mean, come on! I'm the least delicate person!" She rants.

I can't help but laugh.

"Get to the point Rose. You're a tough cookie, I get it."

"I'm glad you do, what I'm saying is that I get that it infuriates you too. Now here's the bit you're not going to like so much. Brace yourself." Rose pauses.

"I'm braced." I snort.

"You're behaving like a brat." She blurts.

I start to protest but she holds up her hand, wiggling her pinkie and reminding me of our promise. I sigh and nod for her to continue.

"So today, I get it. Go off the handle, yell, call them out on their shit. But blaming them for everything that's going on now, well, that's the behaving like a brat part. You got with Austin, not them. You pushed them away. I understand why you did that, but let me explain to you how I see it. You have the most amazing and caring family. They would kill for you, they would go to the ends of the earth for you. Are there shit times? Yes. Are there times that've been dangerous? Yes. Ask yourself this though, who was there protecting you, supporting you, making sure you were safe? It was them. Now that is a sign of good family." Rose pauses. She reaches over and grabs my hand.

"I know what happened with you. I know you were raped and it tore you apart and honestly honey, my heart hurts for you. I'd loved to know where the bastard is just so I can dig him up and stab him all over again. But what happened had nothing to do with club life. He was just a sick son of a bitch who happened to fool everyone and become a part of the club."

"What are you getting at Rose?" I ask.

"What I'm saying is for all the shit that comes with the club, the love and the protection outweighs it all. You know that there is a reason they keep stuff from us, it's their way of protecting us. It does drive me insane but I have to learn to accept that. You may hate me for saying it but you belong in this life. You are one badass biker bitch. I mean come on! You went out there with a gun to save your father!" Rose points out.

"Maybe I want the quiet white picket fence life, maybe I'm not the badass biker bitch you all think I am, and maybe I wanted to give Maddie something different to what I grew up with." I state, peeling the label off of my beer bottle.

"You know you can have that life too, right? Just because you want that life doesn't mean you have to cut yourself of the club. It doesn't mean you have to cut off your family. As much as you may want to distance yourself from them, it's who you are. You can be a badass biker bitch with a cottage and a picket fence. Don't keep throwing shit back in their faces, they all love you so much. Plus, Ax has been recruited now, are you going to leave him behind too?" Rose smirks knowing full well I'm not leaving Axel.

"You can't just throw your toys out the pram and blame them for everything. Today was an unbelievably shitty day. Your ex is a complete cock and has gotten himself involved in so much shit...he is so far out of his depth...he's a dead man walking. You know that. So pull on your big girl panties, go back in there, hug your father because the poor bastard just got shot, and hug your mother because, well, she's your mum and she deserves it. Axel was following orders, but of course you already know that, so fucking hug him too." Rose orders.

I smile and shake my head.

"You know, you're pretty fuckin' badass yourself."

"Of course, you don't get to be the wife of the President of the Satan's Outlaws by being a pussy." Rose boasts.

I burst out laughing as does Rose.

I turn to Rose.

"Thanks for this though, for calling me out on my shit and all. Not many people have had the balls to do it apart from my Ma."

Rose shrugs.

"Anytime. If I see shit, I call it out." She

laughs.

Rose stands and walks back into the house.

"Biker boy, guess what Firecracker said? I'm a badass! Why are you laughing?!" I hear her yell as she walks in.

I smile to myself and continue to watch Maddie squeal with laughter as Mammoth throws up in the air and catches her again.

Rose is right, I've had some shit in my life, but the one thing that's always been there is my family. I brought Austin into this situation and that's on me, not them.

Axel comes out and sits next to me. He reaches over and pulls me on to his lap. I snuggle my face into his neck.

"I'm sorry for being a bitch." I apologise.

Axel takes my hand in his and kisses my palm.

"Already forgiven. You sure you're okay?" He asks.

"I am now, your sister is quite a woman." I admit.

"Oh yeah. Rose don't take no shit, but she would do anything for the people she loves." Axel says fondly.

We sit for a while longer, just watching Maddie. I sigh, feeling content. Even after today's events, I feel happy.

CHAPTER TWENTY-THREE

Axel

Patience has drifted off to sleep on my lap. I kiss her head and smell her sweet intoxicating smell. Maddie and Mammoth went inside for some food a while ago and now it's just me and Patience.

The door opens and Raven steps out. She smiles when she sees Patience.

"Daisy rang, she's taking Miguel back to her and Carter's place." She whispers.

"What? That can't be good for Miguel; he's only been with me for a couple of days." I protest.

Raven smiles and places her hand on my shoulder.

"It's for the best right now, what with everything going on. We all decided it would be best if we keep Maddie here and Daisy and Carter take Miguel. Patience will stay with you. I know you can keep my girl safe." Raven informs me.

I want to argue but I know they're all right. This is probably the safest option right now. I know Daisy will love having Miguel with her and I know he's in excellent hands. I stroke Patience's black silky hair and kiss the top of her head. I will protect her with my god damn life. She is my angel, my saviour, and now it's my turn to protect her from whatever comes our way.

"Axel, you good with that plan?" Raven asks, her lips fighting a smile.

I shake my head, realising I'd switched off.

"Yeah, you're right. It's for the best." I agree.

Raven smiles and goes back inside the house. I slowly stand with Patience in my arms. I try not to wake Patience but her eyes flutter open.

"Hey." She says sleepily.

"We're going home now, I was trying not to wake you."

She yawns and smiles up at me.

"You can put me down solider, I can walk." She teases.

I put her down. She goes to walk back inside

but I grab her hand and pull her to me.

"Axel, what the…"

I don't let her finish what she's saying. I crash my mouth down on hers. I sweep my tongue across her tongue, teasing her. She whimpers and grips my shirt tightly in her fists. I grab a fistful of her hair and gently tug, pulling her head back and breaking our kiss.

"Let's finish this at home baby." I whisper, nipping her plump bottom lip.

Her lust filled eyes are alight and a smile plays across her lips.

"Fuck you're beautiful." I state.

Before we leave Patience gives Maddie hugs and kisses with the promise that she will see her first thing in the morning.

I swear on the ride back my dick is so fucking hard it's about to break through the zipper on my jeans. I just want her in my bed beneath me. Her hands wrapped around my waist and her soft tits pressed against my back aren't helping either.

After the call I got about her nearly being driven off the road and being shot at, my heart felt like it was going to implode. It felt like there was something crushing it. I've been needing to feel her, to be with her, ever since.

I swerve and park outside, making Patience

squeal and giggle.

She gets off and takes her helmet off, shaking her hair out.

I get off and grab her in my arms and then chuck her over my shoulder in a fireman's lift.

"Axel, what the hell are you doing! Put me down!" She giggles.

Once inside I kick the door shut and drop Patience on the couch.

Her eyes meet mine and I pull my t-shirt over my head. I watch as her gaze wanders over my body and she licks her top lip. I reach for my belt and remove it. I kick my boots off and undo the top button of my jeans.

Patience jumps forward, pushing my hands away. She slowly takes over undoing my jeans. She pushes them down my thighs along with my boxers, freeing my painfully hard cock. Her eyes connect with mine as her hand wraps around it. She swirls her tongue teasingly around the tip.

"Fuck baby." I groan.

She smiles playfully before taking all of me deep into her mouth. I grab a fistful of her hair as she sucks and swirls her tongue, taking all of me. She sucks harder and faster, my cock hitting the back of her throat.

"Jesus baby, I'm going to come." I warn.

Patience just looks up at me, her green eyes

bright with desire, and she moans. She pumps me with her fist as she keeps on sucking. My grip on her hair tightens and I can't help but thrust my hips. I can't hold it back anymore, I come hard.

"Fuck!" I moan.

Patience doesn't let up. She continues to suck, milking every last drop of me.

Patience smiles and shimmies out of her shorts and panties. I move quickly, dropping to my knees. I grab the back of her thighs, spreading her wide. I lick her centre. Patience lets out a surprised gasp. I take her clit in my mouth and suck.

"Oh god!" Patience moans, her head falling back. She closes her eyes.

"Open your eyes baby, watch me." I growl.

She opens her eyes and watches as I lick and swirl my tongue. I place my finger inside her and circle that sweet spot.

"Fuck!" She pants.

I smile and continue to lick and tease her clit. Her moans, her taste, are making me so hard. Knowing she is close, I continue circling her sweet spot and take her clit in my mouth.

"Axel!" Patience cries as her orgasm hits her.

I moan, licking every bit of her arousal.

"You taste fucking amazing."

I kiss my way up her stomach, lifting her top over her head and exposing her full breasts. I pull down the cup of her bra and take her nipple in my mouth.

"Axel, please." She begs.

I climb over her, resting between her legs with my cock pressed at her entrance. I lean down and kiss her and as I do I push my hips forward, burying my cock deep inside her. She gasps, but it soon turns to a moan as I slowly circle my hips. I move painfully slowly, making sure to take my time. I kiss and nip at her neck. She moves her hips up to meet mine, her nails digging in my back. I still move slowly, circling my hips.

"Axel, please. I need more." She begs.

"I know you do baby." I say as I swirl my tongue around her nipple.

I start to feel her tighten and I know she's close. I stop moving completely. I watch her eyes fling open.

"Axel!" She whines.

"Say it baby." I demand.

Confusion crosses her face. I reached down and take her nipple in my mouth and suck. Patience lets out a moan. I stop.

"Say it." I smile.

"Say what Axel?" she pants.

I move my hand down between us and circle her clit. Her hips buck and I feel her start to tighten again. I immediately stop. Her eyes snap open with a mixture of lust and fury in them.

"Say what you feel baby." I again demand.

"I'm feeling fuckin' pissed right now Axel." She snaps back.

I smile and take her mouth with mine.

"Tell me you love me." I whisper across her lips.

She gasps.

"How do you know I love you?" She asks, feigning disbelief.

"I feel it. I feel it when you kiss me, when you look at me, when you take me." I say as I thrust.

She lets out a moan.

"Let me hear you say it." I order.

She bites her bottom lip hesitantly. Nervously she whispers the words that I need to hear.

"I love you."

I thrust forward making her moan. Leaning down I take her mouth.

"I love you baby, you fucking saved me.

You're my fucking dark angel." I declare.

"Axel." She chokes. Her eyes brim with unshed tears.

I crash my mouth down on hers and take her. I thrust fast, over and over. I feel her clamp around me. I hear her moans fill the room. I feel my orgasm building.

"Fuck, I love you baby. Come for me." I groan.

I feel her walls clamp around me as her orgasm hits.

"Axel! Fuck!" She cries.

I can no longer hold mine back, I come hard.

We both lay back, catching our breaths. Both of our bodies are slick with sweat.

"I love you Axel Rocke. I know you said I saved you, but it's you that rescued me."

I stroke the hair from her face. Her gaze full of love is directed towards me. I lean down and kiss her softly.

"We're just two messed up people coming together and saving each other." I wink.

"I love you Patience. Heart and fucking soul."

CHAPTER TWENTY-FOUR

Patience

I slowly open my eyes and stretch. My body is aching deliciously from last night. I feel Axel's hand wrap around my stomach as he pulls me against him. He nuzzles my neck.

"Morning baby." He rasps.

I smile and turn in his arms to face him.

"Morning." I beam.

Axel returns my smile before kissing me. His hand grabs my thigh and pulls it over his hip.

"Axel, we have to go and see Maddie." I

breathe.

"Hhmm, hhmm." Axel mumbles while kissing and nipping my neck.

He cups my breast and pinches my nipple between his fingers.

"Axel." I moan.

The next thing I know Axel has jumped out of bed and pulled the covers back, leaving me extremely turned on and naked. He laughs and stands in the bathroom doorway. He's completely naked too.

"Axel!" I yell.

"You said we had to get up, so let's get up."

He smirks when he notices that my eyes have travelled down his hard body and are now fixated on his very big hard cock.

"Like what you see?" He asks as he wraps his fist around his cock, stroking himself up and down.

I bite my bottom lip and nod.

"Then come and get it." He teases.

I scramble off of the bed and practically jump on him. Axel smiles and grabs me. I wrap my legs around his waist and he carries me into the bathroom.

After we'd finished up in the shower I texted

Ma telling her we would soon be on our way. Axel was on the phone to Daisy.

"So he's doing okay? Alright, well that's good. Yeah, we will come by this afternoon. Yeah sure, lunch will be good. See you then." Axel says before disconnecting.

I grab a cup of coffee and lean against the counter.

"Miguel okay?" I ask.

Axel's eyes come to me; they sweep my body. I'm wearing a square necked dark red cotton bodycon dress with a pair of black flat sandals.

He walks to me and grabs my hips, pulling me to him. He takes my cup from my hand and places it down on the counter. His hands come up and holds my face in his hands. His thumb strokes along my bottom lip.

"You're fucking stunning." He states before kissing me passionately.

"If you keep kissing me like that we aren't ever going to make it anywhere." I point out.

"Stop looking so fucking beautiful, then I'll stop kissing you." He returns.

I snort and roll my eyes.

"Ready to go?" I ask.

He nods.

"You're wearing your leather jacket, even with that dress." He adds, grabbing the bike keys off of the counter.

"What? It's like a hundred degrees out there!" I protest.

"Baby, if you want to be on the back of my bike, you wear the jacket. You need some protection." Axel yells over his shoulder.

I huff. I'm going to boil out there.

With the wind through my hair it wasn't so bad wearing the jacket.

We pull up at my parents' place and I can't help but look around and scope the road after yesterday's events.

As soon as we step inside Maddie come running up.

"Mama!" She screams, jumping into my arms.

I shower her with kisses, hugging her tight.

"Hey Cupcake. You having fun with Nana and Pops?" I ask.

"Yeah, I'm Pop's nurse. I'm giving him medicine and bringing him his special juice." Maddie states.

"Ahh, his special juice." I sigh.

We walk into the kitchen and see Pa has been covered in princess plasters.

"Woah! Looking good Pa!" I laugh.

"Ha-ha, yeah. Very fuckin' funny." He says rolling his eyes.

"Calm down pops or I will need to give you more medicine!" Maddie orders.

We all burst out laughing except for Pa who doesn't find it very amusing.

Ma pulls me in for hug and kisses my cheek.

"Go and sit down. Breakfast is ready. Here, take the jug of juice for me." She hands me the jugs.

I turn around to place them on the table, only to see that Maddie has wrapped a bandage around Axel's head.

"Maddie honey, why are you doing that to Axel?" I ask, fighting my laughter.

"Because I am a pwincess doctor and I make people better." Maddie declares.

I take a seat next to them and laugh.

"Maddie that's enough now. We're having breakfast." Ma states placing down a plate full of pancakes.

"Okay Nana." Maddie sighs, slumping into her chair with a huff.

We eat breakfast with the conversation flowing. Maddie finishes and runs off to watch her favourite TV show.

Pa's face turns all serious and he leans in.

"No one followed you on your way over here?" He asks.

I shake my head.

"Not to my knowledge." Axel answers.

"Good. Rubble will be over to install some security cameras today. Also, I want to put a tracker on your bike and truck." Pa states.

"Listen Big Papa..." Axel starts.

Pa holds up his hand, pausing him.

"Call me Jace. Only refer to me as Big Papa when in the club or on the road." Pa interrupts.

"Fine, Jace. I'm not about to let Patience out of my sight."

"I know that, but you're part of the club now. If the club calls for you or needs you it could be ten or twenty minutes until security arrives to watch Patience, at least this way we have her covered. I won't take any fucking risks when it comes to my daughter. You should feel goddamn honoured that I trust you enough to look out for her. I don't just trust anyone." Pa states.

"How long do you think this will go on for?" I ask.

Pa shrugs his shoulders.

"No idea darlin'." He answers honestly.

I sigh; I just want Maddie with me. I hate being apart from her. I want normality. I want to be able to put my daughter to bed at night and have her wake me up in the morning.

As if reading my thoughts Axel reaches over and squeezes my hand. I look up at him and give him a small smile.

"When's the next church?" Axel asks.

"Don't know yet, waiting on Pres." Pa answers.

No sooner have the words left his mouth then his cell rings.

Pa picks up his phone but doesn't say much and then hangs up.

"Mammoth and a prospect will be here in ten to pick us up. We're leaving the prospect here to keep guard of the house." Pa announces.

"What did Rip say?" I ask.

"Nothing darlin', just that church is being called." Pa lies to me.

I can always tell when he's lying because his eyes flicker. I don't call him out on it though, I just accept his answer. I'm trying to remind myself of what Rose said yesterday: it's just club rules. I just hope it's good news.

Axel pulls me to him and kisses me softly.

"You good?" He asks.

I nod and smile.

"Yeah, I am now." I reply.

Axel smiles.

"You know that regardless of the rule, if I thought you should know something I would tell you, right?" Axel asks.

I nod because I know he would. He kisses my forehead.

There is a pounding knock on the door and a moment later Mammoth walks in.

"Morning y'all. Let's get this shit over with, I have things I need to be doing." He booms loudly.

"That thing you gotta be doin', is it a woman?" I tease.

Mammoth smiles and shakes his head.

"No Firecracker, ain't nothin' like that. I promised an old friend I would fix their grandma's porch. She's baking me an apple pie in return" He smiles brightly, patting his stomach.

I wouldn't be surprised if he ate the entire thing in one sitting. Mammoth is a big guy, he's nearly seven foot. He's solid.

Axel gives me a kiss and they leave. I look out of the window and see a young prospect guarding the house. Ma opens the front door to ask him if he wants some leftover pancakes.

He declines and goes back to standing and guarding.

"Well he certainly takes his jobs seriously. Poor boy has probably been threatened within an inch of his life to protect us." Ma snorts.

I laugh, agreeing with her. I look back out of the window, biting on my thumb nail and wondering what's going on at church.

CHAPTER TWENTY-FIVE

Axel

We arrive at the clubhouse and go straight to church. We all sit and wait for Rip to come in.

A moment later Rip walks in followed by Khan. They take their seats. Rip bangs his gavel to start the meeting.

"We have news brothers. Some of it is good and some of it is, well, fuckin' shit. So let's start with the good." Rip announces.

He pauses for a moment, looking at me as if he's warning me to brace myself. I don't have a good feeling.

"So we found Austin, that's the good news. The bad news is he's staying up at the Cartel's place in the next town. There are some big players in that place. It's confirmed that Austin is their puppet. They are feeding him drugs on the promise that they get a way into the club. We know the way Austin is trying to get to the club is Firecracker. Rubble managed to follow Austin. The fucker is on so many different types of drugs that he's unpredictable. I mean he's going around threatening folk with a knife for no reason, the guy is twitching out." Rip informs.

"So surely that works in our favour, right? He's reliant on the drugs, makes for an easy take down." I point out.

Rip shakes his head.

"That's not all, as well as Austin being off the scale high, he isn't just doing dealings with the Cartel. Rubble caught him meeting up with Dreads." Rip states. The guys all groan, clearly knowing who Dreads is.

"Dreads?" I question.

"Dreads is the biggest drug and guns dealer in the south. He's our gun supplier and if we get a shipment we cut him in. We have a good business trade going with him. He's a good guy but never to be underestimated. The problem we have is the Cartel are moving in on our turf. Austin is the Cartel's bitch but he's promised them a way in with us. He's also promised Dreads a way in with the Cartel. That cock sucker Austin is close to causing an all out fuckin' war on our turf. Dreads ain't gonna take to kindly to it. On top of that, Dreads is gonna be pissed that it all comes back to Patience. She's one of our own. It puts us smack bang in the fucking middle of it." Rip states.

He pulls a cigarette out of the packet and takes a long pull.

"If we don't start sorting this shit soon, it's all gonna come around and bite us in the ass. I've requested a meeting with Dreads. I leave in a minute. Khan and Axel, I want you with me." He orders.

"Me? You sure about that?" I ask.

"Fuck yes I'm sure. You're a trained fuckin' killer and we are walking into the lions' fucking den! Dreads will have snipers aimed at us. I need someone who knows where those snippers will fuckin' be in case shit goes bad." Rip fumes.

I nod. Tension fills the room. Rip said it: we're walking into the lions' den. Let's hope this guy Dreads is in a good fucking mood because the last thing we want is for things to get ugly.

"I'm not happy about just you guys going. Dreads has at least fifty men. Doesn't matter how good a shot Ax is, fifty against three ain't exactly good odds." Rubble points out.

"We can't all go in there armed, that declares war. We have to show Dreads respect. He is a smart man and the last thing we want to do is undermine him." Rip states, banging his gavel.

"Church is over." Rip yells, gets up, and signals to me and Khan to follow.

We ride in Khan's truck so we don't attract attention.

Rip hands me a gun and ammo. He checks his knives, running his finger along the edges. It's almost like he's caressing them.

"Are you not taking a gun?" I ask.

"I don't need a gun; my blades are all I need."

"You're in for a treat Ax. You ain't seen nothing until you've seen Pres with his blades. It's like a fuckin' art form." Khan smiles.

I had heard about Rip. I heard exactly what he was capable of with a blade. I don't think many would call it art though.

We drive for around forty minutes until we pull up to a huge white plantation house with a massive amount of land. This guy has money.

Guards with guns walk the perimeter. Khan pulls the truck to a stop and we jump out. A huge black guy is standing in front of the door; he looks familiar.

The guy looks at me and smiles.

"Well shit! It's you! My man that got his ass handed to him! How the fuck you doin' man?" He yells.

I smile. It's Tank, from the strip club.

"You know him?" Rip asks in disbelief.

"Yeah, he was security at the strip club where Patience used to work." I inform him.

I walk up to Tank and shake his hand.

"Good to see you Tank. I'll have to tell patience I've seen you." I state.

"Holy shit! You guys an item now? Well fuck me! It's a damn good thing that she got shot of that white trash she was dating before."

Rip and I exchange a look and Rip smiles and steps forward.

"Tank, I'm Rip, President of the Satan's Outlaws. We're here to talk to Dreads. That white trash has been causing a problem for Patty and for us. Do you think you could take us to him?" Rip asks.

"That piece of shit has been causing Patty grief? That mother fucker! Hell yeah I can take you to Dreads, he's my cousin. Follow me." Tank opens the door and leads the way.

Expensive paintings, ornaments, and furniture fill every corner of the house. The whole house screams money.

"Yo D! Got some guys here to speak with you. Trust me, you're gonna want to hear them out."

Tank yells as we walk through to the back of the house where there's a guy at a table on the extremely large back porch.

He stands and walks towards us. I notice he's wearing an expensive tailored suit to fit his broad frame. His Rolex watch glistens in the bright sun. This is not what I was expecting. The guy screams class and Money. He removes his expensive sunglasses as he comes to a stop in front of us. His dark gaze assesses us. He tenses his jaw. That look alone confirms that this guy is not to be underestimated.

"Rip, what do I owe the pleasure of your visit?" He asks, holding out his hand in greeting.

"Is there somewhere we could talk? Sorry to say man, it ain't good news." Rip states.

Dreads nods and gestures to follow him.

"Tank, get these men an iced tea while I talk with Rip." He orders over his shoulder.

We look at Rip for confirmation that he's good. He gives us a chin lift and follows Dreads.

Khan and I stand outside drinking iced tea and talking to Tank.

"This place is fucking impressive." Khan states, looking around.

"Yeah man! Cuz has done well for himself. Do you know our great grandmother was a slave here when it was a cotton farm? Dreads said he was gonna own it and make all those white sons of bitches turn in their graves that a black man now owns it. He even named it after our Grandmother." Tanks smiles.

"Fucking good for him." I agree.

A few moments later Dreads and Rip come out of the office.

"Tank, can you find me that piece of white trash Austin who seems to think he can mess with me, my god damn business, and my associates?" Dreads growls.

"Yeah cousin, I know him. He is proper white trash, loves a bit of crystal meth too." Tank rolls his eyes.

Dreads curls his lip in disgust. He turns to Rip.

"I will be in touch. I appreciate you coming to speak to me face to face. I know not many men would do that." Dreads shakes his hand and leaves.

Tank shows us out and promises he will hit up the bar soon to see Patty.

"So?" I ask once we're in the truck.

Rip turns around to face me and a smile spreads across his face.

"He's in. If this turns to war we are fighting together against the Cartel. Dreads knows it's in his best interest to get rid of the Cartel. Austin trying to play each of them against each other just gave Dreads a taste for blood." Rip smiles broadly.

"I've got to say, Dreads isn't what I was expecting. I was expecting a Rastafarian with a cannabis farm or something." I admit.

"Dreads is at the top of his game. There ain't many people that have my respect, but he has it. He made himself what he is. He is feared among many and they fucking should be scared. Known a few that went to him expecting what you just said and they underestimated him. Those fuckers didn't even blink before their heads were rollin'." Rip states.

"No shit?" I ask.

"No shit." Rip nods.

"Guessing it's fucking good he likes the Satan's then huh?" Khan adds.

"What's not to like mother fucker? I'm the fuckin' best there is, and I only have the best men for brothers." Rip laughs.

Laughing I sit back in my seat. Something tells me to look out of the back window. When I do I see a black saloon car with blacked out windows.

"Rip, we're being followed." I state.

Rip turns to look out of the back window.

"Khan, lose these mother fuckers!" Rip

orders.

"Yes boss." Khan says smiling.

Khan puts his foot down and takes a sharp right. The car speeds up and follows. I pull out my gun and lean out of the window slightly.

"Keep the truck fucking steady Khan." I yell.

"On it." He yells.

"What you fuckin' doing Ax? You kill them fuckers then you declare a war." Rip barks angrily.

I ignore him and shut out everything else. I take aim and fire, taking out the driver's side tyre. The driver loses control and swerves into ditch.

I sit back down and smile. Fuck that felt good! Never thought I'd miss shooting so much.

"Fuck! That was cool as shit! Your aim man, fuckin' spot on!" Khan hollers.

Rip gives me a different response. He looks pissed.

"I told you not to fuckin' shoot." Rip growls angrily.

I hold my hands up in surrender but I can't wipe the smile off my face.

"You said don't shoot them. I didn't shoot them, I shot their tyre. They aren't dead, hell, they're probably barely even injured. Not my fault they had a tyre blow out." I say, smiling.

"Fuck you're gonna be a pain in my ass just like your damn sister. Neither of you listen to what you're fuckin' told." Rip complains.

"Yeah but admit it, you're glad I shot their tyres out." I tease.

"Fuck I need a drink." Rip moans.

I throw my head back and laugh, Khan does too. This is what I needed, being part of Satan's gives me a purpose. I'm trained to kill, there is no way I'd be able to return to normal civilisation. I've gone past that point. I've seen too much and killed too many.

I sigh, happy that I've found the place I belong.

CHAPTER TWENTY-SIX

Axel

Once we're back at the compound Rip updates the guys and I get Mammoth to drop me back to Raven and Big Papa's place.

I walk in and go straight to Patience. I cup her face and kiss her.

"What's this all about?" She asks surprised.

"I finally feel like I know where I'm supposed to belong outside of the military. You, the Satan's, everything just fucking fits perfectly." I admit.

Patience smiles warmly. She reaches up and kisses me again.

"Come on, let's get over to Daisy and Carter's, I want to check in on Miguel."

Patience nods. We say goodbye to Maddie who makes me promise to take her out on my bike soon.

I love riding my bike on the open road with Patience's arms wrapped around me. It really doesn't get any fucking better than this.

Daisy greets us at the door with a huge smile on her face. She puts her finger to her lips to quieten us. I look at her, confused, and she ushers us inside.

Once inside I see exactly what she wanted us to see. Miguel is cuddled into Carter, giggling at something he's watching on the TV.

My smile couldn't get any bigger. I grab Daisy and hug her tight, kissing the top of her head.

Miguel hears the commotion and turns his head to look at us. He waves and then turned back around to continue watching his show.

Daisy ushers us into the kitchen.

"Okay, what kind of voodoo Mary Poppins shit did you pull?" I ask.

"I didn't do anything, we brought him back here yesterday and he was the same. He was shy and didn't really say anything. We had dinner together, bathed him, and read him a bedtime story. I may have bought him a few extra teddies and toys just to make sure the room he's staying in wasn't scary for him. I led with him stroking his hair until he fell asleep. Then we went to the pond this morning to feed the ducks, and that's it. I swear, no voodoo Mary Poppins stuff going on here." Daisy holds her hands up in surrender.

I smile down at Patience who looks equally as happy as I am.

"I'm just glad to see him relaxing and being a kid again. Are you still good to have him for a while longer? Shit isn't sorted yet and I don't want to put him at risk." I state.

"We're more than happy to have him here for as long as you need. I'm loving having him here." Daisy beams happily.

We are sitting outside eating lunch when the doorbells ring.

Daisy stands up to get the door but Carter puts his hand out, halting her in her tracks.

"I'll get it sweetheart. With what's going on it's the safest thing to do." He states kissing her head.

I brace myself. I'm ready to follow him but soon relax when I hear the commotion.

"Where's Auntie Daisy and Uncle Ax?" Lily coos.

Lily walks into the garden carrying Ivy. She sits down with a sigh as Blake puts down the baby changing bag. It looks like they're packed to move in with the amount of stuff they've brought.

Daisy jumps up and carefully hugs Lily.

"What are you guys doing here?" Daisy asks.

"Well we've just left the hospital and we thought we would swing by on the way home. We heard about what's happening and figured this was the safest option. I'm hanging out my arse and as much as I love you all, I really don't want you all piling around ours. I just want to take a bath and sleep." Lily slumps in the chair with a sigh after handing Ivy over to Daisy.

"Ooo you're so cute." Daisy coos.

"I will text Rose and get them over here with Mum and Dad." I state, pulling my phone out to send a group text.

"Tell them they have precisely two hours and then I'm going home to sleep." Lily yawns.

"Sure thing skin and blister." I smirk.

I send the text and Mum replies instantly with:

Mum: **Ooh we were just about to eat lunch. I made chicken vaginas so I will bring them over to share. It's a new recipe, best chicken vaginas I've ever made!**

I burst out laughing, holding my stomach.

"What?" Lily asks.

I show everyone the message and they all cry with laughter.

"I take it your mum doesn't text very often?" Patience says.

"No, she's trying to get used to her new phone." I chuckle.

My phone pings with another message.

Mum: **OH MY GOD! I MEAN FAJITAS! FAJITAS! WHY IS MY MESSAGE ALL IN CAPITALS? NOW IT LOOKS LIKE I'M SHOUTING. I'M NOT SHOUTING! STUPID DUCKING PHONE.**

My phone pings again with another message.

Rose: **Tell the saggy minge we are on our way. R xoxo**

"Rose says they're on their way." I inform Lily, not repeating exactly what Rose said.

Lily looks at me and raises her eyebrow in question; she knows there was more to that message than what I divulged.

It's not long until the whole Rocke family are here cooing over baby Ivy.

"You getting any ideas sweetheart?" Rip asks Rose, wrapping his arms around her.

"Err not right now biker boy, I'm enjoying our time alone. Also, not being scared to sneeze is a perk." Rose answers bluntly.

"Too much fucking info sis!" I grumble.

Miguel comes over and looks at Ivy in Daisy's arms.

"Hey sweetie. This is baby Ivy, do you want to come and say hello?" Daisy asks while kneeling down.

He comes to a stop in front of Ivy and his big round eyes look up at Daisy. He leans forward and kisses Ivy's little head. The little guy has my heart bursting. He smiles and says "bebe."

He actually fucking speaks. Patience grabs my hand and squeezes it, just as stunned as me. I can see that Daisy is trying to contain her excitement over the fact Miguel actually spoke.

"That's right sweetie. She's a little baby." Daisy says, her voice wavering with emotion.

Then Miguel puts his little arm around Daisy's neck and perches himself on her opposite knee. He places a kiss on her cheek.

"Well that's it, I'm gone. Someone pass me a tissue." Lily sobs.

Daisy stands up with Ivy on one arm and

Miguel on the other. She carefully hands Ivy to Rose and gives Miguel lots of massive kisses.

"You okay?" Patience whispers in my ear.

I turn and smile. Leaning in I place a brief kiss on her lips.

"More than okay." I state.

I watch Daisy and Carter with Miguel as they talk and play with him. I watch the way Miguel cuddles into Daisy and the way Carter can get a snippet of a smile from him. It hits me like a freight train, this is what Miguel needs. He needs a mum and a dad. He needs a stable family, and I can't give that to him right now. I can't expect Patience to instantly take on the role of mum to Miguel. I can't even guarantee I won't have a PTSD episode because I'm only just finding my feet. Daisy and Carter are exactly the stability that he needs.

I decide to wait a while before saying anything, it has only been twenty-four hours and Miguel will be with them for a few more days yet. I can't see the situation with the Cartel easing any time soon. That's another reason Miguel is better off with Daisy and Carter. He is safe here.

A little while later Mum places down her chicken fajitas.

"Don't think anyone wants to eat your chicken vaginas mum." Rose says.

"Oh just piss off! That stupid bloody phone." Mum grumbles.

"You know she told the phone off like it was a person? Like it was a naughty child. Don't even get me started on your grandmother." Dad sighs.

"When is Nan moving over?" I ask.

"Two weeks tomorrow. Her visa has just come through but she wants to be in the final bowls tournament so she can kick Vera's arse before she comes over." Dad says.

Blake and Rip are huddled at the other side of the garden, I look to Carter who also notices. He gives me a chin lift and we both head over to them.

"So is this a private conversation ladies or can anyone join in?" I ask.

"Go fuck yourself." Blake spits angrily.

Shocked by his outburst I hold my hands up in surrender.

"Calm down Blake. This isn't the place for you to be losing your shit." Rip warns.

"What's going on?" Carter asks.

"Shit, sorry Ax. It's Wes." Blake admits.

"Fuck, what's he involved with?" I ask.

"It's not what he's involved with, it's who. You weren't around when it happened but the club and Rose had a bit off a run in with the Cartel and a guy called Luis." Blake pauses.

"So he's involved with this guy Luis?" I ask.

"No, Luis is dead. He's getting involved with his daughter." Rip answers.

"No shit?" Carter asks, shocked.

"No shit. The thing is, Wes is in denial that being with her puts the whole club at risk. She's just using him to gather info on the club. He won't listen and now he won't even answer my calls." Blake sighs.

"What about getting Daisy to speak with him?" Carter asks.

Blake and Rip shake their heads.

"Tried that one before we found this shit out but he refused." Rip adds.

"He will come round. If not to you guys then to my sisters. They're relentless and never take fucking no for an answer." I smile.

I'm just trying to give Blake and Rip some reassurance.

"He's got a point there." Carter adds.

"Shit if you even mention it to them they'll hound him until he breaks. It's definitely an option." Rip smirks.

"Okay but let's leave it a couple of days. Let me settle with Lily and Ivy first before we get her all riled up. Who knows what a lack of sleep will do to Lily! I want to get through to my brother but I don't want her to murder him." Blake laughs.

"Well whatever happens just call. You know we all have your back." I state.

CHAPTER TWENTY-SEVEN

Axel

It had been nearly a week when Blake finally made the call. He was getting restless for Wes to listen. It was also partly because Lily was pissed he hadn't been to see them or his new niece. I would fucking hate to be Wes right now.

I pull up to where the guys tell me to meet. As I pull up outside a nice little house in a quiet neighbourhood, I question whether I have the right address. It's not somewhere you expect the daughter of a Cartel boss to live.

I hear yelling coming from inside the house: Lily. Well I guess I definitely have the right address. I don't even bother knocking, I walk straight in.

"What the hell Wes? Your brother and I have just had our baby daughter and you can't even make the effort to come and see us, to see her! Don't think we didn't notice that you were missing for ages at the hospital when Ivy had been born! I bloody well know Rip had to track your arse down. I might have given birth but that doesn't make me stupid or blind. I still noticed what was going on right in front of me! Why? Why are you being such a prick?" Lily yells angrily.

I stand next to Blake and lean in.

"So she hasn't gotten much sleep these past few days then?" I mutter.

"Practically none, Ivy has had a bit of colic." Blake answers.

I notice he looks shattered too.

"I'm sorry but I've been busy with stuff." Wes answers vaguely.

"Uh oh." Blake and I both mutter.

"Stuff! Stuff! You've been busy with stuff rather than coming to meet and spend time with your niece?! Too busy to see your family?" Lily rants.

Before Wes can answer Rose and Rip walk through the door followed by Daisy and Carter.

"Fuck me, what's this?! A god damn intervention?!" Wes snaps.

"You bet your arse it is. Sit tight Wes because you're about to get a Rocke sister intervention." Rose smiles, sitting down on the couch.

"Fucking Christ." Wes sighs.

Daisy walks up to Wes and something flickers across his eyes as she approaches. They've always had a good friendship and connection. Ever since they met Wes has been protective of Daisy. Everything she went through with that scum hit a nerve with Wes. He was there for all of my sisters, but it was Daisy that pulled at his heart strings.

"Daisy, just don't, alright? I've had enough shit from these guys. There isn't anything you can say that hasn't already been said." Wes pleads.

Daisy doesn't say anything, she just steps forward and wraps her arms around him, hugging him tight. Wes can't hold back, he hugs her tight.

She leans back and smiles.

"Wes, if this woman makes you happy then we are happy for you. You have to understand why there is some concern about her though! Especially because of who her father was."

"Yeah because he was such a bloody delight!" Rose interrupts.

Daisy rolls her eyes.

"What we are saying is, you've got to understand what happened with the club, with Rose. I know you get it because it's embedded in you to protect us. If she's a good woman there is no way she would be keeping you from your family. If you can just bring her to meet all of us, then we can accept that you're with her and we will say no more. We want you happy and to be in our lives. Don't cut us out. We will always be here for when you need us." Daisy tries to plead to Wes.

"Listen to the nice sister otherwise you get another round with either me or Lily." Rose points out.

"Hey, I'm nice!" Lily yells which wakes Ivy.

"God damn it! Now you've made me wake up Ivy."

"See what I mean, all the niceness and goodness went to Daisy." Rose points to Daisy.

"You guys have to trust me. Do you really think I would put my life or your lives at risk for some woman? She isn't what you think, there's so much more to it. You don't even know who she is so how can you know what she's like? Our dad was a wife beating low life and we're nothing like him, so why assume she is like her dad?" Wes argues back.

"To be fair you have a point there. Doesn't

explain why you've been absent though, and let's face it, you've been a bit of a dick." Lily points out.

Wes smiles. It's the first time in a while I've actually seen him with a genuine smile.

"Alright, that's on me. I promise I will stop being such a prick and make sure I'm there more." Wes sort of apologises.

"Great. Now that shit is over, here's your niece Ivy. Now you can actually hold her." Blake states while handing Ivy over to Wes.

Wes takes Ivy and smiles.

"So, when can we meet the mystery lady?" Rose asks.

Wes' smile falls from his face.

"Not yet. Not for a while at least, we're having to keep it under wraps for her safety too." He states.

I look to Rip who gives me a quick glance before stepping forward.

"You know I have the resources and the powers to find out who she is, right? You also damn well know that none of us would tell a damn soul." Rip says sharply.

"I know that but I promised her and I'm not about to break that trust." Wes answers back.

"Fine. We will respect that but only for so

long. You need to convince her that she can trust us. As long as she's open and honest with us, we will trust her." Rip offers.

Wes nods.

"One question, whose house are we standing in right now?" I ask.

"It's owned by Luis, or it was. It's not in his name though. There's no trace of him. I'm surprised you found it. There's no trace of her, not even the Cartel know who she is. Luis only ever told one person about Se...um...her. If it ever got out who she is, who her father was, that would make her a massive target. She didn't even know who her father was until she was sixteen. The papers for the house just show it's rented, there are fake names on the papers." Wes answers honestly.

"Oh I feel for her. There must be no way to live happily with your life being a constant lie." Daisy states.

"Well you know where we are if you need us, if you need anything. You know we'll be there." Blake says with his hand on Wes' shoulder.

"I know." Wes says handing back Ivy.

We all pile out. I stop and chat to Rip and Blake.

"You good now?" I ask.

"For now. As long as no one finds out who she

is or who she's involved with, Wes is safe." Blake states.

"Hang on a minute, how in the hell did you find this place?" I turn to Rip.

Rip smiles.

"I have contacts. Those contacts can see through pretty much any fake paper trail. As long as nothing gives the Cartel the idea to sniff around, they're safe."

We nod in agreement and part ways.

I had to ride to Patience, eager to be with her. It may have only been a few hours since I've been with her, but it's a few hours too many.

I ride, enjoying the winding open roads. I pull to a stop seeing a small stall selling flowers. An older woman smiles as I approach.

"Hey there sir. What can I do for you today?" She greets me warmly.

I smile.

"I want a bunch of your nicest flowers please!"

"Sure thing, are they for your wife?" She asked.

Wife. The word hits me, but not in a panicky suffocating way. It settles over me. Patience being my wife fits, it's like I've finally found that last piece of the puzzle. I'm complete.

"No ma'am, but she will be one day." I answer honestly.

The woman smiles and starts picking up flowers.

"Tulips, red for undying love and passion. Now tell me about her so I know what to pick." The woman asks.

"Um, well she's an angel." I answer.

"Pink, caring. What else?" She asks again.

"She is the most beautiful woman I've ever met. Oh and she has amazing green eyes." I state.

"Variegated, for beautiful eyes." The woman states picking a mixed white and pink Tulip.

"She is the only one to truly get me, and she wouldn't take any shit." I smile.

"Orange, understanding, truest love." She laughs.

"Even after I messed up she still took care of me."

"White, forgiveness, sincerity." She smiles kindly.

She doesn't ask me anymore. She gathers a few more little flowers and arranges them. She wraps them tightly with a bow and hands them to me.

"By the sounds of it you've found the one. Cherish every moment together." She smiles.

I go to hand her the money but she shakes her head.

"Not for true love; true love comes at no cost." She smiles.

I nod and thank her. Carefully I leave some notes next to some of her other flowers.

"Then it's a gift." I shout as I pull away, making sure I've strapped down the flowers so they don't get ruined.

I don't think I've ever brought anyone flowers before apart from my mum on mother's day. I smile to myself. I never thought I'd fall in love and be buying flowers. Joe would be ripping the shit out of me right now.

"Hope you're having a fucking good laugh at me up there brother."

CHAPTER TWENTY-EIGHT

Patience

Ma dropped me back at the apartment. Axel still wasn't back so I pottered around and cleaned up a little. Bored with not much else to do I sat on the couch and watch some daytime TV soap opera.

I feel my eyes become heavy and drift off to sleep.

"Patience, baby, wake up." I hear a deep voice say.

I open my eyes and see Axel crouched in front of me. He smiles when I look at him.

"Hey." I mumble sleepily.

I sit up and rub my eyes.

Axel sits next to me. He hands me a bunch of the most beautiful flowers.

"Tulips." I smile. I bring the flower to my nose and smell their sweet floral fragrance.

"I don't think anyone has ever bought me flowers before." I breathed.

"Well I haven't bought flowers for anyone before either, apart for my mum on mother's day." Axel adds.

I place the flowers down and straddle his lap. I take his face in my hands and kiss him.

"Thank you for my beautiful flowers." I whisper across his lips.

I playfully bite his lip and swivel my hips, making him groan. Axel's hand grips my ass tight. I rise, undoing his jeans and freeing his hard length. I hold him in my hand, stroking him slowly. Axel's eyes are hooded as he watches. I move and kneel in between his legs, still stroking him, my eyes never leaving his. I lean forward and take the tip in my mouth. Axel hisses through his teeth. I smile and take as much of him in my mouth as I can. I suck and swirl my tongue. Axel moans and his head falls back. I take him deeper and moan, feeling him begin to pulse. I continue to suck and tease him with my tongue.

"Fuck baby, I'm going to come." Axel groans.

I don't ease up, I suck faster. I feel him explode down my throat as he comes. I moan and continue to lick and suck.

Axel leans forward and grabs me under my arms and pulls me on top of his lap. He strokes his fingers across my centre and I moan.

"You're already fucking soaked, does sucking my cock turn you on baby?" He asks.

I bite my lower lip and nod.

Axel slides his fingers inside of me, curling them and hitting that perfect spot. He circles them over and over. I roll my head back as my hands grip his shoulders. I move my hips in unison with his fingers.

"Show me those beautiful green eyes baby, come for me. Let me feel you." Axel demands.

My eyes connect with Axel's, his eyes are hooded with desire. I can't hold off my orgasm anymore. My hips move quicker as do Axel's fingers.

"Fuck!" I yell as I come hard.

I stop moving my hips and I watch as Axel takes his fingers and sucks my arousal off them.

He lets out a throaty moan.

"Fucking supreme."

I lift my hips enough to position him at my entrance. I slowly slide down his length. We both groan at the feeling of him slowly filling me.

I start rocking and swirling my hips. Axel lifts my dress over my head and throws it aside. He cups my breasts and pulls down the cup of my bra. He takes my nipple in his mouth. I moan, the feeling going straight between my legs. He grips my ass and thrusts up to meet me. I start riding him faster and harder and his grip tightens.

"Fuck that's it baby, ride my cock." Axel demands.

I'm close. I can feel myself begin to tighten around him. Axel continues to thrust up harder and faster. My orgasm hits me. My hips buck and I cry out, my nails digging into his shoulders.

Axel buries his face in the crook of my neck, biting down and groaning as he orgasms.

We are both panting. There's a sheen of sweat covering our bodies.

"I love you Axel." I breathe.

Axel lifts his head and cups my face, stroking my cheek with his thumb.

"I love you too. I fucking worship you, do you know that?" He states with pure emotion and conviction in his eyes.

I swallow back the tears and kiss him softly.

We stay like that together, connected in each other's embrace, for a while. Axel tells me about each of the tulips' meanings. I feel like my heart is going to explode from my chest it's so full. I don't know what I've done to deserve this man but I know I will never let him go and will cherish every moment I have with him.

"How do you like it?" I ask placing a fresh fillet steak into the pan.

"Medium, but if you're making it I'd eat it even if it came out tasting like a dried up rubber tyre." Axel winks.

"Well lucky for you this girl can cook. Well, a little bit anyway."

I plate up our dinner, steak, fries, and stuffed mushrooms.

We sit down and Axel moans after he's taken his first bite of steak.

"Well now I don't know if it's actually nice or you're just being polite because I cooked it." I tease.

"Oh baby, it's a fucking spectacular steak. I lied, I wouldn't have eaten it if it tasted like shit. I would have feigned illness." Axel says around a mouthful of food.

I throw a bread roll at him. He, of course, catches it rather than it hitting him in the head.

"Easy there Firecracker." Axel goads.

I flip him of and continue eating.

"I'm thinking of asking Daisy and Carter to take Miguel full time." Axel blurts out.

I stop eating and look to him. I immediately reach over and grab his hand.

"Is that what you want or what you think is right?" I ask.

Axel lifts my hand and places a kiss on my palm.

"Both. I saw the way he was with them and around them and the way they were with him. I can't give him that and I can't expect you to take that role on either. Him being with them brings him so much joy and it makes Daisy and Carter happy too. I know he would get so much love from them, he would never want for anything." Axel states.

I get up and move, perching myself on his lap. I wrap my arms around his neck and he wraps his arms around my waist.

"You know I would happily take on that role with Miguel. I understand what you're saying but don't think for a damn second that you couldn't give Miguel that kind of life or love, because you can. Just know that whatever you decide I will be supporting you one hundred percent. I know where I want to be and that is by your side. I'm not going anywhere, whether we adopt Miguel or not." I point out.

"You're fucking incredible. I will think about it some more. Maybe I'll talk to Daisy and Carter about it and see how they feel. I know that if Daisy and Carter want Miguel, I can't deny them that happiness and I know I will forever have Miguel in my life regardless."

I lean in and kiss Axel softly. He groans in his throat and grabs the back of my head, deepening the kiss.

"Now I'm hungry for something else." Axel says while kissing along my neck.

He stands, picking me up, and starts walking to the bedroom.

"What about dinner?" I giggle.

"Fuck dinner, it's you I want to eat." Axel winks.

"Then please do continue kind sir." I wave my hand in the direction of the bedroom, doing my best English accent.

Axel laughs and shakes his head.

"Easy there Dick Van Dyke." He mocks.

I squeal and laugh as he throws me onto the bed.

He kneels at the foot of the bed, placing my legs either side of him.

"Prepare yourself baby, because I'm bloody starving." Axel wiggles his eyebrows.

I start to laugh but my laughter soon dies down and turns into moans as I feel his mouth on me.

Later that night after mind blowing sex, Axel and I led in bed eating cold steak and fries. In that moment, it was the best steak and fries I've ever tasted.

CHAPTER TWENTY-NINE

Axel

Patience is spending the day with Maddie. She wanted to take her to the mall to go shopping as a surprise. Afterwards they are going to see the new princess movie that has just been released. The terms of her being able to do this were that she has a tracker on her phone at all times. If it weren't for Rip coming to an agreement with Dreads, things would still be on high alert. As it is, Austin's double crossing ways have been exposed to Dreads and now to the Cartel. He's a wanted man, a dead man walking. He's wanted by the deadliest people around.

While Patience is with Maddie I go and get

her birthday present. I pull into Denvy's, park up, and walk over to the office.

"Hell, don't tell me you broke her already?" I hear yelled from inside the workshop.

I turn and see Denvy walking out and wiping oil off of his hands with a dirty rag. I take off my sunglasses and smile.

"No, I'm not here for me. I'm here to make a purchase." I state as I shake his hand.

Denvy gives me a look.

"Well come on through to my office." He leads the way.

Once inside Denvy leans on his desk and slams down some paperwork.

I pick it up.

"How the fuck did you know I was here to buy her bike?"

"I may be old, and I may not be fucking bright, but I've got eyes in my damn head. I knew you'd be back. You two had love in your eyes. Believe me, I know that when you fall for the right woman you'll do anything to make them happy." Denvy states before sitting down and pouring himself a shot of bourbon.

"Well you're right. I know it's her birthday in a couple of weeks and I wanted to surprise her, so here's the cash. Can you have it ready with side cart in two weeks?" I ask, placing a large wad of dollars on his desk.

Denvy smiles.

"Abso-fuckin-lutly."

I shake his hand and promise to be in touch. I can't wipe the smile off my face.

I pull up at the club and walk in to see all of the brothers hanging out in the bar.

"Took your damn time. We've been waiting so long we had to have a beer to pass the time." Rubble jokes.

"Sorry, I had to make a stop on the way. Where's Rip?" I look around.

"Sat in his office. I will go and grab him so we can get this church under way." Khan walks off to get him.

We all pile into the room and wait for Rip. I quickly check my phone and see a text from Patience.

P: We've just sat down with our popcorn and we're waiting for the movie. We are fine. See you in a couple of hours. Love you xxx

I type a quick reply.

A: Just at the club, will meet you both here after the movie. Love you too.

I put my phone back in my pocket as Rip

walks in. He's smoking which I've learnt is never a good sign because it means he's stressed out or there is some shit going down.

He takes his seat, looks over the papers he has in his hands, and sighs.

"Pres?" Mammoth asks.

Rip's head snaps up as if he's forgotten where he is.

"Right, yeah. Sorry brothers. I've got shit to tell you and it ain't gonna be easy. Just shut up and listen." Rip pauses, pinching the bridge of his nose.

"Our newest prospect, Jack, was gunned down last night outside his girlfriend's place."

We all look at each other in shock. I didn't know him well. I only saw him when he was keeping guard at Big Papa's.

"Titch? Who in their right mind would want that boy killed! He was only 20!" Khan fumes.

"We spoke to the girlfriend. She said it was a saloon type car and had blacked out windows. Nothing stood out for her to be able to identify them. She also said he was wearing his cut; he never took it off. He was too proud to ever do that. So we know he was killed because of the club, because of his association to the club." Rip puts out his cigarette.

"I thought all the threats were done with

now, or at least for the time being." I questioned.

Rip sighs.

"So did I brother. I've spoken with Dreads and he assured me his men had nothing to do with it and that he will let me know if he hears anything. I'd guess it was the Cartel. Can't be anyone else. The war is building with them and it's just a matter of when, not if. I thought we'd pushed it back and it was under wraps for now but I guess I was wrong. They came onto our turf and shot a brother in his cut. That confirms there was no mistaken identity. This was a planned and organised hit. I know I will not fuckin' rest until I find the fuckin' parasites that did it. I will exterminate every fuckin' one of them."

The feel of anger and loss radiates around the room, the brothers murmur their promises for blood and revenge.

Rip bangs his gavel and yells.

"Alright, enough! That's not why I called you to church. We will find the fucker and gut him, but we also need to deal with this."

Rip stands and puts a load of photos in the middle of the table. I look over and what I see has my blood running cold.

Photos of Patience, Maddie, Big Papa, and Raven. I'm in some of them too.

"Who the fuck took these?!" I bark.

"Calm down Axel. It's just some private investigator that Austin hired. There are more though." Rip places down a few more photographs.

One is of Patience and I when we were in the car park after I bought her shopping. Another is when we were outside getting hot and heavy. The last one is from inside my apartment. It's a picture of Patience and I from the other night and we're fucking on the couch.

"What the fuck?!" I yell, jumping to my feet.

You can't see anything, just Patience with her head thrown back in ecstasy. Judging by the angle it's taken, from the fucker was right at the window.

"That's from the side window. I guess I forgot to close the damn curtains." I say through gritted teeth.

"I've purposefully sent Big Papa to bring in the PI that took these. He's got him and is bringing him in now. Big Papa hasn't seen these for good reason; no goddamn father wants to see their daughter like that." Rip states.

"He will be here in ten, so all round to the shed boys." Rip sneers.

The guys all holler and cheer as they get up, cracking their knuckles. I look to Rip.

"The shed?" I ask.

"Small warehouse out the back. It's sort of our questioning area." Rip smirks as he leaves.

I follow behind him. As I enter the shed I notice a chair in the middle of the room with cuffs attached to it. I smile at Rip, I shouldn't have expected anything less. This is their interrogation room. There are some weapons along the walls, all for the purpose of scaring the shit out of anyone that comes here. Mammoth and Rubble pull out a large polyethene sheet and place it around the chair. I raise my eyebrow in question.

"Oh don't worry brother, we ain't killing him. You can guarantee he will shit his mother fucking pants when he sees this though. He'll probably cry like a baby too." Mammoth laughs.

I laugh too. I want this son of a bitch to be scared. Hell, I want this mother fucker dead. I hate that he took pictures of Patience in that way. I'm the only one that gets to see her like that. I crack my neck and knuckles, feeling agitated and wanting nothing more now than to get my fucking hands on the weasel.

We hear a commotion outside and the door swings open. Big Papa shoves the guy through. He's snivelling like a baby. He falls to the floor and Mammoth practically picks him up and seats him in the chair before cuffing him to it.

The man's panicked eyes dart around the

room. There's sweat dripping from his brow.

"Please, please! I didn't do anything wrong. I don't even know why I'm here." He lies and begs.

At his words I step forward. His eyes come to mine and recognition flickers through them. I smile.

"Do you recognise me?" I ask.

"No, I'm sorry, I don't. I think there's been a terrible misunderstanding." He lies.

I hold out the picture of Patience and I in the parking lot and then the one of me outside of my apartment. I pause and turn to Big Papa.

"Sorry you have to hear this Big Papa." I warn him. Confusion crosses his face.

"So you don't recognise me in the pictures you took of me with my girlfriend?" I ask before showing him the final photograph.

He shakes his head vigorously.

"What about when I'm making love to my girlfriend in my own home? You telling me you weren't the one peering through my god damn window and taking pictures of my girlfriend while she was screaming my name? While she was riding my cock?"

"What the fuck?!" Big Papa yells and I hear a scuffle behind me.

Khan and Rubble hold him back.

"Easy brother. Let Axel have his say and then you can have yours." Rip warns.

I turn back around to face the guy. I stand in front of him.

"You know what I really hate? I'm sorry, where are my manners, what's your name?" I ask.

"Patrick." He rushes out.

"Well Patrick, what I really fucking hate is when people lie to me. You know, when I've asked a question, when I've been nothing but polite, and they've still lied to me. I'm guessing you didn't do your investigating very well or you would know I'm well trained in reading people and knowing when they are lying. I know exactly when that lie slips from their lips. Also, if you'd researched me properly you would know that I'm trained to kill. I'm trained to kill so that there is not a drop of blood or evidence. I mean, this sheet isn't for me, I'm not planning on to killing you. But I can't make any promises for my girlfriend's father over there." I walk behind him and squeeze his shoulders. I lean in and whisper in his ear.

"I really don't want to kill you but I might just cut off your dick and feed it to you."

"Nooo, please, please. I was hired by this guy, he said his girlfriend was cheating and he wanted evidence. That's all he said. He didn't say it was anything to do with the Satan's or believe me I wouldn't have touched the case. You have to believe me!" He wails and begs.

"Thank you Patrick for being so honest with me. I appreciate it. I've got one more question for you. Tell me, did you enjoy watching me and my girlfriend fucking? I mean, she does have the perfect body. Her tits man! Fuck! Don't even get me started on her arse. So I guess you saw all of it, huh?" I ask.

The guy looks confused at my change in tactic. I show him my palms.

"Hey, I know I've got a good thing buddy. My girlfriend is fucking hot. You're only human, right?" I shrug and smile.

"Oh yeah Patty. She's fuckin' one hot piece of ass" Rubble adds.

"Brother, do not make me bury your fucking ass too!" Big Papa threatens.

Patrick, smiles.

"Yeah, she is hot." He doesn't say any more.

"You know Patrick, I think after this little misunderstanding we could be friends. I mean, you were just doing your job, right? You're a red blooded man. I mean come on, we've all watched porn, right?" I ask with fake laughter.

Patrick laughs with me and nods.

"So did you get more than photographs of me and my woman? Film us maybe? Because I wouldn't mind seeing that, seeing her bounce on my cock." I sigh.

I watch as Patrick swallows nervously. That's my answer.

"You did, didn't you? You sneaky bastard." I laugh like it's no big deal but inside I'm raging. My fingers twitch, wanting to kill the fucker.

"So did you give the video to Austin? Or do you keep those personal videos at home?" I ask.

"Oh no. I keep the videos like that at home, locked away." He answers straight away without thinking.

I turn and look to Rip who gives me the nod.

"Well I would love to see that collection sometime Patrick, I mean, they're all hoes any-way right? They can't keep their legs closed! What can I say, I'm a sucker for some good pussy." I laugh and nudge him.

Patrick laughs.

"Yeah, your girl's pussy has to be one of the best I've seen."

I snap. I swing round and hit him so hard his head whips to the side, knocking out a few teeth. I grab him by his hair and hold his head up.

"You vile fucking piece of scum. You're going to regret everything you've said and done. Remember what I said earlier? Well I hope you're fucking hungry because you're about to get a mouthful of your own dick."

I hold him down as Big Papa walks towards him with a knife in his hand, smiling. He doesn't say anything, he rears back his knife and stabs him right in his dick.

"Whoops! I went right through the middle rather than from the top, silly me." Big Papa mocks.

He pulls the knife out and does it again. Patrick lets out another blood curdling scream.

I lean in and whisper in his ear.

"This will be your lasting memory Patrick. No one ever fucking takes what's mine. No one ever disrespects the woman I fucking love. No one should ever disrespect any woman." I don't give him time to respond. I grab hold of his head and using my full strength I twist and pull. The room fills with a loud cracking sound.

"Oh man, that sound." Khan moans.

I let go of his head and it hangs forward.

"Is he dead?" Mammoth asks.

I reach forward and quickly check his pulse.

I nod.

"Just about. He has a really weak pulse."

"I thought that move killed instantly." Khan states.

"Not instantly like in the movies. Sometimes not at all. He's fucking paralysed for life if he does survive. If you leave him like that, bleeding out, he's definitely dead." I shrug.

Big Papa leans over and pulls Patrick's head up. He slits his throat with his knife.

"Well now he's one hundred percent dead." I state.

"Any fucker who messes with my family meets his maker." Big Papa states.

I nod in agreement.

"So do want me to ride on over and burn the guy's house down?" I ask.

"Leave it to the guys. I don't know about you but I need a drink." Rip smiles.

I nod and we all go to the bar, leaving the Prospects and Rubble in charge of the clean-up.

I go to the bathroom first to wash any blood remnants off of my hands.

I join the brothers in the bar.

Rip stands.

"This toast is for Jack. May he be raising hell wherever he may be." We all cheer and toast with him.

I take a large pull of my beer and pull out my phone. No new text from Patience. I look at the time, realising they might still be in the movie. I grab another beer and enjoy kicking back and chatting with the brothers.

Rip pulls me to one side and hands me a piece of folded paper. I frown as I unfold it and see a name and an address on it.

"What's this?" I ask.

"You know I said I have connections? Well that's the name of the guy who ordered your assignment. He owed the Cartel a shit load of money through gambling and the Cartel cashed in what was owed to them: the land of that village. That place is well hidden and not on any maps. It's the perfect place for the Cartel to hold their drugs, guns, and girls." Rip informs me.

I look down at the paper in my hands and feel a surge for revenge.

"The only thing I ask is that if you decide to kill him, you be smart about it. If you need our help we will have your back." Rip states.

I nod. "Appreciate this man."

"I know. You may be able to get some closure from this. Come on, let's get a beer."

CHAPTER THIRTY

Patience

"Mama, I just loved the pwincess! She was so pwetty and she could sing and dance and bake! I think she might be my favouritest." Maddie skips happily alongside me.

"Okay Cupcake. You know you said that about the last princess movie I took you to see, right?" I remind her.

"Oh I know! I just love them all!" She giggles.

I shake my head and smile. I load the trunk with our shopping: more princess dresses. I can't help spoiling her; I'm trying to make up for my mistakes.

Maddie jumps in her seat and I fasten her in. I

give her a kiss.

"Love you Cupcake." I say while blowing a raspberry on her cheek.

"Love you too Mama!"

I jump in my seat and I can't wipe the smile from my face. Life is good. For the first time in a while, my life is going great. I have Maddie back in my life and Axel. My life is complete.

"Mama play my songs! Pwease!" Maddie yells from the back seat.

I hit the button and princess songs fill the car. I inwardly groan but can't be mad when it makes her so happy.

Driving back I realise I forgot to text Axel. I reach for my cell and hand it to Maddie.

"Cupcake, press the call button and ring Axel. Tell him we're on our way." I tell Maddie.

"Okie dokie!" She sings.

"He's not answering Mama." She yells.

"Leave him a message."

"Axel we are sooo close to home. We will see you super soon. Oh and the pwincess film was..."

We are hit from behind which causes the truck to tail fish out of control. Maddie screams as the truck flips into the ditch.

"Mama! Mama!" Maddie cries.

My eyes feel heavy and my head is pounding. I put my hand up and feel blood. My whole body hurts but I need to get to Maddie.

I unclip my seat belt and try my best to manoeuvre into the back with the truck upside down.

"Shhhh, it's okay Cupcake, Mama is here. I've got you, okay?" I say shakily.

I unclip her and her little arms hold me tight. I look around for my cell. Luckily I find it and it's not too cracked. I can still call on it.

"Can you call Axel again for Mama while I break this window to get us out?" I ask Maddie.

She nods and I place her down.

"Stand back, Mama doesn't want you getting hurt."

I kick and kick at the window but it doesn't give. Suddenly there's a gunshot at the window which makes us both scream. Whoever it is kicks the window in.

"Get the fuck out here now before I shoot the gas tank." He threatens.

I immediately know that voice.

"Austin." I whisper.

"Mama." Maddie whispers, scared behind me.

"It's okay. Listen to Mama and do exactly as I

say, okay?"

She nods, her eyes filling with tears, I notice a cut on her head and my heart breaks.

"Bring the cell but keep it hidden, okay? I love you so much Cupcake." I whisper.

I crawl out of the truck, not letting go of Maddie. As soon as we are out I see Austin aiming a gun at me.

"Put the girl down!" Austin orders.

I shake my head. Maddie holds onto me tightly, sobbing.

"I said put the fucking brat down now before I blow her tiny little brains out!" He screams.

I jump and slowly kneel down and place Maddie on her feet. She won't let go of my neck.

"No Mama, pwease No." She sobs.

I need to get her out of here. Austin looks strung out and is twitchy and unpredictable.

I crouch down and lean in, whispering in her ear.

"Cupcake, listen to me. Run. Follow this road and run to the Satan's building. It's just at the end of this road. Keep pressing the call button for Axel. I promise Mama is going to be okay. Be a brave princess. I love you so much." I say, desperately trying to hold back my own tears.

"Okay Mama, I love you." Maddie says wiping her tears.

"Go." I whisper.

She takes off running. I stand quickly.

"Where the fuck is she going?!" Austin yells and aims his gun at her. I don't think, I just walk towards him, blocking his aim and protecting Maddie.

"It's me you want, isn't it? You don't want her so leave her out of this Austin. You have me." I try to reason with him.

He sneers. Reaching out he grabs my hair and yanks me to the ground. I scream in pain. I look up and see Maddie has stopped and turned to face me. I mouth the words go over and over. I'm begging her to keep running. I breathe a sigh of relief when she turns and continues to run.

"This is what you're used to, isn't it? Being on your fuckin' knees, you stupid slut. You fucking owed me! I own you and you defied me and left. Now you've left me in it. You've left me in a shit storm, all the while you're happily skipping along and fucking the army boy. All while I fuckin' suffer." Austin spits in my face.

"You see, your army boy and Satan's have interfered. They have messed up my plans and now I'm wanted by the Cartel and Dreads! If you'd just done as you were told I could've handed you over to the Cartel. They could have used you as bait with the Satan's and then everyone would have been happy. But nooooo, you had to be a selfish bitch!" He screeches.

He's lost everything and he's a wanted man. He has nothing left to lose. This doesn't fill me with comfort. He's a man who has nothing to risk, nothing to lose. It means there's nothing stopping him putting a bullet through my head.

"Talk to me Austin. I promise I will help anyway I can." I offer.

"Trying to sweet talk me? That won't work. There's only one thing your mouth is good for and that is sucking dick!"

I curl my lip in disgust.

"You can't be too picky when you have a gun pointed at your head. I have the fuckin' power now." He pauses, laughing.

"In fact, hell, I can get you to do whatever I damn well please. I'm in charge and while I wait for pick up, I think I deserve a little fuckin' reward." Austin sneers.

I freeze. I look up to see that Maddie is long gone. Thank god she's out of this. I swallow the bile in my throat. I don't think I can live through this again. I finally let the tears I had been holding back fall. I just pray that Maddie gets to the Satan's. I pray that she gets to Axel.

CHAPTER THIRTY-ONE

Axel

"To Jack!" Is shouted again for the third time. Whenever someone fills their drink, we all cheer with them.

I see the outside door open and a scared Maddie looking around the room. I frown in confusion. It's then I notice the cut on her head. I run to her and pick her up. Her little arms squeeze so tight around my neck. She is sobbing and her whole body is wracked with tears.

The guys cut the music and stand around to see what's wrong with Maddie.

"Maddie, princess, where is your mum?" I ask, dread filling my stomach.

She finally lets go enough to lean back.

"The bad man, the horrible man! He, he cwashed us. He had a gun! He has Mama!" She continue to sob.

"Maddie, where? Do you know where?" I ask, my heart beating so hard and fast it feels like it's about to burst through my chest.

"Down the end of the road. Mama told me to run here. I tried calling, Mama said to call." She wails.

At that moment Big Papa comes in.

"What the fuck? Maddie?!" He rushes over.

"Big Papa, take her. Patience needs me." I say, handing him Maddie.

I ignore the brothers. I ignore them calling my name. I don't have time for them right now. I walk out and head straight for my bike, not waiting to see if any of the guys are following. My only concern is that I need to get to Patience in time.

I ride as fast as I can. I see a car pulled up ahead and see the truck overturned in the ditch. My heart lurches. I pull out my gun and make the rest of the way there on foot.

I keep low and use the bushes for cover.

I hear Austin.

"Take it off bitch. I've got the Cartel arriving soon and they will want to see the goods. I've missed it and I deserve a run before them, especially after what you've fuckin' put me through."

I creep with my gun aimed. I can see Patience standing there in her denim shorts and bra. There's a bad cut on her head and it's pouring with blood. Her hands shake as she reaches for the button of her shorts.

Red hot molten lava runs through my veins. As I move forward Patience's eyes land on me and relief flashes through them. I hold my finger to my lips to keep her quiet. Just as I'm about to move the sound of bikes approaching spooks Austin. He reaches forward and grabs her, yanking her by her hair. She screams in pain and the sight and sound rips through me like a knife.

I'm helpless to do anything right now. I follow, keeping low and out of sight. Austin stops in the middle of the road, using Patience as a shield and holding his gun to her temple. Rip, Mammoth, Khan, and Rubble come to a stop. All but Rip raise their guns and take aim.

"Austin, what the fuck do you think you're doing? There ain't no way this can end good for you." Rip warns.

I see his eyes clock my bike to the side. His jaw tenses as his eyes casually scope the surrounding area. He spots me and returns his full attention back to Austin.

"You fucking Satan's think you can have it

all! You think you can rule this town! Well I've been making friends, friends who want to see you dead, and they will be here any minute." Austin threatens.

"Y'all are gonna have to be more specific. See, there are a lot of people that want me and the Satan's dead." Rip snorts laughing.

Austin smiles.

"The Cartel, motherfuckers! The Mexican Cartel! Do you remember what Luis did to your old lady? I heard about that. Oh, and wasn't there some other slut who got what was coming to her at the orders of the Cartel before your bitch wife?!" Austin goads.

Hearing him talk about Rose and Lily like that is like being stabbed in the chest. Hearing what happened to my sisters and not being here to help, to protect them, it killed me. Now I'm watching Patience with a gun to her head, there is no way I am letting anything happen to her.

"Oh silly me, I forgot! I shot one of yours last night. Perfect fucking head shot too! Man he fell to the ground like the sack of shit he was." Austin continues to goad, his hands twitching from the drug use.

Rip and the brothers all tense at those words. They want blood.

The sound of trucks arriving draws our attention and Austin smiles.

"Ahhh, my friends have arrived. I'm so glad you'll get to meet them."

Two trucks pull up behind Austin. The doors open and out step four guys with what look like machine guns and rifles.

Another guy steps out of the truck. He's smartly dressed in an expensive suit. He walks forward and his guards step aside, allowing him to pass.

"Hola mi amigos. I must say, I wasn't expecting such a large welcome party for my arrival." He states with a strong Mexican accent.

"Jesús." Rip sneers.

"Fuck me. It's like looking at the ghost of Luis!" Khan states in shock.

"Ahh yes, I get that a lot. When my padre was alive we often got mistaken for hermanos. Of course I was the better looking one." Jesús brags.

He walks up to Austin and tuts.

"Austin, mi amigo. That is no way to treat a beautiful woman." He says as he makes Austin lower his gun. He takes Patience's hand and pulls her aside and whistles.

"She's a goddess." He states as his eyes sweep over her body.

Patience spits at him and struggles to pull away. She kicks out but Jesús is too strong for her. He grabs her by the waist and pulls her to him, holding a blade to her throat.

"I like a woman with pasión." He states, smiling.

He turns to his men and with a flick of his chin they fire and shoot down Austin. Patience screams and shakes in fear. She's only a few feet away from him.

"What do you want Jesús?" Rip asks.

"I will say it in perfect English so you understand. I want this land, I want this territory, but most of all, I want revenge for my padre." He threatens.

"Those are things I cannot let you have." Rip responds. Tension is high and I feel a war building. One wrong move and there will be a mass shoot out and Patience will end up dead.

"I wasn't asking, mi amigo." He spits.

The angle Jesús is at I could shoot him and take him out, hopefully without causing any harm to Patience. I take aim but just as I'm about to shoot the sound of more bikes and trucks approach.

Rip smirks.

"You want a war Jesús, you've fuckin' got it!"

Jesús' eyes go wide and a flicker of fear dances across them as the rest of the Satan's pull up. Dreads and his men step out of the truck.

They are all armed and all aiming at Jesús and his men. I breathe a sigh of relief at the sight of them.

I look to Patience. She looks at me and I give her a brief nod, hoping she understands what I mean. Thankfully, she does.

She kicks back hard, hitting him unexpectedly in the shin. Jesús shouts out and immediately lets go of Patience. She runs right to me. I take aim and start shooting, taking out his men one by one. Rip and the guys leave it to me but they're ready to back me up if I need it. With my training I've taken out all four of his men within quick succession. I don't need the others to help.

Jesús is on his own. He backs away to his truck.

"This isn't over. There will be a fucking war! I will kill you all!" He shouts as he runs the last few steps to his truck.

Rip gives the nod, smirking. The guys open fire, shooting at the truck as it speeds off.

I reach for Patience and pull her into my arms. Her body shakes as she sobs. I don't say anything, I just hold her tight.

"Maddie?" She asks, wiping her tears.

"She safe, she's with your dad at the club." I answer, cupping her face.

"Fuck, I thought I was going to lose you. I

thought my world was going to end right before my fucking eyes. I can't be without you. I need you like I need my next breath. I'm so sorry I missed your calls, I should have been here to protect you and Maddie. I could have stopped it somehow." I confess, emotion clogging my throat.

Patience's eye brim with tears. She leans in and kisses me so softly. Her lips caress mine.

"I love you Axel. Don't be sorry, you saved me when I needed saving. Without you, my world would have continued to be surrounded by darkness, I would've never seen a way out. You made me see that. Don't ever apologise; you saved me long before today." Patience sobs, tears running down her cheek.

I wipe them with my thumb. I place my lips just barely touching hers.

"Baby, we saved each other from the darkness." I whisper.

I crash my mouth down on her mouth and kiss her with everything I am. I pour all that I have into the kiss.

"Ah man, at least wait until you're in goddamn private before you start fucking!" Mammoth yells loudly beside us.

We break the kiss, laughing.

"Err, brother." Mammoth points to Patience's half-dressed state.

I take off my t-shirt and place it on Patience. It swallows her small frame. She smiles and shakes her head.

I take her hand and walk over to the rest of the guys. Rip pulls Patience in for a hug as do Mammoth, Rubble, and Khan.

"So tell me again why we didn't kill Jesús?" I ask.

Dreads walks forward and crosses his arms over his broad chest.

"We didn't kill him because they would just appoint someone else. It would never end. This way, we go to war and we take out all of them. Can't regroup when there aren't any men left." He states.

"We're off, catch you around Rip." Dreads nods to Rip and leaves.

"Wow." Patience breathes next to me. I give her a look.

"What? I'm sorry but he is one fine looking man! And with his presence! You know he owns it all." She swoons. She damn well swoons!

"Baby! I've just saved your ass! We shared a moment and you're here swooning after Dreads?!"

"Sorry, there's only ever you, I promise. Now take me to see my Cupcake." Patience bats her eyelashes at me.

I growl in my throat and she smiles.

We ride back to the club house and as soon as Patience walks through the door, Maddie comes running.

"Mama!" She wails.

Patience drops to her knees and wraps her arms tightly around Maddie, rocking her back and forth.

"I'm here Cupcake. I'm here." Patience repeats.

"Mama, where's the bad man?" Maddie asks sobbing.

"He's gone and he will never ever hurt us ever again. Axel saved me, he saved us." Patience cries while looking up at me.

Maddie wipes her tears and lets go of Patience. She runs to me, I catch her in my arms and pick her up, holding her tight. Her little body shakes with tears.

"Thank you Axel! I love you so so much." She sobs.

I kiss the top of her head.

"Anything for you. I would go to the end of the world to save you and your mum." I whisper in her ear.

Patience stands and I put my arm around

her. Maddie puts an arm around her too. I hold them both in my arms. I hold my world, my dark angel, my saviour, and her wonderful daughter, in my arms, and I don't ever plan on letting either of them go.

CHAPTER THIRTY-TWO

Patience

In the days that followed Axel wouldn't leave my side. For two days he made me rest, even though apart from my head and a few bruises I was fine.

It's been over a week now and his smothering is driving me insane.

I get up and head to the kitchen. I can hear Axel and Maddie laughing. I stand and watch them from across the room and my heart melts.

Maddie is sitting on the kitchen side with her little apron on. What looks like pancake mix is splattered all over her. Axel has the music on and is doing air guitar with the spatula. All he has on are a pair of low hung trackies. My eyes travel over his ripped body; I can't help but lick my lips.

"I was made for lovin' you baby! You were made for lovin me!" Axel sings while sliding across the tiles.

Maddie roars loud with laughter. Axel puts down the spatula, picks up Maddie, and swings her around. She's giggling so much she is red in the face. She still has the whisk in her hand and the pancake mix is flicking everywhere, it's all down Axel's back.

I can't contain my laughter. Axel stops spinning Maddie around and his eyes land on me. His smiles almost bowls me over. I love seeing him this happy, seeing him smiling like this. God, he kills me!

I walk over to them both and run my finger down Axel's back, scraping off some of the pancake mix.

"Whoops." Maddie giggles.

"Whoops is right, Cupcake." I laugh.

Axel wraps his arm around me and leans in to give me a kiss.

"Morning baby." He smiles across my lips.

"Nice moves." I respond.

"Mama we were going to make you breakfast in bed!" Maddie says excitedly.

"We still will princess. We just need to clear this mess up first. Mama can have a shower while we make it and then we can still surprise her, okay?" Axel looks at me and I nod. I give Maddie a kiss before I turn around and leave to get in the shower.

Once showered I put on a plain navy thin strapped dress. I sit on the bed and wait for my surprise breakfast from Axel and Maddie.

I don't have to wait long before Maddie comes in. She's carrying some fresh flowers that she's obviously just picked from outside. Axel is carrying the tray. Both of them still have flour on their faces. God, they look so cute!

"Mama, these are for you." She hands me the flowers.

"Thank you Cupcake." I kiss her head and pull her onto my lap.

Axel climbs on the bed and puts down the tray.

"Breakfast is served!"

I burst out laughing. On the tray is a takeout breakfast from the local drive thru.

"Yeah well, it turns out we lost a lot of pancake mix and I'm not a great cook. Taadaa!" Axel laughs.

I pull him in for a kiss. I sweep my tongue against his and he moans. I smile, breaking the kiss.

"I will thank you properly later." I whisper in his ear.

Axel's eyes heat with desire. He lets out a low growl which makes me laugh.

"Are you ready for today?" I ask, changing the subject.

"Yeah, I have all of the paperwork. Do you think they will go for it?" He asks.

"I think they will be beyond honoured that you've asked them." I reassure.

"Go and get showered and dressed and let's head over there. They will be expecting us."

Axel gives me a brief kiss before jumping off of the bed and getting in the shower. I sigh. Today he's taking over the adoption papers to Daisy and Carter and asking them to adopt Miguel. It's a big jump. They think we're picking Miguel up today. Axel knew just by talking to them that they were gutted to be seeing Miguel go, even though they didn't voice it. Axel knows that Miguel loves them, that he has loved living with them. It all just reaffirmed to Axel that his choice was the right one.

Once Axel and Maddie are dressed we jump in Axel's new truck and head over to Daisy and Carter's. I reach across and place my hand on his thigh to reassure him.

We pull up to the drive and park. I turn to Axel.

"It will be okay, I promise."

Axel pulls me in for a brief kiss.

As soon as we enter the house we are greeted by all of the Rocke family apart from his parents. They've gone to the airport to pick up Penny's mother.

"Hey Miguel." Axel kneels down to his level and Miguel smiles and gives him a hug.

Maddie runs straight to him, twirling around and showing him her latest in princess dress. He already looks bored.

After the greeting Axel and I ask to speak with Daisy and Carter privately.

Once we are outside on the decking Axel holds out the envelope to them. Daisy opens the envelope and pulls out the adoption papers.

"Axel, what is this?" Daisy asks. Carter gently squeezes her neck, looking over Daisy to see what they are.

"I would like for you both to adopt Miguel." Axel rasps.

I take his hand in mine for support, although I can already feel myself having to fight back the tears.

"What?" Daisy asks, her voice breaking.

"What I mean is, if you wanted to adopt him, I'd like you to. Miguel has been through a lot. He's seen his whole village get murdered. I held him in my arms while his mum begged me to keep him safe, to take good care of him, and I will. I will take damn good care of him, but seeing the way you are with him, the way he is with you, I know this is where he needs to be. This is where he belongs. The boy deserves a stable dad like you Carter. He deserves a mum like you Daisy: kind, caring, and unbelievably giving. In the short time he's been staying with you, you've become a family." Axel swallows the lump in his throat.

Daisy's hands shake. Tears stream down her face.

"Axel...I...I..." She sobs. Carter pulls her to him and kisses the top of her head.

"I don't mean to force this on you and I meant what I said. If you don't feel right about having him I will happily look after him. I just didn't want to be the one that broke up what appears to be an already loving family. I know how long you've wanted a family, Daisy. I just... I don't fucking know...I just wanted to try and do the right thing for Miguel and for you." Axel sighs.

I wrap my arm around Axel's waist and wipe

away my tears.

Daisy looks up to Carter and he cups her face, gently caressing her cheek and wiping away her tears.

"Sweetheart that boy has worked his way into my heart, and I know he has yours. I want nothing more than to have a family with you and while we're still trying for our own I reckon we have a lot of love to give. We have a lot of love to share. Sweetheart, I know you'll be the best goddamn mum there is." Leaning in he kisses her gently.

Daisy smiles while wiping her tears.

"You mean it? Once we sign these papers, he's ours. He will be all ours." She beams.

"Where's the damn pen?" Carter asks, smiling.

Axel pulls out a pen and hands it to them. Carter signs and then hands the pen to Daisy. Her hands shake as she signs the papers. As soon as she's done she jumps into Carter's arms.

"We're parents! I can't believe I'm a mum!" She sobs into his neck.

"Shhh, I know sweetheart. You'll be the best fucking mum." He croaks.

I let out a sob and Axel looks at me. I notice a lone tear fall down his cheek. He smiles.

"I just helped to give my sister the one thing

she thought she could never have: a family. She has wanted this for so long." He croaks, swallowing back his emotion.

Daisy turns to Axel and pulls him in for a hug.

"Ax, thank you so much. You have no idea, none. You've given us a family. I am a fucking mother!" Daisy screeches joyfully, making us all laugh.

"Oh shit, I probably shouldn't swear. Do mums swear?" She asks.

"All the fuckin' time, we just mutter it under our breaths." I smile.

Daisy jumps back into Carter's arms.

"You're a Daddy." She smiles up at him.

"Yeah sweetheart, I fuckin' am." He smiles proudly.

Carter reaches out his hand and pulls Axel in for a guy hug. They slap each other on the back.

"You want me to call Miguel out so you can talk to him?" I ask.

Daisy and Carter both nod.

"Yeah because once our family get a hold of this news there ain't no way they'll keep quiet." Axel snorts.

I call Miguel and he comes running over. I take him out to Daisy and Carter.

"We will leave you too it." I say as Axel and I turn to leave.

"No, stay. This involves you guys too." Daisy adds.

We stay. I watch as Daisy and Carter crouch down low to Miguel's level.

"Sweetie, how would you like to stay here forever, for us to look after you forever?" Daisy asks. Miguel doesn't say anything for a while.

"Para ser mi madre y mi padre?" He asks.

"Yes, if you want us to be your mum and dad." Daisy answers cautiously.

Miguel stands silently for a moment. I can see the worry in Daisy's face.

Miguel smiles and jumps into Daisy's arms.

"Yes!" He yells.

Carter envelopes them both in his arms and I let out another sob.

Axel smiles and pulls me into his arms.

"What on earth is all this secret meeting crap that's going on?" Rose asks bluntly, opening the door.

Daisy stands with Carter holding Miguel.

"We've just adopted Miguel! I'm a mother!!" She yells proudly.

"Oh my god Daisy! Lily, get your arse here

now!" Rose screams excitedly.

"What?" Lily asks in confusion.

"Daisy and Carter have just adopted Miguel." I inform her.

"No shit?!" Lily asks shocked.

"I'm a mummy!" Daisy yells.

"Ahhhhhhhhhhhhh!" Lily screams, wrapping her arms around her sisters.

"Mum is going to lose her shit." Rose says smiling and wiping tears from her face.

Lily and Rose shower Miguel with kisses which makes him giggle.

"This is a celebration now!" Lily shouts.

CHAPTER THIRTY-THREE

Axel

"Oh my god!" Mum cries. "I have a new grandson!"

"Oh well bugger me! That's just lovely. I have a new great grandson!" Nan claps excitedly.

"Well, I'll remortgage the house ready for Christmas!" Dad teases.

"Ben!" Mum slaps his arm.

Dad walks over to me and pulls me in for a hug. He pulls my head down and kisses it.

"Bloody proud of you son, of what you've done for your sister." He says with emotion.

"It was the right decision to make." I add.

I hand Dad a beer and we clink bottles.

Blake walks over, holding Ivy.

"Fuck me! It's mad to think that this time last year I'd only just met Lily!" He shakes his head and sighs.

He stops mid movement and his eyes go wide.

"Shit, what date is it?!" He asks.

"The fifteenth, why?" I answer.

Relief washes over him.

"I thought I'd forgotten our anniversary. Shit, she would have had my balls in a vice." Blake says while adjusting his balls.

Dad and I laugh.

"Of course she would son; the Rocke women are not to be messed with, believe me." Dad warns.

"What's this?" Rip asks as he and Carter come over.

"Blake just shit himself because he thought he might've forgotten their anniversary." I state.

"Holy shit. Yeah, you do not want to do that. I forgot to put the toilet lid down once; fuckin' christ she chewed me a new asshole." Rip moans.

We all laugh.

"You're alright, you got the timid sister." Rip

points out to Carter.

"Ha! She still has that Rocke sister streak, believe me." Carter adds.

Suddenly Ivy starts screaming at the top of her lungs.

We all look at each other.

"The Rocke gene." We say in unison.

"Good luck with that son, you're in my prayers." Dad slaps Blake's back and walks over to mum.

I look up to see Nan chatting to Patience. I don't know what Nan is saying but whatever it is, Patience's cheeks are blushing and she's laughing. Oh Christ, I bet it's something that no grandma should be saying.

"So then I said Albert, I don't think you should have taken that much Viagra! I mean, it looked so angry dear. In the end I was right and he had to go to the hospital. I took the nurses some biscuits. Oh and they were having a right old giggle at his giggle stick!" Nan snorts.

"His giggle stick?" Patience asks, laughing.

"Oh yes sorry dear, I forget that Americans have different names for things, we call his penis a giggle stick because, well, as soon as you see it you giggle. I mean it was a tiny little thing, no bigger than my pinkie finger." Nan wiggles her pinkie in the air.

"Oh christ Nan! I don't need to hear that shit." I groan.

"Well Axel, this was a private conversation with your lovely girl here." Nan pulls Patience in for a side hug.

"Well Nan, I hate to break it to you but we have to be getting back. It's getting late and Maddie needs to get to bed." I say, kissing her head.

"I'm happy for you Axel. Now go. Now that I'm going to be living out here you'll see me all the time. Plus I feel absolutely bloody shattered." She yawns.

We go to say our goodbyes and Maddie begs us to let her sleep over.

I look to Daisy.

"Of course. Caden can too! We will have a sleep over, I'm sure Miguel will love it." Daisy smiles.

"You're having Caden overnight?!" Rose asks.

Daisy laughs and nods.

"Biker boy, take me home and have your wicked way with me. Tonight we are child free!" Rose says, putting on a posh English accent.

"God Rose!" Dad grumbles.

"Whoops sorry Dad, my bad, forgot you were here." Rose apologises.

Rose and Rip practically run out of the door

as we say goodbye to everyone.

"Fuck Baby! I can feel you coming. Hold it back, wait for me."

I thrust faster and harder, filling her to the hilt every time. Her perfect soft tits bounce with every thrust. I feel her walls clamping around my cock. She is desperate to come and I can't hold it back anymore.

"Fuck yes! Come now." I roar as my orgasm hits. I feel her walls tighten and she screams my name.

I roll us to one side. Both of us are trying to catch our breaths.

"I fucking love you." I mumble.

I stroke her dark hair from her face and her bright green eyes light up.

She smiles.

"Love you too."

"You excited to be officially patched in to-morrow?" She asks.

"I can't wait." I say sarcastically.

"You're secretly looking forward to being a member of something again. I know you; you miss that brotherhood, you need it in your life." She calls me out on my bullshit.

"Hmmm, maybe you're right." I say sleepily.

I feel her walls tighten around my cock.

"Don't do that Baby." I warn.

"What's the matter? You don't have it in you to go again, soldier?" She teases.

I growl and roll her over so she's straddling me. I put my arms behind my head.

"I will take that as a challenge. Let's see who gives up first, shall we?" I say as I thrust up, causing her to gasp.

"Oh the challenge is on." She winks and swivels her hips seductively.

Three hours later we are both spent. Our bodies are covered in a sheen of sweat. Patience has fallen asleep, her head on my chest. Fuck! I fucking love this woman. I smile to myself before falling asleep.

The next day everyone is at the club for a massive cookout in celebration of me being patched in.

Khan whistles to get everyone's attention.

"Brothers, biker bitches, and biker brats! It's time to hand over to our boss man, the man we adore, President Rip!" Khan cheers.

Everyone laughs and cheers. Rip gives Khan a thump as he stands on the bench.

"I know this isn't way we normally we do things, but we're the Satan's and we rebel against the fucking normal." Rip laughs.

"Ax came to us when we needed the brothers most. He has proved his worth and loyalty to the club and let's fuckin' face it, he has skills that are invaluable to us." The brothers cheer.

Patience smiles as she wraps her arms around me. She's one of the only people outside of the club who has witnessed my 'skills'.

"So when we were voting Ax in and the road name came up, there was only one fuckin' name that fit. Ax, get your ass up here and get your cut!" Rip orders.

I hand Patience my beer and everyone cheers as Rip hands me my cut. I look at the patch with my road name and smile.

"You're gonna be happy as a pig in shit riding with us and having our back. Welcome to the mother fucking Satan's Outlaws, Hitman." Rip slaps my back.

He points to my patch and yells.

"Welcome Hitman! Now let's get fucked up!"

The brothers all cheer and laugh. I walk back to Patience. Her eyes are alight. She grabs hold of my cut and pulls me in for a kiss.

"Hitman, huh?" She says running her fingers over the patch.

"Yeah Firecracker. You're Hitman's property now." I say across her lips, sliding her cut over her shoulders.

She gasps and puts her cut on. She traces the 'property of Hitman' patch and smiles.

"You know I never wanted to be an old lady? I damn right detested the idea, but seeing this patch and belonging to you, I couldn't be fuckin' happier." She breathes.

CHAPTER THIRTY-FOUR

Patience

This last week has been incredible. What might just be normal everyday life for most was a dream for me. Living with Axel and having Maddie with us was everything I longed for. Love, support, and a happy loving environment for my daughter.

I laugh at how utterly fucked up Axel and I were. We shouldn't have worked. We should have spiralled, drowning in each other's darkness, but instead we were the missing piece of each other's puzzle. We were that vital piece we needed to put ourselves back together.

Today is my birthday. Axel and Maddie brought me breakfast in bed and this time they managed to keep the pancake mix in the bowl. I'm just finishing up my make up. Axel warned me not to wear a dress today as we would be riding his bike.

I decide to wear my black high waisted denim shorts with a white lace bodysuit. I pair it with my heeled biker boots and grab my Satan's cut. I add some silver bangles and my favourite choker chain necklace. I decide to hell with it and add deep red lipstick. It is my birthday after all! Walking out of the room I reach for my sunglasses.

"Okay I'm ready to start my birthday." I state, twirling around.

"Fuck me." Axel groans. His eyes sweep my body.

He walks towards me until my back hits the wall. He sweeps my hair from my neck and places soft kisses.

"Hhmm baby. You smell and taste as delicious as always." He moans. I gasp as he nips my neck.

He pulls back slightly, his eyes full of lust. They drop to my lips.

"You don't fight fair." He groans.

"I only play dirty." I whisper.

Axel crashes his mouth down on mine and I moan as his tongue teases mine.

But all too soon, he stops.

"We can't be late. We'll get back to this later; I have plans for that mouth of yours." Axel smiles.

I bite my bottom lip and smile.

"Let me make sure my lipstick isn't smudged." I say. Leaning forward I kiss him briefly before running to check my lipstick.

We ride to the club along the quiet open roads with the Texan heat beating down on us. I sigh. This brings me so much peace, so much freedom. Now things are working out in my life, I can dare to dream again about getting Darago.

We pull up and park at the club. There is loud music playing the smell of the fire pit and barbeques. Axel takes my hand. He leads the way and as soon as we turn the corner everyone shouts 'surprise!'

I gasp and hide in Axel's chest. The whole club is there and all of Axel's family. I turn to Axel.

"You arranged this?" I ask.

"Yeah, it's just one of your surprises." He

smiles.

"Hey, what do I have to do around here to get a hug from my favourite girl?!" I hear yelled.

Recognising the voice I swing around and see Tank.

"Oh my god, Tank!" I walk up to him and he envelopes me in his big arms.

"Damn, happy birthday girl!" He says and kisses the top of my head.

"It's so good to see you Tank, how are you, the club?" I ask.

He smirks.

"It ain't the same without you, when are you coming back?"

I shrug.

"I don't think I will be, Tank. I'm really happy with Axel and I don't think he would be too happy about me working there. He definitely would not want me dancing there." I answer honestly.

"What about running the joint? There's a new owner and they need someone with your knowledge and experience. The new owner has big plans for the club. He's having it made all classy! What do you say?" Tank asks.

I feel Axel come up behind me.

"I think she would fucking love to." Axel answers for me before I get a chance.

I spin around, shocked.

"You wouldn't mind?" I ask.

"No. It's not like you're performing and I know you enjoyed working there. Tank told me all about the new owner and the job offer. If you want it, go for it."

"Okay, yeah, I'd love the job. Who's the new owner?" I ask.

Tank and Axel exchange a look before Tank answers.

"It's Dreads, but before you get all twitchy and shit, he will be more of a silent owner. He wants someone else to run the club. He doesn't want any hassle, just the profits it brings." Tank pauses, waiting for my reaction.

"Why wouldn't I want to work for a tall dark handsome man?" I tease.

"Very fucking funny." Axel warns.

"Set it up Tank! I'm in!" I say excitedly.

"Fuck yeah!" Tank cheers.

"Right, I'm off to tell Dreads the good news. Have the best birthday and I will see your fine ass at the club." Tank kisses my cheek and leaves.

"You sure you're happy about me working for the very handsome Dreads?" I ask, teasing him.

Axel pulls me into his arms.

"Baby, you're mine. I trust you and I know you'll be safe with Dreads. Now come and enjoy your party because there are more surprises to come." Axel winks.

I chat and dance with everyone. I watch Axel play with Miguel and Maddie and they both wrestle him to the ground.

"Baby girl, I can't tell you how happy I am for you to have found your happily ever after." Ma states wrapping her arm around me.

"Me too Ma, me too." I sigh.

Rip walks up to Axel and whispers something in his ear. Axel's eyes are alight and he walks towards me. He holds out a bandana; I frown in confusion.

"Turn around baby, I need to blindfold you." Axel smiles.

Ma takes my drink. I bite my lip, excited at what the surprise may be. Axel places the bandana over my eyes and ties it at the back of my head.

"Take my hand and I will lead you to your next surprise." He whispers in my ear.

I smile wide and everyone starts to quietly mumble, following behind us. I hear a few gasps as we come to a stop. The excitement causes a belly full of butterflies.

"Happy Birthday." Axel whispers as he removes the bandana.

I squint as my eyes adjust to the light. That's when I see her: Darago. The chrome is glistening in the sun.

"Ax...I..." I gasp, stunned.

I reach out and my hand shakes. It's as if I'm dreaming and she will disappear when I touch her. I run my fingers over the magnificent marbled paint work. She's really here. I squeal when I see the side cart with matching paint work. Placed on the seat is a child's leather jacket and helmet.

"Axel." I sob.

He stands behind me.

"Just liked you wanted, your dream."

I spin around and jump into his arms. I wrap my legs around his waist.

"You really have made my dream come true. I fucking love you Axel the Hitman Rocke!" I yell.

Everyone cheers and whoops as I kiss Axel. I pour all of my love into it.

"Ah fucking hell, I'm crying again!" Lily sobs.

"Alright you two, a father doesn't need to see this shit." My Pa groans.

We break the kiss, laughing. I rest my forehead on his and catch my breath.

"I would give you the damn world if that was your dream. Now I know you're dying to get on that bike. Go and take her for a spin with Maddie but be quick because I'm not done with the surprises yet." Axel winks.

He places me back on my feet and I jump with excitement. I call over Maddie and put her jacket on her. It has her name stitched on and the Satan's Outlaws badge on it.

"Mama! I'm a biker chick!" She giggles, twirling around.

"You sure are Cupcake. Come here and put your helmet on." I say, holding out it out to her.

It's bright pink and covered in glitter. Maddie loves it.

Once she's all strapped in, I start up Darago. Her engine roars to life and I can't wipe the smile off my face. I pull the throttle and ride out of the parking lot.

My skin prickles with goose bumps and the hairs on the back of my neck stand on end; she's finally mine.

Maddie squeals and waves her hands in the air. I laugh.

"Hold on Cupcake!" I yell as I pick up the speed.

"Weeeeeeeee! This is so much fun Mama!"

Maddie screams with delight.

I turn around at the end of the road and ride back to the club. Everyone is standing around waiting for us.

I come to a stop and Axel unclips Maddie and lifts her out.

Maddie takes off her helmet and holds it under her arm.

"Come on boys, let's go play. Look at my cut! I'm a biker chick now." Maddie says attempting to click her fingers at the boys.

I burst out laughing. Axel's concerned gaze comes to me.

"I don't know why you're laughing, that sass will be a teenager one day and I can't go around killing teenage boys." Axel complains.

I get off Darago and walk to him.

"Don't worry, we can take the killing of teenage boys in turns." I wink.

I go to walk off but Axel grab my hand.

"Final surprise. We're going away for the night." Axel states.

"Are you serious?" I ask in disbelief.

"Deadly." Axel points to Khan placing a holdall in the side cart.

"Lets ride baby."

I give everyone a quick wave, not having time for proper goodbyes, because Axel is already on his bike. Excited I jump on Darago and start her up. Axel looks over his shoulder and gives me a wink, then rides off. I laugh and quickly follow.

As we ride, side by side, with the early evening sun and the wind in my hair, I can't contain my emotions. My heart is so full it feels like it's going to burst. I take a deep breath, trying to hold it all in.

We pull up to a small cabin that has a sign hanging from it which says Olson's Holiday Lodges. Axel holds his hand up for me to wait while he runs inside to collect our key.

I don't have to wait long for him to come back out. He doesn't say anything, he just climbs on his bike and starts to ride. I follow.

I follow him around the winding dirt track until he turns off and comes to a stop outside of a beautiful little log cabin surrounded by trees.

I get off my bike and stretch, aching a little from not having ridden for that long before.

Axel takes my hand and pulls me to the cabin.

"What about the bags?" I ask.

"The bags can wait, there's something I need

to show you first." He says excitedly.

I smile and follow him through the little cabin, which is cute and rustic inside. He stops in front of the sliding glass doors, opens them, and pulls me out onto the decking.

I gasp. I never would have expected the view that greets me.

The cabin is suspended high up, almost like a tree house overlooking a massive lake. The sun is setting over the tree tops and the warm orange and red sky reflects in the clear water of the lake.

I can't contain it anymore, I let silent tears fall. I let out a little sniffle and immediately Axel becomes concerned.

"Baby, what's the matter?" He asks while cupping my face.

I smile and shake my head.

"Absolutely nothing; it's perfect. These are happy tears. I just...there is so much love and happiness in my heart right now I feel like it's going to burst. You have made all of my dreams come true. I don't care if life is a pile of dog shit from here on out, today's memories are enough to keep me happy for an entire lifetime." I sniffle and smile up at Axel.

Axel leans in and kisses me.

"I will make sure you're living your dreams every fucking day. I will go to the ends of the mother fucking earth to make you happy." Axel declares.

Feeling his words I pull his mouth down on mine. I kiss him hungrily, needing him. I try to go inside and find the bedroom but Axel holds my hand and pulls me back to him.

"No. I'm going to make love to you right here with this view and that damn sunset." Axel states before taking off his t-shirt and kicking off his boots.

I watch as he undoes his jean buttons one by one. I clench my thighs together and lick my lower lip whilst watching him undress.

His eyes are hooded and on me as I walk towards him.

I take his hard length in my hand and stroke. I lean forward and kiss and nip along his chest and down his stomach until I am on my knees taking him in my mouth. I moan as he thrusts his hips forward,

"Fuck, that's it baby, suck my cock." He groans deep in his throat.

Unbelievably turned on I slide my hand between my legs, eager for some kind of release.

Before I can register what's happening I'm on my back with Axel yanking off my shorts. His mouth is on me. I cry out as he sucks my clit, circling it with his tongue. I grip his hair and buck my hips, feeling my orgasm build.

"Fuck Axel, yes!" I scream as I climax.

Axel takes off my top and throws it across the decking. He leans down and kisses me, the taste of my arousal on his tongue.

He grabs my thigh and hooks it over his hip as he slowly slides in me, filling me to the hilt. We both let out a throaty moan.

He moves his hips slowly taking his time inch by sweet inch, filling me. I bring my hips up to meet his and he kisses and bites along my neck and shoulder. Kissing over my breasts he takes my nipple in his mouth and sucks.

"Oh fuck." I cry out.

I arch my back and close my eyes, feeling my orgasm build.

"No baby. Open your eyes. Watch us. Watch me fucking you." Axel orders.

I open my eyes and lean up on my elbows and watch as Axel moves in and out of me. His thrusts become harder, deeper, and I can no longer hold myself up. I lie back down, feeling my climax climb higher and higher.

"Axel! I'm gonna come Axel!" I scream as I can no longer hold it back. My orgasm hits me so hard my body bucks.

"Fuck, so fucking tight." Axel moans, finding his release.

Axel cocoons me in his arms, stroking my hair from my face.

"I fucking love you Patience." Axel says, his voice gravelly.

I reach up and cup his face.

"I love you too."

We get up and Axel gets our things from the bikes. We curl up with a beer on the bench swing and stare out into the night sky.

CHAPTER THIRTY-FIVE

Axel

Looking up at the star filled night sky with Patience across my lap, my thoughts wonder to Joe.

As if sensing my shift in mood Patience reaches for my hand and places a gentle kiss on my palm.

"What is it?" She asks with concern in her eyes.

"I'm sorry, my mind just wondered off for moment. I was thinking about Joe." I sigh.

"Tell me about him." She demands.

I smirk.

"Well he was a cocky, filthy minded, pain in my arse. You would've liked him." I laugh.

"He was my best friend. Being through and seeing what we saw together created a bond like no other. He was the glue that kept me going through each mission, through each battle. I was the serious one and he would always crack a joke or make light of whatever situation we were in to distract me, to distract both of us. He kept us human." I sigh.

"He sounds like he was a really great guy."

"Yeah, he was. I feel guilty you know? I feel guilty that I'm now living this amazing life with you and he never got that. He never got to see his son go to school, go with his son for his first legal pint in the pub, see him get married, or even hold him in his arms. He was the best there was, and he deserved better. He deserved to have a life like this." I grit, swallowing back the lump in my throat.

Patience sits up in my lap and cups my face.

"You deserve this. Joe was a good guy and he would've wanted this for you. Your life isn't less important than his so don't ever feel guilt over what happened that day. You could have never known what you were walking into." Patience kisses me softly.

"Sorry, I didn't mean to bring a downer on your birthday." I apologise.

"Don't ever apologise for talking to me about you."

I take her mouth and kiss her slowly and softly. She lets out a little whimper and I smile against her mouth. I stand. Lifting her with me I carry her inside to the bedroom.

We lay there, Patience spread across my chest. I stroke my hand up and down the soft skin of her back.

"Marry me." I state.

"What?" Patience whispers, leaning up on her elbow.

"Marry me. You're my life, my world, I don't exist without you. I can't fucking breathe without you. You're mine and I'm yours. Marry me?" I ask again. I tuck a strand of hair behind her ear. Her beautiful green eyes fill with tears.

"Yes." She whispers. I roll her on to her back.

"Yes Axel, I will marry you. I love you so much, I can't bare the thought of ever living without you. You're everything to me, to Maddie." Patience sobs.

"Fuck me. You've just made me the happiest man alive. I love you Firecracker." I whisper across her lips.

◆ ◆ ◆

I sit in my truck outside his house and watch as he waves off his wife and kids and returns to the house. I walk around to the back of the house and straight through the sliding doors. The son of a bitch doesn't seem to have considered security. Why would he when he lives in such affluent neighbourhood? I walk down the hall to his office, knowing exactly where I am going. I'm not stupid, I'm playing it smart; I've been scoping out and watching his family for weeks.

I pull out my gun and open the door. His head whips up in shock and I watch as his face pales when he sees my gun. I kick the door shut behind me.

"Wh-ho are you? What do you want?" He stutters.

I smile and remove my shades.

"What, you don't recognise me?" I ask, walking closer and keeping my gun aimed at his head.

"Maybe you'll recognise my brother in arms, Joe." I state laying a photograph of Joe on his desk.

"I'm sorry, I don't. Is it money you want?" He

asks, chucking dollar bills on his desk.

I feel the heat and the rage creep up inside me; he doesn't know who I am. He had no idea who we were. It was just an order to him, a way of repaying his debt.

"I'll refresh your memory. See a while ago now you ordered a special operation to take out a secret underground drug operation in Mexico." I pause and I see it, I see the moment it registers.

"But, you see, I know the truth. I know that you owed the Cartel. I know you ordered that ambush and killed a village of innocent people." I seethe.

"I haven't killed anyone." He shakes his head.

"You gave that order, you killed those women and children, you killed Joe. All because you have a gambling issue and owed the Cartel money. You don't just have blood on your fucking hands, you're drowning in it!" I yell.

"Now I have to kill you. I have to kill you for the poor innocent people that died at your hands. I have to kill you for Joe." I state.

"Please...I'm sorry...I didn't know...I was in a bad place and I...I promise I will compensate you. I have a family, I have children." He begs.

I smile and click my neck.

"I know. I've done the decent thing here and waited until they left. Now you're going to write a letter explaining what you've done and why you can't live with the guilt any longer. You're going to explain why you're taking your own life." I order.

He writes a letter, his hands shaking. He's sobbing like a baby. Even now he isn't sorry, he only cares about himself. Once he's finished writing the suicide note, I hold out the rope and smile.

"Get on your desk and tie the rope to that hook up there." His eyes follow where I'm pointing and he climbs onto his desk.

"Where did that hook come from?" He asks.

"I put it there last week, but I wouldn't worry about that now." I smirk.

He ties the rope onto the hook and places the noose over his head and around his neck.

"Now, to ensure you take that leap off your desk, I'm going to make a little call to your friends at the Cartel. I need to let them know you've been running your mouth off. The difference between me and the Cartel is that I have a heart; they don't. They will burn your mother fucking house down while you and your family sleep." I state and pull out my phone.

"Wait! I'll do it." He yells.

I smile.

"Well come on then, I haven't got all day." I

state tapping my watch.

He sighs and closes his eyes and then steps off of his desk. He splutters and his face turns bright red. His body is desperate for oxygen. I stand and watch.

"Who are you?" He gasps.

I smile.

"I'm the mother fucking Hitman." I answer as I watch the life drain from his eyes.

I pick up Joe's picture and walk out of the house to my truck. I drive off, feeling a weight leave me. Justice has finally been served.

"You can sleep peacefully now Joe. Rest in peace brother." I mutter to myself.

The battle is finally won. I can live my life free from the darkness that plagued me. I can live my life with my saviour, my dark angel.

I am free. The war within is over.

THE END

EPILOGUE

It's been a busy few months for Patience and I. She started her new job which had her working at all hours and she loved every minute of it.

Maddie recently started her new class at school and I'm waiting to pick her up. I enjoy picking her up from school because she's always excited to see me. I've missed her.

The only thing I hate about picking her up is the looks of appreciation I get from the other mums in the playground.

"You know that bitch Melissa is totally eye fucking you right now." Rose mumbles beside me.

"I don't give a fuck. I'm not even looking at her." I sigh, come on teachers, let the kids out already.

"She is! She does it to Rip too. She thinks I don't notice, the filthy whore. She can't find a single man so she has to go around trying it on with guys who are taken." Rose gripes.

"Oh watch yourself, she's coming over." Rose warns.

Please fucking Christ, just let the kids out.

"Hi Axel."

"Melissa." I grunt.

"Listen I wanted ask you a little favour. Could you possibly fix my bike? I know you're good with mechanics and things and, well, I just don't know what I'm doing." She whines in that way that some women think sounds attractive. She definitely does not sound attractive. Her voice is like nails running down a chalk board.

Before I can answer I hear the sound of heels marching their way over. My lips twitch, knowing exactly what's about to happen.

"Hey Hitman." Patience purposefully states and pushes herself between Melissa and I. She leans up and kisses me.

"Oh hey there Melissa! Sorry, I didn't see you there. How are you? You still having that little issue?" Patience points to her vagina area.

Rose snorts back her laughter.

"Because if you are, I'm sure there's a surgeon who can help. I mean, just look at the wonderful things they do to help burns victims! I'm more than sure they would be able to cut back your giant hoo-ha!" Patience snaps.

Rose is doubled over laughing her arse off at this point. I lean in and whisper in Patience's ear.

"Easy Firecracker." I warn.

"So Melissa, as I was saying, surgeons work wonders. Not sure what they'll be able to fix after I'm done with you though. So don't let me ever catch you coming on to my man again. Am I clear?" Patience smiles sweetly.

"You're insane." Melissa whispers.

"No sweetheart, I'm a Satan's Outlaw, and I protect what's mine. Now fuck off." Patience fumes.

Fuck! I love it when she gets fiery.

"Mama!" Maddie shouts while running down the steps.

It's as though someone flips a switch: Patience turns from wanting to murder Melissa to being warm and loving.

"Oh Patty, I swear I think I'm falling in love with you." Rose wipes tears of laughter from her face.

"Okay that's enough. Come on, we have to be somewhere." I flip Rose off and lead Patience and Maddie to the truck.

I bite the inside of my cheek, feeling a little anxious about where I'm taking them. I pull up outside a farmhouse with a white picket fence.

It's a five minute drive from Maddie's school.

"Where are we?" Patience asks, looking out of the window.

I don't say anything, I just get out of the truck. I walk up to the front door and wait for Patience and Maddie to join me.

I pull out the key and unlock the door and gesture for them to go on in.

Patience's eyes scan the living room. There's a large rustic fire against the wall. She wanders through to kitchen and I follow.

She opens the large glass sliding doors and Maddie runs straight out and jumps on the brand new swing set I built for her.

"What is this place Axel?" She asks.

"I brought it for us. It's ours." I state, awaiting her reaction.

She doesn't say anything, she just watches Maddie play on the swing set.

"Patience. Say something." I beg.

She turns to me, tears flowing down her cheeks.

"When will you stop making my dreams come true?" She sobs.

I smile, pull her into my arms, and kiss her.

"I will never stop. I'm going to spend my life making sure your dreams always come true.

Messed up attracts messed up, after all. You're this missing piece of my life's puzzle. Now I've found you I'm never letting you go."

This is the 4th and final book in the Rocke series.

The Rocke family will pop up from time to time in future planned series. Thank you so much for reading. I hope you enjoyed reading the series just as much as I enjoyed writing it.

Keep up to date with my latest releases by following me on Facebook, Instagram, Twitter, Goodreads and Amazon.

Releasing later this year: Tiers Of Joy.

A standalone novel.

Planned for early 2021. The Satan's Outlaws series.

Printed in Great Britain
by Amazon